TIGER'S NIGHT OUT

ASHLYN CHASE

Tiger's Night Out

By Ashlyn Chase

This book is a work of fiction. Names, characters, places, and incidents are either products of the author's imagination or are used fictitiously. Any resemblance to actual events, locales, or persons is entirely coincidental.

Cover by Syneca Featherstone

www.syneca-originalsyn.com

© Ashlyn Chase

Published by Imagination Unlimited

Edited by Peggy McChesney

Proofread by Dianne Donovan

Sign up for my newsletter, right on the home page of my website:
http://www.ashlynchase.com

This book is dedicated to the wonderful people of India (and to Mr. Amazing, who took me there.) It's true that I had the 5 star experience, but that's only a small part of why I heart India!

CHAPTER 1

Before the summoning

Four thirty-something friends met for their drinks at a Manhattan restaurant on a busy Friday night.

"Look, Haley. That tall, blond guy is staring at you," her friend Maura said.

Haley raised her focus over her friend Ronda's curly brown hair, past the other tables, and located the hottie in question leaning against the bar. "You're imagining things," she whispered to the redhead sitting next to her. "He couldn't be older than twenty-five."

"Oh, yeah." Barb sported that evil grin that meant she was picturing somebody naked.

"Don't look," Maura said. "He's coming over."

Haley took a quick glance to confirm it. The cougar bait was grinning and heading their way. "Act cool, everybody—or try to, please?"

"Why wouldn't we?" Barb, queen of the fitting first name, sputtered. "But think of the gorgeous blue-eyed, blond children you could have with him."

Haley wanted to tell her friend to shut-up, but she'd just be rising to the bait. The outcome wouldn't be pretty and she wanted to look her most attractive.

Ronda who, thank God, hadn't whipped around to stare in his general direction said, "I hope he's bringing friends with him. Four to one odds are great for him, not so much for us."

Maura ducked her head and whispered, "No, he's staring right at Haley. I'd say there's no competition."

Haley sucked in a deep breath and watched the fair-haired hunk approach, glide by, and land at the table behind them. No longer caring how uncool she appeared, she craned her neck and risked a look over her shoulder. *Fuck. Not again.*

"A table full of college girls. Figures." Ronda muttered.

"Fan-friggin-tastic," Barb added.

Haley stared at the electric candle flickering in the middle of their table. "I'm never going to have someone to come home to, am I?"

Maura grasped her hand and gave it a squeeze. "Oh, honey. There's plenty of time for that."

"You have me," Barb said. "I live right down the hall."

"It's not the same. I mean, you're nice and everything…"

"No, I'm not. Now that I think about it, you probably wouldn't come home at all if we lived together."

Haley tried not to sigh. "That's not true. It's just that…you know what they say. When you lose your family, you have to create a new family."

"You want to be part of the gigantic, annoying, Italian Russo family?" Barb asked. "Hell, I don't even want to be one of them."

"My big, Irish family will adopt you," Maura said. "You'll just have to take your turn working at the bar and get used to a lot of ribbing, which sometimes lead to fights. But don't worry. "Da" throws the boys out onto the street when that happens."

"I thought your father died, Maura."

"Yeah, but my uncle sort of adopted me. He even wants me to call him 'Da,' which is the Irish way of saying Dad."

"That's why you and Barb will never know what I'm talking about—and try to be grateful for *having* a family. As crazy as you think they are, you'll never be dead a year without anyone noticing."

"What are you talking about?" Ronda asked. "Oh, wait. I know. There was an old Hollywood actress found dead in her home, recently. They think her corpse had been there for over a year."

Maura slapped her drink on the table. "That's it. I've had enough."

Pulling her hand away in time to miss the slosh, Haley asked, "Enough of what?"

"Enough of hot guys passing over quality women like us for some bubble-headed babes barely out of diapers."

"Like there's anything we can do about it?" Barb crossed her arms, openly pouting.

"Look, you guys are going to think I'm crazy, but there *is* something we can do." Maura glanced to her left and right, then leaned forward and lowered her voice. "Promise not to react *at all* until I finish my story."

The other two nodded their ascent. Haley wasn't known for holding in her immediate reactions, so she didn't make any promises.

Maura crooked her finger and Haley watched as Barb and Ronda leaned in.

"Don't you want to hear this Haley?" Maura asked.

Haley shrugged. "What is it? Another makeover weekend? A promising on-line dating site?"

"Nope. Nothing you've ever heard of."

Her tone and mischievous eyes caught Haley's attention more than her words. The redheaded imp had something up her sleeve.

Scooting her chair closer, Haley joined the huddle, thinking they looked as if they were planning a political overthrow. The only conspiracy she was interested in was how to manipulate the stock market in her favor—for once.

"Like I said, this is going to sound nuts, but I swear it's true. My cousin told me about a spell she and her friends performed, and it worked!"

A spell? "Are we talking about witchcraft?"

"Not exactly. My mother's ancestors were druids. There's all kinds of magic passed down through that side of the family. Now, don't interrupt, and let me finish the whole story. Okay?"

Haley, Barb and Ronda all glanced at each other.

"Oh, what the hell," Barb said. "What do we have to lose?"

Ronda propped her chin on her cupped hand. "Go ahead, Maura. We're listening."

Maura wove the most fantastical story Haley had ever heard. A story about wizards, and vampires, and shapeshifters of every ilk. Apparently, she believed they existed! Barb would stop her any minute now...

But she didn't. Haley watched in fascination as her two very grounded friends seemed to be absorbing Maura's entire speech.

"So, you see?" Maura finally said. "Immortals would appreciate women like us. *They* are the group of men we should be looking for. The only problem is, they're pretty rare and they don't want to be found out."

"Naturally," Barb said. "The population would panic if they knew these creatures lived among us. Neighbors would be scrutinizing their *strange* neighbors. The government would probably want to get their hands on them for research…"

Haley straightened. "Barb? Ronda? Are you actually buying this?"

Maura sagged back in her chair. "I knew at least one of you would doubt me. I just didn't expect it to be you, Haley."

"But, this is nuts. You can't be serious. Have you met any of these so-called immortals?"

"Yup. My cousin's husband. Well, they're not actually married. He's more like her common-law husband. He doesn't have a birth certificate so they couldn't apply for a marriage license—not a real one anyway. I mean, how would that look? The guy is about a thousand years old."

Haley burst out laughing. She shot a look between Barb and Ronda and was shocked to discover they weren't laughing with her.

"Ladies?" She waited for one of them to jump in and say the whole thing was a prank. That they all got together and planned this elaborate joke on her.

"Do you have any better ideas, Hale?" Barb asked.

"Yeah, how about we go shoe shopping?"

Ronda let out a long sigh.

"Wait a minute…" Haley reached over and grasped Ronda's hand. She was the most objective of the three, and even though she was a blurter, at least she was honest…A well-balanced Libra. "Ronnie? You're falling for this bull-crap too?"

Ronda shrugged. "I don't pretend to know everything. If Maura's right, and these guys are out there—just hoping some interesting, intelligent woman doesn't need to be convinced of their existence, maybe…I don't know. Maybe there's some hope for us. I mean, aren't you desperate? I hate to admit it, but I'm desperate. I think all of us are."

Haley leaned back in her chair. Her mouth gaped open as

she realized, no one was going to pop out of the woodwork with a hidden camera. She was not being punked. She was being offered the chance to summon an immortal lover who might actually want someone with the maturity that comes with age and experience. All she had to do was believe. *Yeah, that's all. Just toss everything I know out the window and put my faith in a demented cousin of a friend.*

She shrugged. "Why the hell not?"

"Great!" Maura nearly shrieked. She glanced around sheepishly. "Sorry, it's just that because we don't know exactly why or how it works, we have to replicate the spell *exactly*. The original group consisted of four females, so I needed three more."

Ronda lifted her glass. "And we're the lucky three, I guess. Frankly, I hope this works. I'm tired of waiting for Prince Charming—although I could totally go for a royal wedding, you know? Imagine wearing a real diamond tiara, and handling the crown jewels!"

Ronda never realized when she was setting up the perfect double entendre. Ordinarily, Haley wouldn't let it slide without a good teasing, but she had more important things on her mind at the moment.

"Hold on," Barb said. "Is there anything that can go wrong? I mean, you know, could we all turn into toads or something?"

Maura chuckled. "You don't know anything about magic, do you?"

"Nope. I sure don't."

"Well, it's nothing to be afraid of, as long as you're trying to do something beneficial. Because you ask that the wish only be granted if it's for the good, it either works or it doesn't."

"Are you sure?" Ronda asked.

"I have it on good authority that as long as you don't use

magic to harm anyone, you can do whatever you want with it."

Barb looked over at the giggly girls and Mr. Handsome again. "I guess if it keeps me from beating the shit out of those baby bimbos..."

Haley snorted. "You wouldn't harm a bleached hair on their heads, and you know it."

Barb shrugged. "Hey, I can fantasize, can't I?"

Maura pushed her hands down a couple of times, as if to say, *keep your voices down.* You'll need that power of visualization. I was told that's very important. You need to see the outcome as clearly as possible in your mind's eye."

Barb smirked. "Oh, I can see them all right—black eyes and all."

"Leave the bimbos out of this, Barb," Haley said. "If these idiot guys want shallow girls, they can have them. I'd rather find a man who appreciates a real woman with experience and sophistication."

Maura grinned. "So, it sounds like we're all agreed?"

The other three took one last glance at each other, the guys only hitting on younger woman, then nodded.

"Great. I have it all written down at home. We have to do this outdoors under a full moon. The original four did it in Central Park at midnight."

Barb took the sparkly comb out of her hair. "When is the full moon?"

Maura looked at her watch. "In five days."

"You have a moon watch?" Haley asked.

"No, it's just the day and date, but I think the next full moon is on the twenty-seventh."

"So, is there anything we need to do to prepare for this?"

"Just show up in Central Park on the night of the twenty-seventh. Let's meet at the artist's gate at eleven. We can find the right spot from there. Oh! And come shit-faced."

Barb chuckled. "Excuse me?"

"You heard me. The original four women were all bombed out of their minds, and like I said, it has to be repeated *exactly*."

Haley chuckled. She could hardly believe she was going to do this with her friends, but hey, she had done some pretty crazy things before. Risk was her middle name—literally. It was her grandmother's maiden name and fit her even better than it did her grandmother. "Hey, what's one more humiliating attempt to find love? Why the hell not?"

"I'm so embarrassed, I could die! Maura, are you one hunnred percent sure you knew what you were doing?" Ronda grabbed her bra off the branch and slipped it back on. She had a hard time with the clasp and slurred curses under her breath. "Well?"

Maura cringed and steadied herself so she could step into her panties. "Shh. Like I said before, don't talk so loud. At least not until we get dressed and out of these woods."

Despite their inebriated agreement with her earlier, the women had suddenly freaked out when a bolt of lightning split the clear, black night. Maybe they didn't believe in Maura's ability to summon immortals, but they went along with it.

Barb let out a huff, then whispered loudly. "A lightning bolt came out of the cloudless, starry sky and could've fried us. That was weird and everything, but no immortals were riding it to earth. Couldn't you have screwed up?"

Haley pulled her tummy slimmer halfway up and staggered, barely staying upright. "I can't believe you made us get naked and dance under the moon. What kind of dumb ceremony is that?"

Ronda added, "I think you just wanted to see how far we'd go to find decent men."

Maura snapped. "I'm not sure of anything except that mortal men are not worth the trouble and heartache anymore. If you think immortals might appreciate an older, wiser woman and want to date one, you have to summon. And I tried to do it—for all of us."

Barb snorted. "Is that what you call summoning? To face in the general direction of Romania and mutter, 'Where the hell are you, damn it?'"

"Look, I tried the nice poetry from my memory of Irish summoning circles, but I was a kid. My grandda made all kinds of magic stuff happen."

"Like pulling a quarter from behind your ear? My grandpa did that," Ronda said

"No, silly. Things you wouldn't believe—like talking in Gaelic to little people I could swear now were leprechauns. Maybe immortals have to hear each of us speaking our own language."

"Irish celebrations, huh? No wunner. They wa prob'bly as shtonkered as we are." Ronda's bra clicked into place. "Ah, I finally got it."

"Look, Barb, you have your ways and I have mine. You faced the east and spoke to the gods, right?" Maura reached for her camisole and swore when it wouldn't fall off the branch where she'd tossed it.

Barb pointed an accusing finger at her. "Yeah and all I got was some immortal ass's wrath. When I sober up, I'm going to be really embarrassed, not just about the nudity, but for getting suckered into this. Why the hell did we have to take our clothes off again? We didn't even undress in front of each other in college, roomie."

Ronda answered when Maura didn't. "She said we had to

come to the high-and-mighty ones pure to show our commim… com… commiment."

"The word is commitment," Haley said. "As in all of us committed to Bellevue mental hospital if the cops catch us and I'm pretty sure that none of us are pure. Besides, I'm with Barb on dying of embarrassment tomorrow. Commitment's not all we showed by running around buck-naked under the moon."

"No kiddin'." Ronda let out a nervous giggle.

"It's called sky-clad and I'm not exactly proud of my butt without a body shaper, either. Look, I didn't force you to do it, did I? We're all sick of successful men, our equals, going after the little babes with big boobs, leaving us flourishing older women alone, feeling like rejects." Maura couldn't free her camisole from the branch to save her life. She stood there in only her bra and panties frowning at the branch.

"'Flourishing.' Good word," Haley said.

"Maura's right, everyone." Ronda mumbled the words from under the blouse she had somehow decided to pull over her head instead of unbuttoning it. "She didn't hold a gun to our heads."

"Hey," Barb cried. "That's my blouse!"

"I'm going to have to climb that friggin' tree," Maura muttered.

"Don't." Barb reached up and touched the branch. "Look, you aren't particularly tall or athletic. Let me do it."

"Is that your way of calling me short and fat?"

"Of course not. I never said that, for god's sake! I'm just trying to help."

"Maura, your body is perfectly normal for a thirty-eight-year-old woman. You have nothing to be ashamed of."

"Thanks, Haley. But I still wish I could find that friggin' fountain of youth."

"Sorry I got mad at you before," Ronda said to Maura.

Haley smiled. "Yeah, me too. I really love you, man."

"I really love you, man, too." Barb hugged Maura. "Now let me get your top."

"Well…" Maura eyed the branch. "Are you sure? I mean, I know we're the best of friends and everything, but you don't have to risk your pantyhose for me."

Barb shrugged. "What else is new? Friends to the end, right?"

CHAPTER 2

West Bengal, India

"Thank the Gods and Goddesses the monsoons are finally ending," Jamir said.

His brother Shahid agreed, telepathically. He stretched lazily, his muscles bunching and relaxing behind his orange and black fur.

Jamir thought his brother looked positively majestic sitting atop the reddish steps that led to the temple. He turned around a few times in the tall grass—dry for a change. When he was satisfied that no snakes hid in the area around his paws, he settled down and rested his powerful jaw on his front leg.

After so much rain, the grass grew high and bright green. Later in the season, the jungle grasses would dry to a wheat color and allow for better camouflage. But, even then, the brothers didn't blend with the isolated ruddy temple.

Jamir sensed no danger, so he chose to lie down upon the soft earth rather than the unforgiving rock.

Shahid suddenly whipped his gaze toward the opposite side of the temple.

"What is it?" Jamir asked.

"I thought I heard footsteps."

Jamir lifted his head and sniffed the air. "If anyone is about, their scent must be wafting away from us, upwind..."

Crunch.

Jamir's senses ratcheted to high alert. "I heard it too. Stay here. I'll investigate the perimeter."

Shahid nodded his large orange head, his gaze never wavering from the edge of the temple wall.

Jamir crept off to the side where the breeze was blowing toward him, so his scent would not give him away. Placing each pad carefully, he was able to move around in near silence.

Shahid rose cautiously, ready to have Jamir's back if danger presented itself.

What came into view astounded them both. All three of them, actually, for a young woman dressed in a long, white dress, holding a parasol against the midday sun, froze in place as soon as she spotted the adult male tigers.

Jamir had never seen such an ethereal creature. Her hair was light yellow, like the sun, and some curled beside her face while the rest was piled atop her head. Her lips and cheeks, pink against her fair complexion suddenly drained of color. Her eyes, the color of a clear blue sky, widened. Fear pulsated off her, until she closed her eyes and crumpled to the grass.

"By the Gods! What sort of creature is this?" Shahid exclaimed.

"I have never seen anything so rare...or so beautiful," Jamir said, breathlessly. "But our animal forms frightened her, brother. We must shift to humans before she wakes."

The brother tigers bounded into the temple, transformed, then donned and fastened their loin cloths. Just as they rushed to the woman's side, her eyes fluttered open.

Jamir extended his hand and she grasped it, raising herself to a sitting position. Her gaze darted around the terrain.

"What—where?"

"You are safe," he managed to say. His English was not perfect, but he had been given the gift of many languages. English to protect the temple from the recent influx of British, who would exploit their wilderness. Yet a woman alone had never entered their midst.

"Where did you come from?" she asked.

Jamir shrugged. "Here."

"B—but the tigers!" Her wide eyes searched the landscape once more.

"Gone," Shahid said quickly, and he shot his brother a meaningful look. In their animal forms they were able to communicate telepathically. As humans all their senses changed to dull and limited. Vishnu did not approve of telling the woman what they really were...immortal tiger-human shapeshifters, charged by the Gods with the responsibility of protecting the temple for eternity.

The woman appraised the brothers. Jamir still knelt by her side, holding her trembling hand.

At last, she smiled. "You saved my life. Thank you."

Shahid extended a hand and she grasped his too. The two of them lifted her to her feet. She teetered a bit, so Jamir placed a steadying hand at the small of her back.

"My father will want to reward you for saving my life. Will you escort me back to the plantation?"

Ah, so she came from the tea garden at the base of the rolling hills. "We need no reward, but one of us will walk with you to your home."

"Considering the proximity of wild animals, I would be very grateful...and so will my father. Perhaps if you'll take no reward, he could pay you to be his guide. He'll surely want to hunt down and destroy the tigers."

A gasp lodged in Jamir's throat.

Shahid bristled. "There will be no hunting. This land is sacred, and so are all the creatures put here by the Gods."

His anger silenced her.

She dropped Jamir's hand and strode down the hill. He caught up with her easily. Matching her stride, he said. "You have nothing to fear. We protect the temple you saw. The tigers will never bother you as long as my brother and I are here."

She gave him a sidelong glance. "How can you be sure?"

He had to think of an explanation that would keep their secret hidden. The Gods must have had a good reason to keep it small and tucked into the landscape.

Instead of answering her question, he distracted her by asking one of his own. "What made you wander so far?"

"I..." The long pause that followed told him she had secrets too.

"Wake up, brother!"

Jamir opened his eyes and scrambled to his feet. "What is it, Shahid? I sense no danger."

"You were having a dream that upset you. I thought I would do you a favor and wake you out of it."

"I was not upset."

"But you were back in 1913 again, weren't you?"

"Yes."

"With Lady Helen Hastings?"

"Yes."

"I thought as much. What have I told you? What does the Gita say? You must let go of emotional attachments."

Jamir sighed. "I cannot control my dreams, Shahid."

"If you had truly let go of the past, you would not still be dreaming of her."

"But what if she has been reincarnated, brother? I cannot help feeling the Gods would never be so unkind as to tease me with love, snatch it away, and then leave me to mourn for eternity."

Shahid shrugged. "It is not ours to guess the ways of the Gods. It is only our duty to them that matters. We guard the temple. That is all."

"Then I had better get some sleep in order to do my job well. Wake me for my shift."

"I will."

Jamir laid down in the grass and thought about what his brother had said. He was right, of course. Still, Jamir could not help feeling as if someone—specifically another incarnation of Helen—was fated to find him again. She was his soulmate, of that he was sure. Soulmates were not meant to be apart.

Jamir sat atop a rock, thinking about the delicate English woman who kissed him so sweetly. When he had told his brother what happened, Shahid had cheered him with a rousing, "Shabash!"

Apparently she hadn't forgotten him either, because he heard his name in a feminine voice on the wind.

"Shahid, we must shift, quickly."

"Why?"

"Helen Hastings is calling my name."

His brother bounded into the temple right behind him. Their powerful bodies shrank and morphed into two humans on their hands and knees.

"I didn't hear anything, Jamir. Are you sure it wasn't wishful thinking on your part?"

They rose quickly and affixed their loin cloths to cover their nakedness.

"You're getting old, Shahid."

"Doubtful, considering we never age."

"In that case, your ears need cleaning."

Jamir flashed him a teasing smile, then rushed out of the temple and descended the stone steps two at a time. He hoped he wasn't mistaken about the voice. He could almost feel the beautiful Lady Helen in his arms again.

As he sprinted toward the crest of the hill, he realized he would have to convince her to allow him to drop the word, lady, before her given name. He wanted the intimacy of using the Englishwoman's first name.

His heart beat fast as he peered down the hill. Yes! It was no trick of imagination. She was standing several yards below him, wringing her hands.

"I am here, Helen," he called down to her. "You are safe."

Her worried expression relaxed and she broke into a wide smile when their eyes met.

"Jamir." Her voice was breathy and soft as if relieved or spent from exertion. She lifted her long skirt and began to climb the hill.

"I will come to you," he said. "Stay where you are."

When she nodded he bounded down through the tall grass. As soon as he reached the flat terrain, he picked her up and twirled her.

She squealed but continued to smile.

He grinned at her and set her on her feet. "I am happy to see you, Helen."

Instead of asking permission to use her Christian name he decided to just go ahead and gauge her reaction to it.

She hesitated. Her hands were still braced against his shoulders. He wanted nothing more than to repeat the kiss they had shared, but what if her feelings had changed in the last few days?

She lowered her gaze. It seemed to be fixed on his loin cloth. An erection was beginning to tent the soft leather.

Her face flushed. "Is this all the clothing you have to wear?"

"Yes. Is my form displeasing to you?"

"No! Not at all, it's just that..."

Confused, he studied her face. She turned to the side but didn't remove her hands from his shoulders.

"If my body embarrasses you, perhaps you could bring clothing to me and I will wear it."

She nodded. "That would be more appropriate."

He sighed.

Helen was quick to add, "Not that your body is displeasing. On the contrary..." She blushed and couldn't finish her sentence.

Typical of the repressed English. Perhaps in time she would find less clothing more fitting to the Indian climate. Her layers of long fabric didn't appear comfortable, even if the garments were beautiful.

"Get up, Jamir. It is your turn to guard the temple."

Jamir stretched and tried not to resent the empty hours ahead. He would do his duty and guard the temple, but if his mind wandered back to 1913, and the woman who stole his heart only to disappear with it a year later, well, so be it.

Helen had managed to slip out to see Jamir frequently. Her father spent most afternoons at the British India club in the nearby town.

Each time the couple met they grew closer. They talked at length about her home, hobbies, and dreams, as well as the plans being made for her by her father. She was betrothed to marry a wealthy Englishman—one she didn't love, for she loved Jamir, and he loved her.

He knew she'd leave him one day, perhaps without warning.

And that's exactly what happened—in 1914 when the Indians rose up against the British, she vanished without a word.

Jamir had pined for her. If not for Shahid, he'd have wasted away to nothing. His brother hunted for him until, eventually, his despondency passed.

He'd never forget Helen, however. Even though they never consummated their love, she was his mate. His destiny. The timing was all wrong, but Jamir prayed that someday she would come back to him. He would wait for her. The Gods would not be cruel enough to part them forever. Jamir would see his Helen again—in this lifetime or the next. He was sure they would be reunited.

"Why does my butt hurt?" Barb gently lowered herself into a chair at Haley's breakfast table.

Haley couldn't help laughing as she watched her friend rubbing her rear end.

"You don't remember last night, do you, Barb?"

"After all the scotch you poured down my throat? Not bloody likely."

"Oh, sure. We forced you to drink it."

Barb caught her rolling her eyes and scowled. "Okay, fine. I drank the damn pint, but only because of Maura's insane plan. Would you have gone through with it if you were sober?"

"Not bloody likely, as a certain non-Brit I know would say."

"So, I stole an expression. Do you have to be so anal about the American-English language?" Barb sat down gingerly and scratched her head as if trying to stimulate her lost memories from last night.

"The words you're looking for are anal retentive. No one is purely anal."

"Wanna bet? You're an ass."

"Teaching English is what I do for a living," Haley said. "What do you expect?"

"I expect you to tell me why my butt hurts!"

"Because you fell out of a tree, dumbass."

"Now look who's butchering the language. Asses can't be stupid or intelligent, smartass. And, by the way, what tree?"

"You want to know the exact one out of all the trees in Central Park?"

Barb sighed. "Of course not. I just meant, what was I doing up in *any* tree?"

"Trying to get Maura's blouse down for her."

"Oh shit." Barb slapped a hand over her eyes. "Do I want to know?"

"Might as well. You must remember that Ronda, Maura, you and I got together and went 'sky clad' as Maura called it to perform a summoning ceremony, right?"

Barb groaned. "We actually went through with it, didn't we?"

"Yes. Maura tossed her blouse in the air and it never came down. When we looked up, it was hanging from a branch, rippling in the breeze."

Barb laughed, despite—or perhaps because of the embarrassing memories flooding back.

When her giggles subsided, she said, "So, I climbed the tree and got it down for her? Wow, what a good friend I am."

"No, you never reached it. You fell out of the tree and landed on your ass before you could grab it."

"So what did Maura wear to get home?"

"She had on a blazer over the blouse originally, so she just buttoned the jacket and showed a lot of skin."

Barb shook her head at their combined idiocy. "Let's never speak of this again, okay?"

"It's a deal."

"But, did it work?"

"I thought we weren't going to speak of—"

"Oh, for frig's sake, Haley. Did the damn summoning work or not? Did any immortals show up?"

"Not sure. A bat zipped overhead. We teased Maura about that being her vampire. I don't think it was though."

"I seem to remember a flash of lightning. Did that really happen?"

"Yes, indeed. And there wasn't a cloud in the sky. I took that to mean we had been heard, so maybe, if you're lucky, some Greek God from Mount Olympus is on his way as we speak."

"Yeah, right."

"You still don't believe it could happen?"

"That we'd call up immortal lovers who will appreciate women of our age?"

"Yeah. Didn't we all agree we were tired of losing quality men to the twenty-somethings?"

"Yeah, I remember listening to everyone bitch about that."

"Hey, no one bitched louder than you."

"Whatever. So, are you sure all I did was fall out of a tree and land on my ass?"

"Yup. Some guy called a cab for us, and I saw you go into your apartment—alone. That was before I staggered down the hall to mine and made it to my own bed before I passed out—thank God, or should I say, "Thank the Gods?"

CHAPTER 3

Back in her apartment, Haley did three days-worth of dishes and reflected on the evening before. The only reason Haley had gone through with the ritual was because deep inside, she believed in things she couldn't see or explain. Maura called it magic, and there might be something to it.

Sharing her spirituality was something she'd learned not to do. In college, any time she expressed any kind of faith, her friends would ridicule her for it. Why couldn't she have gone to Boston College like Maura and Barb had? Oh, yeah, because she wasn't raised Catholic. Not that a Catholic school would have been the right place for her either. She didn't believe in a white-bearded man in the sky. She didn't believe the Pope was his buddy on Earth and had the right to ban birth control. She didn't know what she believed, and attending NYU didn't help her in that area either.

Maybe college had nothing to do with it. Some kind of order in the universe had tugged at Haley since middle school. Her friends thought she was wacky whenever she spoke of the visions she'd had, so she quickly learned to keep them to herself.

Over the past few weeks she'd dreamed of a faraway land.

A place with a red stone or brick temple she'd never seen. Or were they dreams? She was usually in that twilight state just before sleep when the visions startled her awake.

And there was more. Often visions of a smiling brown skinned man with thick black curls, or huge orange tigers lounging in the sun, were in this mysterious spot. She'd have thought seriously about trying to find the temple, if it weren't for the tigers. Their powerful jaws when they yawned gave her the willies.

As she finished the dishes and wiped her hands on a towel, she happened to glance down at the dishwater. *What the hell?*

The man of her dreams appeared. His caramel colored face seemed familiar, but she knew she'd never met him. He stood on a grassy bank, wearing nothing but a loin cloth. Powerful thigh muscles flexed as he stepped closer.

He dropped to his knees and gazed back at her. She recognized his eyes. She had never seen this man, but inexplicably she knew those eyes. Despite seeing nothing but kindness in them, she blinked hard and when the vision didn't disappear, she shrank away. She dropped a coffee mug, which shattered on the floor.

When she regained her balance from the shock of her vision, she looked again. His image had faded and there was nothing left but dirty dishwater. And a broken mug. She wondered if her brown skinned man was the immortal she had summoned. Would he be coming for her? If all he wore was a loin cloth, he wouldn't get very far.

After cleaning up the ceramic shards and hanging the towel on its peg to dry, she noticed her hands. Pasty and less supple than they used to be, they were beginning to betray her age, *dammit*. Thirty years of washing dishes, helping her mother from the age of nine on, seemed to be taking its toll. One of these days, she'd empty her savings account and move to a place with a dishwasher...or take a sabbatical and go backpacking–one or the other.

As she thought about the likelihood of a man in a loin-cloth coming to New York City for her, the backpacking idea rose considerably on her priority scale.

Haley turned on her ancient laptop and waited until it reacted to her password, the level she called its point of cooperation—it seemed to have arthritic joints and needed a moment or two to warm up and work properly.

Having thought long and hard about where that temple might be, she typed *India* into her search engine. Offerings from Wikipedia to travel sites popped up. *Oh boy, where to start?*

She pursued the travel sites that had their own search functions and lots of pictures. Searching the word *temples* produced almost as many confusing choices as *India* itself had.

She sighed and scrolled through the pages anyway. Nothing looked familiar. She was about to give up when she brilliantly thought to seek out places where tigers and temples might occur together. She didn't know much about tigers, but they were called Bengal tigers, right? That was a province or part of India… Sheesh, she knew next to nothing about India too. Well, it was time to learn.

Bengal, India temples. Finally she felt like she might be getting somewhere. Unfortunately, there wasn't a town named Bengal. There was *The Bay of Bengal* and *West Bengal*, which she gathered from the map, was a state. Fan-fucking-tastic. A whole state to search.

Haley started to slam the cover closed but stopped herself, and not only because the piece of electronic junk would probably die just to spite her. Part of her knew she was on the right track.

Should she check the flight and accommodations? What

the heck, she was already on a travel site, and it wouldn't hurt to look.

Okay, here goes nuthin'. She decided to check round trip flights from New York to Calcutta—only now it was called Kolkata. Okay, that was the first step.

Now she had to insert something in the space marked *Dates.* New York winters were brutal and her favorite time to get away, but she might be looking at their monsoon season. Besides, she couldn't wait until her Christmas break. She knew India could be a little hot in summer, but thank Goodness the area she was planning to visit was in the north. How bad could it be?

Summer vacation was fast approaching, and that was pretty good timing. She had planned to teach a summer class, but if she could begin her sabbatical right away, perhaps she'd return before the new semester—immortal lover in tow. If she didn't find him in three months, she should probably give up. But what if she did find him?

I'll fill out the necessary paperwork tomorrow.

Excitement coursed through her as she realized she was really going to do this. Haley looked at her calendar and typed in the day after the semester ended. Summer brought with it loads of tourists in the city, so she'd escape that too.

She hit the enter button and up popped the flights and prices.

"Eighteen hundred friggin' dollars? Holy crap!"

Haley didn't have enough to get there and back, *and* stay in decent hotels where she could drink bottled water and eat the mildly spiced food made for tourists, who weren't used to setting their tongues on fire.

Sorrow set in as she wondered how she could possibly swing this. *Damn.*

Jamir leaned over the quiet pool that formed near a bend in the river. He was going there to wash his face when a shocking picture formed just under the surface. A beautiful, pale woman with blue eyes stared back at him. Short tousled blond hair framed her heart-shaped face. A startling recognition hit him. It's her eyes! Helen's eyes. He whipped around hoping she was standing behind him.

Alas, no. He was as alone as always.

He could have sworn the look of surprise on her face meant she saw him too. Jamir stared into the water again and took a long look, but she had faded from view.

Was he dreaming? Since it was the middle of the day and he was still upright, he doubted it. He reached into the pool and splashed water on his face, neck and chest. When the water became still again, he stared into it and waited.

No more visions appeared. Disappointed, he turned back and shuffled his feet all the way to the temple.

"What is it, brother?" Shahid asked.

"What is what?"

Shahid smirked. "Your face is so sad. I would imagine the river dried up, except for the fact that you are wet."

"I saw her, Shahid."

"Who?"

Jamir couldn't answer around the lump in his throat.

Shahid's eyes widened. "Helen?"

Jamir nodded, still looking at the hard ground.

"Oh, no. She must have been with another man for you to be so unhappy."

Jamir glanced at the temple. "No, I—I just saw her reflection in the pooling water. Except when I turned around, she wasn't there."

"You must have been daydreaming."

"No. I was not even thinking about her."

"For once."

"Yes, for once. I had finally decided to accept the truth. She is gone. I was ready to put her behind me. Perhaps the Gods are telling me not to give up."

Shahid entered the temple. "I wish I knew what the Gods wanted. All I know for sure is they sent this gift, and we must protect it at all costs."

Jamir approached the strange object that fell out of the sky one day. It had definitely been sent by the Gods. It was like nothing he or Shahid had ever seen. Its smooth, white surface was made of a material that didn't exist in their world.

"Yes, we have been trusted with an important responsibility. Since Vishnu made us immortal and told us to protect the temple, this is the only direct communication we've had."

Shahid added, "I cannot help but wonder if the temple itself had been built specifically for this purpose, and they had to see that we would guard the temple with our lives before they sent this special object to house in it."

Jamir let out a big sigh.

"What is it, brother?"

He hung his head. "I might never be able to leave here and look for Helen."

Shahid stood next to him. "She found you once. If it is meant to be, she will find you again."

Jamir nodded and wandered out onto the temple steps. He scanned the landscape, watching and waiting for any glimpse of his beloved—just as he had for a hundred years.

Shahid came to sit beside him. "It pains me to see you so sad, brother. You know the road to happiness and enlightenment is spiritual, not tied up in the physical world, do you not?"

"Yes, I understand. But—"

"But nothing. Jamir, you need to live in the world as it is, not as you wish it to be."

Jamir hung his head, but whispered, "I know she is out there. We are connected."

"You're going to India? What part?"

"Kolkata. That's in the Northeast."

"Why? Are you teaching English as a second language? I thought you had signed up to do that here." The dean's eyes narrowed as if suspicion warred with curiosity.

"It's personal," Haley said. *Although teaching English might be a great way to make some more traveling money. Thanks for the idea, Dean Cranky-Pants.*

"Personal. Do you have family or friends over there?"

"Not exactly."

The dean shook her head slowly as if wondering about Haley's sanity. She didn't blame her. Haley was wondering the same thing about herself.

She had decided to let fate make the decision. If she had her sabbatical approved, she'd go. If the dean tried to talk her out of it, she'd assume it wasn't meant to be. At least not now. The temple tour she wanted to sign up for would begin in two weeks. That should be enough time to get her reservations made, some cash changed to rupees, and ask Barb to feed her cat.

Surprise didn't begin to describe what came over her as the dean signed the form and checked the *approved* box.

"Fortunately I had someone else interested in teaching English this summer." She shrugged. "Well, have a good trip and bring back some nice souvenirs."

"If I can afford any," she said, before she thought about it.

"You're not prepared financially? Are you sure should go?"

Haley sighed. "Can we ever be sure of anything?"

The dean eyed her doubtfully. "India can be a dangerous place—especially the north. I hope you know what you're doing."

So do I. Haley rose and shook the dean's hand. "Thank you. I'll be sure to send you a postcard."

As she strolled back to her office, she second guessed herself for the umpteenth time. Her boss hadn't tried to talk her out of it...or had she? It was difficult to tell. Haley replayed the conversation in her mind and couldn't remember being asked not to go. *Okay, then. The fates have spoken.*

Ronda and Barb were already sitting at the bar when Haley strolled in.

"Is Maura coming?"

"No, she had other plans," Ronda said.

Barb picked up her drink and swirled it. "You called us kind of at the last minute. I assumed we'd all be staying home, recovering from the summoning. So why did you want to go out again so soon? Did you need a little hair of the dog?"

She smirked. "No, it's too late for that."

Ronda raised her glass. "I wouldn't blame you. This is making me feel better."

"Hey, I'm just glad to see you're alive." Haley smirked. "No, what I really need is a reality check."

Barb plucked a pretzel out of the snack bowl while Ronda continued the conversation. "Did you have trouble remembering what happened that night too?"

"No, I remember it, though I'm not surprised you don't. You passed out cold on the asphalt."

"So I was told." She shot a look at Barb.

Haley chuckled. "Don't let her make you feel bad. Ask her about the bruise on her butt."

Ronda's gaze whipped to Barb's face, then her butt, then back to her face. "Oh? What happened to your butt?"

"Gravity poisoning," Barb snapped. "Now, can we get back to you, Haley? If you need a reality check, then you weren't as sober as you pretended to be."

"I never said I was sober. I just didn't black out like you did. Look, it's not about the night before last. Well, it is, but it isn't."

The bartender finally glanced her way and strolled over. "What can I get you?"

"Orange juice, please."

"Want any vodka in that?"

She groaned. The bartender chuckled, no doubt recognizing the symptoms of regret. "Not tonight. Thanks," Haley said.

While he bustled off to get her juice, she drummed her fingers on the bar. *How can I word this so my friends don't think I'm totally insane?*

"Come on, out with it," Barb demanded.

"I think I need to go to India."

"Huh?" Ronda tipped her head. "Do they outsource professors to India now?"

"No, but teaching English over there might give me some extra income while I'm on sabbatical."

"Sabbatical?" Barb exclaimed. "Aren't those long-term? I thought you were going on vacation for a week or two."

"Actually, I don't know how long it might take. If I don't have any success in two weeks, I'll probably come home."

Realization dawned in Ronda's eyes. "Wait a minute...you said this had to do with the summoning. Are you looking for your immortal over there?"

Barb gasped. "You didn't take that nonsense seriously, did you?"

"I wouldn't have, if other things hadn't fallen into place after the ritual."

Barb licked the salt from the rim of her Margarita. "What other things?"

"You'll think I'm nuts."

Barb snorted. "We already do."

"Thanks a bunch."

"Come on, Haley," Ronda encouraged. "Just ignore her and tell us what this is all about."

"I'm going to India to meet my immortal. I'm almost positive he's there."

Her friends stared at each other.

Barb spoke first. "Is this something you've been thinking about doing for a while? You didn't just dream up this harebrained idea in the past two nights, did you?"

"No, it's been a dream of mine for a long time." *Depending upon how one defines the word, dream.*

"Well, that's a relief." Barb sipped her drink. "If you had said you were going over there *just* to meet your immortal, I'd have had to buy you a designer straight jacket."

"Hardy har har."

CHAPTER 4

"Shahid, do you ever think she'll come back? I've all but given up hope."

Shahid walked beside his brother and rested a hand on his shoulder. "Perhaps not."

Jamir glared at him. "That's all you have to say? Perhaps not?"

"I have never been in love, so I do not know how you feel. I used to envy you, but after watching you mope for over a century, I think perhaps I am the lucky one."

Jamir could have flogged himself for not boarding a ship to England long ago. How could he have let his soul mate slip through his fingers?

As if he'd read his mind, Shahid said, "I suppose it would be impossible to find her now. It's been a hundred years. Her soul must have transitioned into another body—perhaps more than once."

Jamir stared at the sunset, thinking how nice it would be to share it with his Helen. If only she'd return. He had sent out prayers to the various Gods and Goddesses, hoping at least one of them would answer his plea.

"I would recognize her soul if I spoke to her and looked

into her eyes, but scanning the world for a woman who looks like Helen would be fruitless. She could be anywhere. She may look similarly and have a similar name, but I think my best chance of ever finding her again is by staying right here. Surely some kind God or Goddess will guide her back to me."

Shahid shook his head slowly. "I certainly hope so. If I have to listen to you sulk much longer, I may have to eat you."

Haley picked up the phone, to call Barb and ask her to come down the hall to join her for a cup of coffee. She changed her mind at the last minute and dialed Maura instead. If she discussed her visions, Barb would only ridicule her, and she needed to talk about them seriously.

She called her spiritually sympathetic friend, Maura, who picked up on the third ring.

"What time is it?"

"What? No hello?"

"I have caller ID, Haley. I think we can skip the 'Hi, it's me, Haley' part of the conversation. Why are you calling in the middle of the night?"

"It's not the middle of the night. It's six-thirty in the morning."

"Like I said."

Haley sighed and wondered if she'd called the wrong friend after all. "Sorry if I woke you. I forget some people don't get up until five minutes before they open their store."

"Well, I'm awake now, so let me make a cup of coffee while I'm talking to you...or while you talk and I listen. I'm too sleepy to talk."

"Fine. It may take a little explaining."

"Go ahead. You don't mind listening to me pee, do you?"

Haley thought, *Oh, gross* immediately, but remembered she'd just gotten her friend out of bed and she hadn't hung up on her. "Sure. Whatever you need to do."

"Women sometimes go to the bathroom together, but this is ridiculous. Boy, you must really need to talk."

"Yeah, and you must really need to pee."

Maura laughed and said, "Let me put you on hold for a minute, okay?"

"That'll work."

Haley heard a soft click and waited. Sure enough, about one minute later, Maura clicked back on.

"So, what's the emergency?"

"It's not exactly an emergency— just a weird experience."

"Now you're talking my language," Maura said, sounding mildly excited for the first time since their conversation began.

"Yeah, I figured you'd be the best person to share this with. Last night I was washing dishes."

"Wow, that *is* weird."

"Hardy har. Listen, I've never told you this before, but I have visions."

"Cool. What kind of visions are we talking about? Premonitions or little green men in your bedroom? Do you have a tin foil hat?"

Damn, maybe Maura isn't going to believe me either. "Don't make fun, okay? I really need to tell this to someone, and I stupidly picked you."

"Hmm…I'm so flattered."

"So can you suspend disbelief for a second and listen to what I have to say or not?"

"Of course. I'm sorry. I'm just a little grumpy when I don't get my beauty sleep."

Haley snorted. "A little?"

"Fine, I'm a total bitch first thing in the morning. I'm sorry. Now, stop stalling and tell me about your visions."

Is that what I'm doing? Stalling? Maybe so. Haley took a deep breath and launched into it. "I've had visions and signs since I was a kid. My parents just laughed them off, but the visions persisted. They help me make decisions, if I interpret them correctly and listen to what they're trying to tell me."

Maura murmured a quiet, "Uh huh." After a long pause, she said, "Keep talking."

"Okay, well, I've dreamed about and seen a guy in my visions—always the same guy. Last night I saw him in my dishwater and I swear he saw me too."

"Is he cute?"

"He's gorgeous."

"Finally, this is getting interesting. Tell me about him."

"He looks a little wild. Black shaggy hair. Brown skin. Muscular. And he never wears more than a loin cloth."

"Ooo...*really* interesting! Does he talk to you?"

"Talk? Don't be ridiculous. It's a vision and it lasts only a few seconds."

"Hey, I thought you wanted me to be open-minded. Spirits sometimes speak in dreams. It could happen."

Haley sighed. "You're right. Well, so far he hasn't spoken to me. In fact, I usually see him going about his day to day activities. He never looked directly at me—until last night."

"Got it. So what do you think it means?"

"I don't know," Haley wailed. "The only thing I can piece together is that he hadn't looked at me until we did your summoning spell."

"Oh my God, that's it! He's your immortal."

"That's what I was hoping, but how do I know for sure?"

"I guess you can do what I'm going to do."

"Which is?"

Maura chuckled. "Don't judge, okay?"

Haley quickly said, "This is a non-judgment zone. Go ahead, spill."

"Okay, well, I'm not going to sit around and wait for my immortal to come to me. I think I know where I'll find him, so...I'm going to Romania."

"You're what?"

"Hey, you said no judging."

"I wasn't judging. I was just surprised."

"Your voice sounded kind of judgy."

"Well, it wasn't. Why Romania?"

"Okay, this is going to sound *super* crazy, but I think my immortal is a vampire."

"Holy shit! After the summoning, I thought Barb was teasing you about the bat that swooped over us being your vampire. She was kidding, right?"

"I'm sure she was. But you know what they say about truth spoken in jest..."

"Yeah. I suppose so. By why would Barb think that when she's the least likely to know anything about immortal or paranormal beings?"

"She knows my reading taste. I absolutely adore vampire romances. Ever since we were roommates in college I've been reading everything *Vampyre* I can get my hands on. At first it was Anne Rice. Lately everyone and her sister writes vampire stories—and I still eat them up."

"Interesting. I guess I understand your trip to Romania now."

"Exactly. I wish I had your visions, so I'd know him when I saw him. Instead I...well, never mind. So what are you going to do about your mystery man?"

"I'm going to India."

"India? That's a friggin' long trip."

"Romania isn't exactly around the corner, either, Maura. I've seen a temple and tigers in my visions too. I'm as sure he's in India as much as you're sure your guy is in Romania."

"Fuck," Maura muttered.

"What?"

"Tigers? That sounds dangerous."

"And looking for your lover in *vampire central* isn't?"

"I'll take my chances with a vampire any day."

Haley laughed. "I guess we're built differently where that's concerned." She stroked her tiger cat, which had jumped onto her lap and curled up into a contented fur ball.

"So who's going to take care of Visa while you're in India?"

"I'll talk Barb into it."

"But she doesn't like cats."

"I know, but she'll love Visa when she gets to know her. How can you not?"

"I don't know. I thought she was more of a dog person."

"Just because you called her a bull dog?"

Maura laughed. "Pit bull. And that's just the way I tease old friends and previous roommates. She knows I'm kidding."

"I hope so. Anyway, I think I'm set to go. I have my sabbatical, my mail is on hold, Barb will be my cat sitter and plant waterer. I can't say I'm not a little nervous though. Aren't you?"

"I'm more excited than nervous. I think I'll sign up for a tour so I won't get lost or have to use an English-Romanian dictionary all the time."

Haley slapped her forehead. "That's what I'm doing too. I'll bet the tour operator would do the translating and steer us toward restaurants with bottled water. But if I don't find him during the two week tour, I may be out of luck. I have crap in my savings account."

"Everything's cheaper in India. Hey, bring me back a sari!"

"Are you willing to pay for it?"

"Um, how about a cheap pair of earrings, instead?"

"How about if I don't starve or land in a hospital?"

"Well, when you put it that way, skip it. Besides, I'm hoping to bring loads of stuff back from Romania for my store."

Haley humphed. "Yeah, and you'll probably triple the prices."

"I always triple the prices," Maura said without a drop of shame in her voice.

"Must be nice."

"It is when business doesn't suck."

"Oh. Isn't the store doing well?"

"It's as if there's a black hole in front of my store. Even tourists aren't coming in like they used to. I'd close the store and only sell online, but that's really tricky with Vintage Clothing. What used to be a size ten is now a size six. There was never a size zero before. So, people really have to try things on."

"You're going to Romania even though you can't afford it?"

"I can't afford not to. We're talking about finding true love. How can you put a price on that?"

Haley sighed. "You have a point. Well, I have to get off the phone and talk Barb into helping me with my crazy plan."

"Good girl. Let me know when you're going."

"Oh, I will. And if I can afford it, I might send you a post card."

"You'd better."

"My love," she whispered. *"I have waited so long for you."*

Jamir cradled her blond head in his hand and kissed the woman from his vision. "I am simply happy to hold you in my arms again."

"We have so much more to share. So much love to express."

He lowered her gently to the grass and lay beside her. "I cannot wait to show you how much is in my heart."

"Let us not wait another moment," she said.

Jamir wanted to take it slow, but he could not. She aroused his animal nature with her loving words and willing body.

He rolled her onto her stomach and lifted her to her hands and knees. She had been dressed in foreign clothing a moment ago, but now she was gloriously naked. He did not question a situation he was simply grateful for.

She wiggled her backside and begged, "Please..."

He groaned, unable to hold off another moment. He had to be fucking her, immediately. He sunk his lingham into her warm, wet channel.

Nothing had ever felt so wonderful. He thrust and withdrew, thrust and withdrew, all the while concentrating on the erotic sensations of every stroke.

She murmured words of love and encouragement. He wanted her to feel as marvelous as he did, so he added a clit rub. She moaned in delight and breathlessly asked him to fuck her harder, faster.

He lost himself. Increasing urgency ramped up his rhythm without his even thinking about it. Soon he was pounding into her as she was shivering and crying out in ecstasy. His climax hit suddenly, shaking him from his head to his to his toes as he ejaculated.

Jamir awoke alone. At least his brother had not witnessed this dream. The precious sensations felt so real, he still luxuriated in the afterglow. It must be a premonition. His reincarnated Helen was coming closer and closer. He could sense the truth without being told it was so.

CHAPTER 5

Haley exited the plane in Kolkata, and after eighteen hours in the air, she wanted to kiss the tarmac—until she took a good look at it. Layers of dirt coated the grimy pavement.

Instead she followed the other weary travelers to the customs area. She had been warned by a fellow traveler not to use her credit card often or volunteer too much information. There were thieves who would grab the number, then sell the information online. Before you knew what had happened, you'd have paid for a train from Moscow to St. Petersburg. She had heard of that happening even in nice hotels in the US, so she vowed to use cash whenever possible.

A sign in English informed her that she was to fill out the form on one of the many waist-high tables and proceed to a customs officer.

Sure. If I have to.

She wrote her name and address in the proper spaces, then came across the section that wanted to know, *Purpose of your visit, and where you will be staying.*

She paused, tapping the pencil against her lip. Should she tell the truth and write, *looking for my immortal soulmate and*

leaving a tour to stay wherever I can find shelter when I'm close?
Yeah, that would go over big.

Instead she wrote *tourist, staying where the tour guide booked us.* Confident that wouldn't raise suspicion, she strolled up to one of the counters and presented her form. The person who checked her form greeted her politely, then scanned it.

"What brings you to Kolkata?"

"Uh, I'm a tourist."

He offered her a patronizing expression that looked like he meant, *No shit, blondie.*

"For how long are you staying?"

By now, she must look like a deer in headlights. "It depends."

He frowned. "On what?"

Should she tell him she didn't know how long it would take to find her true love? A man she'd only seen in dreams and visions? Obviously not. While she was trying to come up with a better answer, he asked another question.

"Where are you staying?"

"Um…" Haley couldn't remember the name of the hotels on the tour, and the tour didn't start for another couple days. She tried to think fast, but a quick answer wasn't happening. Instead she stalled for time by pretending she didn't understand the gentleman's accent. "Excuse me? Can you repeat that please?"

He repeated the question with obvious annoyance.

"Oh, sorry. Yeah, the Taj Mahal. We're staying at the Taj Mahal."

His eyebrows rose. "*The* Taj Mahal?

"She nodded firmly, figuring she'd better stick to her story and make it convincing. "Yes, the Taj Mahal."

"You must be mistaken. The Taj Mahal is a mausoleum—a burial place."

"Oh!" She giggled. "I meant the Taj Mahal hotel." *There had to be one of those somewhere right?*

"The one in Agra?"

Damn, I wish I had taken a course in Indian geography.... She nodded.

"And where are you staying on your way to the Taj Mahal hotel?"

"Huh? What do you mean, 'on the way?'"

He tipped his head and studied her. "If you were planning to make it to Agra today, you would be boarding another plane, not disembarking here. It would take days by train or auto to get there from West Bengal."

"I, uh..." *Shit.* She had to come up with something plausible. "We're supposed to meet up with the tour guide outside the airport. I don't know what he has planned for us yet. I was told to look for a sign with my name on it, and that would be my guide."

Finally seeming satisfied, he nodded and stamped her passport.

Whew!

As she walked through the gate, she could feel his skeptical eyes following her.

The first thing she had to do was get horizontal and catch a long, jet-lagged nap! They probably had all kinds of local accommodations right outside the airport. Right? *Right?*

Wrong.

Heat and humidity hit her chest like a shock wave as soon as she stepped outside. She scanned signs and billboards, hoping for some kind of hint as to what she should do next—hopefully in air conditioned comfort. Nothing was in English. She might love the beauty of Indian Sanskrit, but trying to look up squiggles in a Hindi to English dictionary just wasn't gonna happen.

Oh well. There must be cab drivers who could take her to

a hotel—any hotel at this point. She might as well get used to less than three star accommodations. Somehow, she knew her dream lover wouldn't have central air in his temple and her shoulders sagged.

Jamir lay down and curled up in the grass as he always did. In his tiger form, he lazed in the sun most of the day, taking quick cat naps, but today he slept in human form while his brother stayed awake on guard duty.

Before long his eyes grew heavy and closed on their own.

Helen appeared over the ridge as she had a hundred years ago, except she was dressed in different clothing. His cock twitched as he noticed how much less clothing. Short pants revealed most of her shapely legs, and two tiny straps held up a clingy white top, leaving both arms completely exposed. Her heavy breasts were gloriously outlined under the fabric.

Her hair was different too. Short, straight, and it stopped at her jaw line.

Jamir stared as she approached him with a confident smile. Yes, those were his Helen's eyes and her smile. How had she... Never mind. He was just overjoyed she was finally here.

He rose and ran to her. She grinned and met him with open arms. Did he dare kiss her? She tipped up her chin, as if expecting it. His breath caught in his throat as he cradled her head in one hand and lowered his lips to hers.

Their long, sweet kiss turned passionate. Without even realizing how and when it happened, they were lying together in the tall grass. He flipped her onto her back and lifted his head enough to look into her eyes. She exhibited no shock or inhibition. Perhaps the Gods had left her wanting him as much as Jamir had been burning for her all these years.

He skimmed his hand up her side until he reached her breast.

She simply smiled and nodded. He was tempted to look toward the sky and cry out his joy and gratitude. But no, that would have to wait until he and his Helen had finally consummated their love. It seemed as if she wanted that as much as he.

He kneaded her breast and kissed her—long, deep, slow kisses. Before long the burning passion took over again and their hands were everywhere, groping, touching, squeezing.

He had little clothing in the way, but she had an odd metal fastener running from her waist to the apex of her thighs. He balanced on his elbow and studied that odd contraption. She seemed to understand his dilemma and reached for a hidden tab. She drew it down and pealed back the fabric.

Oh, Gods.

Seeing how it freed her hips, he pulled the fabric down with a hard tug. A quick look around showed they were completely alone. She kicked the garment over her feet and lay before him wearing only the thin top. He pushed it up and exposed one breast. He traced the perfect areola with his fingertip and she cupped the back of his head, pulling him down. His breath caught as he realized he had permission to suckle her.

He captured a nipple between his lips and sucked—gently at first, then more firmly. She writhed and moaned, but kept her hand on the back of his head, as if telling him not to stop. He didn't think he could anyway.

When at last he lifted his head and prepared to shift to the other breast, she took the opportunity to pull the string of his loin cloth and free his erect lingham. He almost growled as she grasped him with her hand and stroked.

Oh, ecstasy! The mounting sensation left him panting, heat coursing through him. He caressed her skin, sliding his hand down at the same time as he leaned over to lavish attention on the other breast.

When his fingers reached her yoni and the sweet spot adjacent to it, she arched into his hand and moaned. He wanted her so badly, he wouldn't be able to wait much longer. He tested her wetness and discovered she was as ready as he was.

As he positioned himself over her, she opened her legs in welcome. How long he had waited for this! She bent her knees and lifted her pelvis off the ground as if offering herself to him.

He had no intention of disappointing her—or himself. He sunk deeply into her slick channel. She sighed and hugged his shoulders. Wrapped in a loving embrace, he began his rhythm. She lifted her hips to meet his every thrust.

The magnificent pressure built to a fevered peak. As he reached his climax, he let out a roar. Her inner muscles clenched in spasms and she cried out simultaneously. He collapsed in a heap on the ground—only his Helen wasn't there.

"Jamir!"

His shoulder shook. He opened one eye and saw the worried expression on Shahid's face.

"Jamir, are you all right? Did you have a troubled dream?"

He sat up slowly noticing his loin cloth had never come undone. "No, brother, I had another wonderful dream. It's waking up that disappoints me."

But somehow he knew Helen was close and coming closer.

Cabbies lined up outside the airport. Unfortunately, Haley was told there were no hotels, no subways, and no busses within walking distance. *You're not in New York anymore,* she reminded herself. She hated springing for a cab all by herself —apparently they didn't believe in sharing either—but she had little choice.

Haley asked her cab driver to recommend a decent place

to stay before she passed out from jet lag. He seemed to understand and said he knew exactly where to take her. As they were driving, she stared out the window at the bleak landscape. When they began to pass signs of civilization, she became alarmed.

"Was there an earthquake here?" she asked innocently.

The cab driver tilted his head back and laughed. "No. You are American?"

"Yes." *How did he know that?*

She hadn't even discovered the sidewalks yet. Taking a better look at those, she saw crumbling materials of all different types. Some concrete, some stone blocks, and some heaving packed dirt.

She was just about to mentally pronounce the place a shithole, then it occurred to her they may have been the victim of attacks. Hadn't parts of India been bombed in recent years? Instead, she mentally pronounced herself a shithead for sounding like yet another American diva.

She remained quiet for a while as the traffic became thicker, louder and crazier by the minute. It seemed as if lanes were merely a suggestion. The number of motorcycles surprised her too. They appeared to be the preferred mode of transportation in the city. Not surprising since bikes were the only things that would fit through the tiny holes in heavy traffic. What astonished her more was the number of woman wearing saris, riding sidesaddle. *What the... How?*

A motorcycle carrying a family of five zoomed past them and took the next corner expertly. The father was driving with junior sitting between his legs. Mother was sitting behind father, holding a baby in her arms. At first Haley didn't see the toddler squished between mom and dad, but when she did, her jaw dropped. She shook her head sadly as she thought about families with minivans back home. Heck, some of them had two minivans!

Everyone was leaning on their horns—like that would make them go faster. Talk about pollution! The noise pollution was as bad as the smell of petrol.

CHAPTER 6

She checked into The Tag Bengal Hotel, a place she couldn't afford, but she realized why the cab driver thought she'd like it. The building was beautiful and catered to westerners. Everyone at the polished mahogany check-in area spoke perfect English.

The tour didn't start until tomorrow, but she *had to* sleep. Even napping on the plane hadn't been possible due to constant turbulence and ridiculously close quarters. If she relaxed and her head tipped a little to one side, she'd wind up leaning on someone's shoulder.

Her money would be tight after this, but the thought of fainting on the grimy sidewalk scared her even more, so she handed over her credit card.

She had brought only a duffle bag, easily slung over one shoulder, and a fanny pack, good for concealing what little cash she had.

The bell man stepped up to her. "Allow me to carry your bag for you."

"No, thanks. I packed light." Actually, she didn't want to tip him and lose any more cash unnecessarily.

"But it is no trouble," he insisted and grasped the strap.

Haley practically wrestled her bag away from him. "I got this!"

Finally, he stepped away with his hands raised. What did he think she was going to do? Whack him with it? Yeah, well, the thought had crossed her mind.

Hefting the bag over her shoulder, she tried to strut to the elevator just to demonstrate her strength and independence. When the elevator doors whooshed open, three men in business suits stepped out.

My God, what a teeny elevator. I'm surprised all three men fit inside.

She and her duffle bag nearly filled it.

Okay, room 223. It has to be on the second floor, right? She blew out a deep breath, partially due to physical relief when she lowered her bag to rest on the floor, but mostly because she was afraid of heights. Second floors she could handle, especially if she stayed away from the windows.

Oddly, the elevator seemed to take longer than she'd expected to ascend one floor. Struggling to extract her big bag from the small elevator, another gentleman in a suit held the door for her.

"Looks a bit heavy," he said with an English accent. "May I help you carry it to your room?"

Haley looked him up and down. He was yummy, but she was on a mission and dare not get sidetracked. "No, that's all right. As soon as I get out of the here—" Her bag popped out behind her. "I've never seen such tiny elevators."

He laughed. "You must be brand new to India. They're all this way."

"Even in the nicer hotels?"

He grinned at her. "This is nicest hotel around."

You're kidding. "Well, thank you for holding the door."

"Not a' tall." He gave her a slight bow and took her place in the elevator.

She looked for her room number, and took a right. As she wandered down the corridor she noticed a window at the end. Her room was right next to it. Just for the heck of it, she glanced out the window.

Eek. This isn't the second floor at all! She checked the room numbers again, and sure enough, they all began with 2. But the drop to the ground looked to be at least a three story leap.

With shaking fingers she tried the card key in the lock, and the door opened. *Okay...*

Thank goodness the curtains were closed. She could pretend she was only one story off the ground and pray for a safe night without the building catching fire.

She kicked the door behind her, dropped the duffle bag and went straight to the phone book. Flipping through it, she looked for youth hostels. She knew those would be much cheaper.

She made the mistake of sitting on the bed with the phone book before locking the door. One glance at her phone and she knew the battery was dead. *Damn.* She sagged against pillows and slumped to one side in exhausted oblivion. Her eyes closed as the door opened.

Something caused Haley to stir. Her face prickled as if someone was watching her. Opening one eye against the desperate need to sleep, she took a moment to react. When she realized she wasn't dreaming and the man who stood at the foot of the bed with a screwdriver in his hand was real...

"Aaaaahhh!"

She bolted upright.

He jumped about a foot in the air and landed with his butt against the small desk.

"Wha—what are you doing here?"

"I fix the telephone. It was reported broken."

"Oh." *Terrific. I can't even call security until the intruder fixes the damn phone.*

She stood and demanded her rubbery legs take her to the chair tucked into the corner. "Go ahead, but make it fast. I really need to get some sleep."

He nodded and picked up the receiver. Apparently he affirmed it was out of order, because he hung up, dropped to his knees and followed the cord.

"Ah," he said. "I see the problem." He poked his hand behind the mini fridge, and suddenly the lights went out.

Oh no! Haley scrambled as far back in the chair as physics would allow. *Did he decide to make the room dark before he kills me?*

The man glanced over his shoulder at her and frowned.

Oh, no. This is it. Goodbye cruel world. My only regret is never having found the man in my visions...even though the whole thing was unlikely.

He stood and strolled to the curtains. "Power surges are common here." With one hand he drew back half of the curtains, letting natural light filter into the room. Haley stayed glued to the back of her chair. It was bad enough to be trapped in her room with a strange man, but now she could see out the window and had to fight the urge to look down. She shifted her gaze to the door.

He returned to his work. As he fiddled with something behind the fridge, the lights came back on.

Maybe he unplugged the lights instead of the phone and was too embarrassed to admit it.

Soon he was on his feet, lifting the telephone's receiver. "Ah, it works now."

"That's nice. Would you mind shutting the curtains before you leave?"

The light began to flicker and she held up a hand. "Never mind. I'll do it later."

"Are you sure? I—" He did that bobble-head thing.

"I'm sure."

"Okay. I go now."

"Bye."

As soon as he exited the room and closed the door behind him, Haley bounded out of the chair, hurried to the door and hung out the *Do not disturb* sign. Then she checked the lock just to be sure it was working and slid the chain across.

Haley's dream man came to her as if their being together was the most natural thing in the world. The vision was so realistic that her body reacted to the impossible, as if the encounter were actually taking place. She was in that strange state between wakefulness and sleep—still aware of who and where she was, but accepting the disjointed thoughts that drifted through her mind.

"Helen," he murmured as he strode to her and hesitated. "I've waited so long for you to return."

In the far recesses of her mind, Haley knew her own name, but his calling her Helen seemed oddly right. For some reason she didn't correct him.

He smiled, but didn't say anything more. Why did he seem suddenly shy?

"I know you," Haley answered. "But how?"

The man held out his hand to her. "Come with me. I will show you."

Haley slipped her hand in his, and warmth filled her. She sensed her previous knowledge of him was genuine. Yet, she had never heard his voice before. The rumbling baritone affected her deeply. She loved his sexy voice almost as much as his sexy body.

He wasn't terribly tall—maybe five feet ten, but plenty taller than her five-four. His broad shoulders and body seemed filled with quiet strength. His smooth coffee-colored skin shone in the sun.

He led her toward a stand of brush. As they cleared the thicket, the most incredible scene met her view. A low, reddish colored temple nestled in a hollow kept the domed roof level with the surrounding ground. I know this place, Haley thought.

"Come and meet my brother. You are as safe with him as you are with me, and I'd gladly protect you with my life."

That seemed like an odd thing to say. "Why?" she asked.

"Because I love you."

Without thinking twice, she stepped into his arms and raised her face. He interpreted her intent and lowered his lips to hers. The kiss they shared was the most magical moment of her life thus far. Love burst in her heart.

As he let their lips part, she sighed. He rested his forehead against hers and smiled. Those deep brown eyes shown with a devotion she knew she could trust.

"Feel my heart." He took her hand and held it against his chest. A slow, steady beat thrilled her fingers. "I want to make love to you, Helen."

She should tell him her name was Haley, dammit. She needed to be honest—even if this was a case of mistaken identity. Helen was one lucky woman. "My name is Haley."

He nodded in easy acceptance.

"Why don't you make love to me if you want to?"

"You never permitted it before."

"Before?"

She sensed her experiences and his words were out of sync, but she didn't want to question that now.

He stroked her hair, leaned in and whispered "You and I have been together before. Many times. I have missed you so much."

She had often sensed something was missing in her life, but she couldn't identify it. Perhaps this man was the answer. She had never felt so peaceful. She wanted to curl up next to him and—

A knock disturbed her. Where was it coming from? She slowly opened her eyes and realized the joy she had just experienced had been a dream. Profound sadness overcame her as she trudged to the door of her hotel room.

She opened the door to reveal a short Indian man, smiling. "It is past checkout time. So you will be staying another night?

Another night? "What time is it?"

He glanced at her strangely. "It is two p.m."

"Two in the afternoon?" *Shit. The tour bus was supposed to leave at eleven a.m.*

Suddenly her stomach rumbled. When had she last eaten? She arrived at the hotel at about dinner time and needed to sleep more than eat. "Are you saying it's May 20th and I slept all night and half the next day?"

"Yes it is May 20th. I don't know if you slept through May 19th. Either way, the front desk needs to see you."

That was it. She had to get out of there. She spun toward the room and located the duffle bag she'd never unpacked. "I'd rather not stay another night."

"Because you insisted on paying cash, the front desk is waiting for you. So you will need to stop there whether you're staying or not."

"In that case, not."

Haley grabbed her duffle bag and fanny pack and rushed out of the room. She didn't care what she looked like. Vanity wasn't worth another seven thousand rupees, even if that only amounted to about one hundred and fifty dollars. She needed what little cash she had left and whatever was in her debit card account.

As soon as the elevator door opened, she ran from it and

bypassed the front desk. A couple of men looked up, but no one tried to stop her.

Whew! Made it.

Unfortunately, without the help of the front desk, she didn't know where or how she'd catch up with the tour.

"Shahid, I'm going to take a good look around the perimeter."

Jamir's brother flicked one of his orange ears and snorted. *"You mean you're going to look for Helen--again."*

"What if I am? She's near. I can sense it."

"It's wishful thinking, brother. I have seen you go through this many times."

Jamir ignored his brother's truthful remark and lumbered to the farthest point along the ridge where he could still see the temple. The tea plantation below was devoid of workers, so he didn't have to worry about scaring anyone and triggering a tiger hunt. Had anyone been there, he'd have hunkered down and scanned the people for a light skinned woman. He didn't know how she'd be dressed. Some of the men's clothing choices had changed over the centuries. Perhaps western women were no longer wearing long, white dresses.

Jamir turned around a few times, intending to lie in the wheat-like dried grass. On his last revolution, he spied movement in the bush beyond. He ducked and watched, shielded from view.

Another majestic orange and white striped animal strolled into his territory. Jamir had to quickly assess the threat—another tiger or another *shapeshifting* tiger? They knew of no other shapeshifters in their area. Movement and a human scent from behind distracted him from his original foe.

Gods. Had hunters followed a lone tiger to the temple's sacred area? If so, he had to get back to Shahid without being spotted. Their only mission for eternity was to protect the temple and the mysterious gift enshrined there.

The human scent wafted his way again and seemed familiar.

Gods, could it be? He glanced toward the other tiger and back to the blonde hair cresting over the ridge.

Should he change back to human so he wouldn't scare her? Or would a hungry tiger decide to attack them both. Jamir pondered for what seemed like minutes. In truth it took mere seconds. The other tiger was apt to attack her, if he didn't intervene immediately. He bounded toward the interloper, growling. When the tiger didn't retreat, he pounced on it. The two giant animals growled, rolled, bit and clawed. Even in the midst of the fracas, Jamir was acutely aware of his Helen. She exuded fear, but he didn't hear her scream or run. Perhaps she had simply fainted like she did a hundred years ago.

He had to drive off this wild animal. It was apparent that he was dealing with a non-shifter. The tiger tore at the flesh on his arm. Jamir, roared, bit the animal's leg hard, then fought as if Helen's life depended upon it. It very likely could.

At last the other tiger broke free and limped off in the direction from which he had come. Jamir waited on high alert until he disappeared from sight.

He whirled around and searched the landscape for Helen. He couldn't see her and assumed she'd crumpled to the ground in an unconscious heap. He had to shift before she came to.

Concentrating on his human form, his powerful body shrank. He rose on steady feet and gazed in Helen's direction again. She wasn't unconscious. She was hunkered down in the grass, her blue eyes huge and round.

"Helen..." he said. He didn't know how she would react to what she'd witnessed. He had never confessed his secret to her in the long ago past. Plus he was butt naked.

She rose and stood quite still. At last she cocked her head and said, "The name's Haley, and you're my immortal I presume?"

CHAPTER 7

The gorgeous man from her vision bounded toward the temple, yelling "Shahid!"

Haley placed a hand on her hip. "Okay, that's weird."

She had traveled all over West Bengal to locate the man in her visions and now he was running away? *What the heck?*

Haley marched in the direction to which he'd fled. "Damned if I'm going to come all this way just to find a handsome man with commitment issues. I could have had dozens of those at home."

She heard his voice in the distance. "Shahid, she's here. Helen is here! Hurry!"

Hurry? What do they have to do? Put away the Playboy magazines and throw out the beer cans? And why is he still calling me Helen?

Soon two men, her commitment-phobic immortal and a handsome nearly nude stranger, appeared. And now they were both wearing loin cloths. *Damn. Why'd he have to get dressed?*

"Helen...Forgive me, I mean Haley, I'd like you to meet my brother Shahid."

She was actually meeting both of them, but perhaps her immortal felt as if they'd already met.

She extended her hand to the one called Shahid and said, "Nice to meet you. And you…" she said, focusing on Jamir, "What's your name?"

"Oh." He slapped his forehead. "Of course, you must not remember. I am Jamir."

He stepped close to her. Too close…not that she felt uncomfortable with a man's nearness. She hadn't bathed for days and must smell ripe. She'd love nothing more than to dive into his arms and kiss him senseless, but first impressions were important.

She backed up a step. "Uh, do you happen to have a shower or tub? I need a bath, baaaad."

His face fell as if he was disappointed. Was he so used to life in the wild he didn't notice her earthy odor? *You'll thank me later, Jamir, believe me.*

"Yes, I will take you. There's one safe place, and you'd be best to stay near the riverbank."

"Safe? What do you mean, 'safe'?"

"Where snakes and crocodiles almost never go."

Haley's jaw dropped. "Almost?"

"If you are not too modest," he added, quickly, "I can watch the river, so you can submerge yourself in the pool and bathe completely."

She nodded, still stunned. "That's very kind of you. And no, I'm not too modest. I'd bathe in front of the president right about now."

"This president of whom you speak would be a lucky man." He grinned and extended his hand.

Haley was sure he'd enjoy the show, but she smelled herself and didn't care if he did. "Let's go. I don't suppose there's a waterfall nearby. I'd kill for a shower."

"Waterfall? When the monsoons arrive water will fall for a moon cycle or more."

Haley sighed. "Okay, the pool it is." She placed her hand in his. He gave it a slight squeeze and led her beyond the temple. As they passed it, she said, "What a beautiful place. This isn't a mausoleum, is it?"

His eyes widened. "A mausoleum? No. It's a place of worship. Vishnu ordered it to be built centuries ago and asked us to guard it for all time."

"You and your brother...or are there more?"

"Only the two of us. We can protect it well, because..."

When he hesitated, Haley helped him out. "Because you're big-ass, scary tigers?"

He stopped walking, abruptly. "You know?"

"I saw you shift. My dreams finally made sense. Sometimes I saw a man and other times, a tiger or two."

His posture relaxed. "My brother and I have two forms. We were originally mortal men, but Vishnu gave us the ability to shift into tigers and instructed us to protect the temple at all costs."

"Including eating an intruder?"

He chuckled. "Only if we can't scare them off."

"So that other tiger I saw...he was a gatecrasher you scared away?"

Jamir hesitated, then nodded. "Yes. They rarely visit, and even when they do we usually ignore them. I had to drive off the hungry male in order to protect you."

"You knew I was there?"

"Yes, I smelled you."

"Oh." *Too late to pretend I don't stink to high heaven.*

When they arrived at the river, Haley surprised Jamir by

stripping down to tiny panties and a thin bra. Her nearly naked body took his breath away. He hadn't thought her skin could get any lighter until she exposed her upper legs and stomach. His Helen from a hundred years ago hadn't shown much more than a wrist. But then again, Helen bathed at the tea plantation.

Jamir picked up the long branch he used to check for snakes and raked the water with it.

"What are you doing?" Haley asked.

"Making sure you are alone in the pool." He gave her what he hoped was a reassuring smile. If he wasn't mistaken, her skin grew even paler.

She straightened her posture and lifted her chin, probably in an attempt to look brave.

"There. No snakes. No crocodiles. I will wait a little further up river to be sure nothing passes by."

"Thanks. I don't suppose you have any shampoo back at the temple."

"Shampoo? What is shampoo?"

Haley sighed. "Didn't think so. Never mind, I'll use soap."

She rummaged through her backpack until she withdrew a transparent case. From that she took a green bar with white striations. Holding it up, she smiled and said, "Irish Spring." The strong verdant scent surprised his sensitive nostrils.

She tested the water with her toes and must have decided it was all right. She plunged in and stood still. "Ahhhh…" The pool came up to her waist. After taking a quick peek all around her, she splashed water under her arm pits.

He hated to scare her any more than necessary, but he had to warn her. "It is better if you stay as quiet and still as possible. Noise can scare off some predators, but attract others."

She froze. "Fuck."

"It is all right. There are no dangers now. I will continue to keep watch."

Even though he meant to watch the river for movement every second, he had a hard time tearing his gaze away from her.

She was different from his Helen. Not as petite, but not large, either. She seemed healthier, less delicate. Gods, she hadn't even fainted when she discovered tigers nearby, and seemed to take it in stride when he turned human before her eyes. Helen would have keeled over had she witnessed that.

Haley ducked her head under the water and scrubbed her scalp. Then she burst through the surface and slicked back her hair.

She was beautiful—and real. At last! Jamir's cock twitched. *Is it too soon to have these feelings for Haley?*

She grinned at him. "I just remembered something."

Hopeful that she had some memory of him or her life as Helen Hastings, he leaned forward. "What did you remember?"

"Well, it's more like something I forgot. I forgot a towel." She stood in the thigh-deep water with rivulets of water running down her slick, goose-bumpy skin. Her peaked nipples were quite visible under the wet scrap of fabric she wore over her breasts.

His mouth dried, and he had a hard time forming coherent words. "We usually lay in the sun to dry."

She shrugged one shoulder, "I guess that'll do." Without waiting for him to turn around, she strolled to the low river-bank and hiked herself up onto the grass. Did she know her brown curls were noticeable beneath the lower piece of fabric?

Haley scooted a few feet into the grass and lay on her back. Propping her head on her clasped hands, she glanced at Jamir. "You look like you've never seen a woman before."

"I—I've never seen so *much* of a women before." His cock hardened.

She levered herself to a sitting position. "You mean you're a virgin?"

"I...uh. We do not discuss such things."

"Oh. That's right. You're culture is fairly modest." She reached for her backpack. "Well, I suppose I should put some clothes on."

"No!" He coughed to cover his enthusiasm. "I mean, you'll get your clothing wet. It's all right to dry like that. I—I don't mind."

She smirked. "I didn't think you would."

He stared at her dark areolas under her thin top. His temperature rose. Then his eyes wandered again to the light brown thatch beneath her thighs.

"Like what you see?"

He could no longer contain himself. The animal inside him demanded he mate, and he pounced on her, kissing her senseless. She responded with as much excitement as he felt.

Haley reached under his loin cloth and grasped his erect cock. She squeezed and stroked it, as her other hand found and manipulated his balls.

Filled with lust, Jamir growled.

Suddenly she let go and her eyes rounded. "You don't turn back into a tiger when aroused, do you?"

He rasped the word, "No."

"In that case, I'm getting rid of the bra and panties." She removed her panties and popped open her bra.

Jamir yanked the bra off her shoulders and flung it, heedless of where it landed. He drank in the sight of her nude body, still glistening from her bath.

"You are so beautiful."

"So are you." Haley cupped the back of his head and drew him down to share another long, passionate kiss which involved their tongues mating. Her mouth tasted savory and spicy.

When he came up for air, Jamir said, "I need to be inside you."

Haley parted her legs and he scrambled between them.

"Not much for foreplay, are you?"

Jamir panted. "Not right now. We can play later."

"I didn't mean literally, 'play.' I simply meant kissing, touching and cuddling. You know, making out for a while first."

"Soon I will not feel so desperate and we will take our time."

Haley smiled. "Well, then. Do what you gotta do."

Jamir positioned his cock at her entrance and plunged home. For home is exactly where he felt himself to be.

Haley arched and moaned.

"Did I hurt you?"

"Oh, no. Feels good. Go ahead. Let's fuck."

That was an English word Jamir knew—some slang picked up by the locals. And thank goodness he knew what it meant. He thanked the Gods for her easy consent and thrust, withdrawing almost all the way and driving into her core again.

She moaned, but he understood it to be a favorable sound this time. Her breaths grew shallower and more frequent the more he fucked her.

"You…"

He ground into her pubis and she abandoned speech in favor of a groan.

"Me?" He prompted as he rose up on one elbow and slipped a finger between them to stroke her clit.

She arched and gasped. She seemed to have forgotten what she wanted to say in favor of surrendering herself completely, luxuriating in the moment.

At last she bucked and cried out—her inner muscles spasmed, squeezing his cock. Her climax continued along with her squeals until her thighs vibrated against his sides. At last, she seemed to melt and her noise died down to a pant.

He knew she didn't want it to be over quickly, so he held back his own climax. Withdrawing his finger, he continued fucking. Pleasurable sensations built steadily until he sensed himself at a breaking point. Haley met his thrusts whole-heartedly. He tried to sense what she was feeling. He wanted her to enjoy the experience too. She seemed to be fully engaged in the activity, letting out little moans of pleasure again.

Finally, he let himself plummet over the edge into a blissful state he'd never reached before. He jerked with powerful sensations and rode them to the last aftershock.

His elbows weakened and he rolled off her, then pulled her to his side.

This was it. He had to find a way to keep Haley with him forever. He knew he should be willing to go with the flow. Let her stay or leave as she saw fit, but how could he? They had waited so long to be together again.

Would she be willing to live off the land and eat raw meat? Could he allow her into the temple when the monsoons came? Vishnu had specifically told them not to allow anyone inside the temple. He assumed this was even more important now with the sacred object that fell from the sky housed inside.

Why hadn't he thought this out before?

Gods! Now that I have her, I don't know what to do with her.

A few minutes later, Haley's stomach growled. She clapped her hand over it and chuckled. "Man, I'm starving and I'm down to my last granola bar from home. Is there a restaurant around here?" She quickly added, "You know, the kind that caters to sensitive American tummies?"

Jamir pulled back far enough to study her face. "If you need food, I can provide for you. It's time I hunted anyway."

A slow horrifying realization made Haley's stomach roil. "Hunt. You mean like, you want me to ear raw gazelle meat?"

He laughed. "Of course not."

"Whew!"

"We have no gazelles here."

Oh boy. I so didn't expect this. She needed to make sure she didn't offend his macho pride, but really? Raw meat?

"Look, I appreciate your wanting to be a good provider and all that, but I'm kind of off raw meat. I—I need more veggies and fruits and stuff. Is there a place where I can buy groceries?"

"Groceries?"

"Yeah, you know…bottled water, food and supplies to cook with. I passed through a village on my way here. Maybe I could go back there and they'd know what I mean."

"Ah, the village. I doubt anyone there would know what you mean, since no one would speak your language."

"Someone did. How do you think I found you after my phone's battery ran out?"

"The Gods did not guide you back to me?"

"Gods? Maybe. It was some little old man in a white robe. I know some people think God looks like that, but…no, he didn't glow or anything. I don't think he was that special. He seemed to think I was crazy for wanting to find the temple with the live tigers. No, if God had wanted me to find you, he'd have sent me a friggin' map."

Jamir scrubbed a hand over his face. "You say a lot of things I don't understand."

A growl rumbled from the bushes.

Haley couldn't find her feet. She scrambled on her hands and knees and hid behind Jamir.

"Relax. It is only Shahid."

She stared at him in wonder. "You can recognize his growl? Are you telling me one tiger's growl is different from another?"

"Most definitely. Besides, I can smell him." He grinned.

"Oh. I hadn't noticed."

"Shahid. Come."

Shahid, in tiger form, strolled lazily around the clump of bushes. Haley grasped Jamir's arm and held her breath. It wasn't that she didn't believe Jamir...it's only that she hadn't been face to fang with a giant Bengal tiger before.

"You are safe, Haley. Shahid would never hurt you."

"Uh, okay. That's good to know. You can understand, I hope, that without a good sized fence between us, I might be a little nervous."

"All is well, Haley. Shahid simply offered to hunt, taking my turn so we can spend more time together. I will need to stay by the temple should trouble arise."

"Trouble? What kind of trouble? I think the uprising against the British ended a long time ago."

Jamir's lips turned down. The opposite of what she expected. She had hoped that by making a joke, she'd lighten the mood a bit.

Shahid bounded off in the opposite direction. Jamir rose and held out his hand. "Come. We must wait at the temple until he returns."

"Okay. I guess we can split that last granola bar until he gets back. Then, I don't care how far away it is, I'm going to find a grocery store."

CHAPTER 8

A few minutes later, Shahid loped back to the temple with two dead rabbits dangling from his powerful teeth. He dropped them, shifted, and said, "I'm sorry I didn't see anything else nearby. I can go back—"

Haley jumped to her feet. "No! I mean, don't go back on my account. I'll be getting my own food, but thanks." She averted her eyes from Shahid's nakedness.

Shahid glanced between Jamir and Haley, waiting.

"She is not much of a meat eater. I told her I would take her to the village after you returned."

His brother shook his head and picked up the rabbits. "Fine. More for me." He grabbed the knife they kept hidden beneath the first temple step and sliced through the skin of each at the midsection. Then he pealed back both ends to expose the meat in the middle.

Haley turned her head and gagged.

Jamir hoped she'd get over that. They all had to eat and tigers didn't live on fruits and vegetables.

"Look, guys. I'm sorry. I know you're carnivores. You eat meat every day, and I don't want to change you, but maybe you could try what I make after I get some—um, *other* food."

Her expression brightened. "I'm a pretty good cook. I bet you'll like it."

Shahid snorted. "I doubt it."

Jamir rose and took her hand, helping her to her feet. "I will give it a try." Glancing at his brother, he added, "You never know unless you try."

Shahid simply sank his teeth into his lunch, tore off a piece of raw meat and chewed his rabbit with gusto.

Haley's color drained. "Come, sweetheart. We will go to the village now." Jamir strode off and she hurried after him.

Haley seemed more relaxed as they walked hand in hand toward the village. Jamir was worried about her reaction to Shahid in tiger form. Both of them would have to shift occasionally.

He didn't relish the idea of her witnessing the two of them frightening off an intruder of the human variety. Shahid was often tempted to forgo the hunt whenever that happened and say that dinner had come to them. But they both knew men would be missed and others would come to find whomever they ate.

The idea of going to a marketplace where a variety of food could be procured easily, keeping their bellies full without killing appealed to Jamir, but he should be the one providing for her. Not that he had any rupees like she did. Perhaps he could trade with the villagers. Now all he had to do was think of something to trade.

Frustration replaced his pensive mood when he realized he had nothing the villagers would want except the meat he and Shahid hunted for themselves. Would Shahid agree to give part of it away?

If he couldn't provide for his woman, would she leave him? Jamir knew he couldn't survive that loss again.

"Haley, I need to speak with my brother. If I take you to

the village and let you shop, then return later to walk you home, will that be all right?"

Her eyebrows rose. "Home?" She worried her bottom lip a little then said, "Yeah, about that...we need to talk at some point. But sure, I can wait until after you come back."

Apprehension invaded Jamir's gut. What did she need to talk about? The word 'home' had triggered some anxiety in her expression.

He squatted and sat in the grass by the side of the dirt road. "We can talk now."

She batted her lashes in surprise, but settled on the ground next to him.

"Okay...I guess this is as good a time as any," she began. "Home—*my* home, is New York."

"New York? Is that near New Delhi?"

"No. It's far away. So far away you can't walk to it or even ride to it. You've seen airplanes in the sky, right?"

"Yes. We did not know what they were called, but airplanes seems as a good word as any."

"Well, you have to get on one of those and stay on it for about a day and a half as it flies across the sky."

He tilted his head. "Why are you telling me this? You are not going back to your home, *are* you?" Deep inside, he vibrated with fear. He'd just found her. How could she leave him? What had he done wrong?

She plucked a few blades of grass as she spoke. "I'm not leaving right away. But I can't stay. I had hoped that as soon as I found you, we'd buy you some clothes and go back to New York, for good."

He reared back and stared at her open-mouthed. "You want me to leave here? I cannot! Shahid and I have a sacred duty to protect the temple at all times. I cannot leave Shahid alone or he would die. One of us must hunt to live. The other must guard the temple."

She held up one hand. "I get that. Really, I do. But if you can't leave here and I can't stay here, Houston, we have a conundrum."

"A what? Who is Houston? One of your Gods?"

"Oh, hell no."

"You speak irreverently, Haley."

"Yeah, my manners suck."

He took a deep breath and asked what he didn't want to know. "Why can you not stay?"

"And live how? Sleeping in the grass? Eating it when I run out of rupees?"

"I will provide for you. A man always provides for his family."

She cleared her throat. "Uh, I think we're getting ahead of ourselves."

Oh no. This is a disaster. Can't she see and accept that she is meant to be my soul mate throughout time?

Jamir's heart ached. He wanted to gather her in his arms and explain. Tell her about all the years of waiting and yearning—and then never let her go. But how could he force her to stay?

He bent his head and stared at the grass.

Haley watched his face fall and saw a blade of grass beneath him bend with a tear. *Oh, shit! I made a big, freakin' Tiger-man cry.*

She stroked his back in gentle circles. "I'm sorry. I didn't mean to upset you. I just think we should be honest with each other. I like you. I really do. You seem like a nice guy. Sweet. Handsome. Great in b—well, grass…"

He stared up into her eyes and she saw the misery there—even felt it.

Holy crap. What have I done? I should have stayed in New York.

At last he moved so that he faced her and took both of her

hands in his. He rubbed her palms with his thumbs. He didn't say a word. He didn't have to. His touch felt so good. So right. Being with him felt right. Maybe she was over-thinking things?

She almost burst out in a snort. *Yeah, Haley Hunnicutt over thinking something? Like a friggin' trip to India without knowing the language, the area, or how I was going to convince my immortal to come home with me... I should have known he'd have some kind of divine duty or an important job, other than just waiting for me to show up.*

She wanted to kick herself. "Please don't worry. We'll figure something out."

He glanced up at her as if he totally didn't believe her.

"I—I don't have to leave soon or anything. I took the whole summer off and I've only been gone two weeks. We could spend more time together. Get to know each other..."

"Then it will hurt even more when you go."

Fuck. I can't win.

She rose. "You know what? I'm getting really hungry. I should continue on to the village and get what I need. You don't have to come back for me. I'll be fine." She gave him what she hoped was a confident smile. "I found you once. I'll find you again."

He blew out a deep breath and rose to his feet. Looking deep into her eyes he said, "I hope so."

Judging from the intense look, the phrase was loaded with more meaning. She stepped into his space and kissed him gently. He kissed her back. Before she realized it, he had engulfed her in his arms and crushed her to his chest. His possessive kiss grew hot and passionate. He opened his mouth and she parted hers. He swept her tongue and wrapped his around it. Swirling. Tasting. *Claiming.*

Haley's head clouded. All that existed in that moment was Jamir and his intoxicating kiss. She could become addicted to kisses like that. The man showed his tiger soul whenever he was sexually aroused. His arm slid down and squeezed her buttocks. It hurt a little—just enough to say he was angry with her, but not enough to think he would really hurt her or wouldn't forgive her.

Jamir let her go abruptly. He stepped away from her and his chest heaved with heavy breaths while he clenched and unclenched his fists.

At last he spoke in such a low, calm voice it scared her. "You should go."

Confused, she started to move, then stopped. "Do you want me to come back?"

He stalked off without answering.

Shahid tried to comfort his little brother, but he knew this would happen. Perhaps the best thing he could do was refrain from saying, "I told you so," and simply listen.

"How can I make her understand she belongs with me?" Jamir whined. "She knows nothing of her former life...of our connection. She doesn't even believe the Gods brought her back." Jamir paced in front of the temple steps like a captive tiger.

"Perhaps she will in time. You should try to be patient, brother."

Jamir halted, dragged in a deep breath and let it out on a sigh. "I hope you are right. A moment later he said, "Perhaps I should go after her. I was upset when I left."

"Where is the patience I recommended?"

"In someone else's loin cloth." Jamir smirked.

Shahid stifled a chuckle. "Give her some time and space to think. She cannot realize how much she will miss you, if you are always together."

Jamir frowned. "I know you are right, but what if something has happened to her?"

"She was on her own for many days without anything happening, and you didn't even know she was in India."

"But, I did."

Shahid scrutinized his brother. "How did you know?"

"I saw her—in visions."

His mouth opened, but at first he had no words. "Visions? I thought you merely spoke of dreaming about her. You never told me you had waking visions."

"Yes, I know. I believed you would not understand—that you would say it was my wishful thinking."

"That does sounds like something I would say but as a kindness—to prevent getting your hopes up, only to have them dashed."

"Perhaps you should not be so kind. As you now know, these visions were not wishful thinking. They were real, and she saw me too."

That news surprised him. "Yet still she questions your connection?"

"Yes." Jamir's misery showed plainly on his face and in his bent posture.

A rustling in the bushes interrupted their conversation and startled them both into alertness. The wind was blowing in the wrong direction to identify the threat.

Haley emerged with a large sack slung over one shoulder. She smiled when she saw them, blissfully unaware how close she had come to staring at their tiger forms. "I should have brought my backpack," she said. "They don't have grocery bags."

Well, it wasn't a declaration of love and undying devotion, but his brother had never looked happier or more relieved. He dashed down the slight incline to meet her.

"I am sorry I became so upset and left you, Haley. Can you forgive me?"

Shahid rolled his eyes. *He is chasing her like a cub, but if I tell him to act like a man, it will not make a bit of difference.*

She placed the bundle on the ground and slipped her arms around his back. "I'm the one who should apologize. I didn't mean to hurt you…especially since we just found each other."

He pulled her tight to his chest and nuzzled her neck.

Shahid was glad to see them making up, but how long would it last? Their lives had been so uncomplicated up until now. Hunt. Eat. Protect. That was just about the extent of it. Shahid was satisfied with the knowledge that he was a servant of the God Vishnu. But that had never been enough for Jamir. *Would he leave me here alone if this woman demands it?*

No. That was a ridiculous thought. He would have to leave the temple unguarded or let Shahid starve until some animal wandered into his camp. Jamir would never let that happen. *Would he?*

CHAPTER 9

Jamir held Haley's hand as they strolled beside the river. Neither of them spoke again about leaving or staying. He had watched her prepare a meal and had eaten something sweet with a grainy texture. He wasn't sure what he thought of it. It reminded him of the foods he had eaten as a mortal man. A lot of trouble, but worth it on occasion.

She seemed pleased with herself, and he was glad. Her happiness here meant she might be persuaded to stay. And that, to him, meant everything.

"I was lucky to find a pan, some bottled water, and some matches. I don't know how I would have cooked the rice otherwise. It was good with spices and honey in it, right?"

"Yes, it was very good."

"I'm not sure how long the fruit and vegetables will keep. I might have to go to the village every other day."

"What if you grow some of the things you need?"

She tipped her head. "That's not a bad idea. I'll look for some seeds when I'm there next time. Or maybe I can plant the pepper and tomato seeds that I was going to throw away."

His relief at hearing this made his heart swell. She was planning to be here long enough to grow crops. "I will help you plant your garden, drag water up from the river, protect your plot from the weather and pests…you will be well taken care of, Haley."

She smiled at him. "I believe you."

"Haley," he said, and stopped walking.

She halted beside him. "Yes?"

He pulled her into his embrace and kissed her soundly. He hoped to convey how much he loved her without scaring her off. The depth of his emotions were such that he imagined the intensity might frighten her. All he could do was show her how much she meant to him and hope he could keep his tiger's hunger for her under control.

In truth all he wanted to do was push her to the ground, rip off her clothing and plunge his cock into her core. At least he knew enough not to do that—yet. He hoped someday she'd be open to letting his animal nature come out and play anytime he wanted her body.

He continued to kiss her and she wrapped her arms around him tighter. He wanted to roar with the power of his sexual need. Instead, he purposely gentled his touch and ran his hand down her torso and then up her thigh. He cupped her bottom and yanked her up against his erection.

"Wow. You're hard as a spike," she teased.

"I hope you can help me with that problem."

Haley grinned and dropped to her knees. The tie of his loin cloth came undone with one tug and fell onto the ground. She gazed at his jutting erection and licked her lips.

She grasped and stroked his shaft from balls to tip. The electric jolt of pleasure surprised him with its intensity. He tossed back his head and moaned.

Haley held the base and swirled her tongue around the head several times. Finally, she took his length into her mouth and applied suction as she withdrew. He could barely breathe. She lowered her lips down over the base again and sucked harder while he pulled back and plunged in.

She grabbed his glutes and held on as he fucked her mouth.

He sucked in air through his teeth and expelled it the same way, creating a hiss.

Haley let his cock pop out of her mouth and frantically glanced around the area.

"What's wrong, my love?"

"Are you sure we're safe here? We won't be interrupted by snakes or other predators?"

"As safe as we can be. I can smell any threats from behind us with the wind blowing our way, and as I said before, there are rarely predators in this part of the river. I will keep my eyes open to be sure."

Haley took one more look around. "Okay. You're positive you can smell something even if you get distracted?"

He gave her a sly smile. "Why don't you distract me and we'll see?"

"Yeah, yeah. I can take a hint." She smiled up at him though and resumed what she had been doing.

Thank the Gods.

The pleasure built again and before he knew it, he had to stop before he spilled his seed down her throat. He withdrew sharply and dropped to his knees in front of her.

"Thank you," he said, breathlessly, then he angled his head and kissed her hard. She met his fervent kiss and returned it. Without stopping, he laid her down in the grass. His hand wandered over her soft skin as if it had a mind of its own.

Eventually, he pulled away and slid down her body, kissing and nipping along her ribs. She giggled as he swirled his tongue in her navel, and then kissed his way down to her mound. He tapped her legs apart and kneeled between them.

He licked her slit, and she jumped when his tongue touched her clit.

He grinned. "You are sensitive."

"Hell, yeah. You turn me into one big nerve ending."

"I think that is good." He resumed making love to her labia and thighs, occasionally nipping her skin. When she began to wriggle, he knew what she wanted. He'd make her ask for it...beg for it.

"Jamir, please..."

"Please what?"

"You know..."

"I may not. Tell me."

Instead of answering him, she grabbed his head and stuck his nose right at her clit.

Well, I guess I didn't specify "in words." Jamir chuckled to himself.

So as not to encourage rudeness, he ignored her non-verbal demand and said, "Tell me what you want."

"A little cunnalingus please."

"Ah, see? Now there can be no misunderstanding. "

"There was no misunderstanding before. You just wanted to drive me crazy and make me beg.

He winked. "Perhaps." He licked slowly at first, like a tiger licking his fur. She let out a low moan. As he increased his speed, she moaned louder and writhed. At last he flicked the little bud as fast as he could and she grabbed onto the grass and cried out her release. He didn't stop, or even slow down, and she rode the orgasm, yelping until she was hoarse.

Jamir backed away, then stalked around her, like the predator he was. Haley noticed his animal nature far more during sexual encounters. They'd only had two, but each time she had seen his eyes glint and an arrogant smile curve his lips.

"Roll onto your hands and knees," he rumbled.

Haley complied immediately.

He tapped her inner thighs and she spread her knees further apart. She felt him right behind her, stroking her buttocks. He tested her wetness, then eased his cock into her sheath.

"Ohhh…" she moaned. "Feels so good."

He didn't say anything. Instead, he started his rhythm. *Mmm…action is a better way to communicate anyway.*

She matched his rocking motion and he thrust deeper. They mated for several minutes. He would occasionally touch her clit, bring her close and then back off. Haley growled. She wanted to hit him. If he didn't have the ability to turn into a big-ass angry tiger, she might have. Finally, she begged.

"Finger my clit, Jamir. Please. I need to come."

He chuckled. "Since you asked so clearly and nicely, I'll do as you bid."

He rubbed her button until she was quivering. The pleasure spiraled up to a desperate need for release. At last she crashed over the edge and screamed out her climax as she shook.

His motions behind her became jerky and he grunted. When she had finally come back to earth, he pulled out, collapsed beside her and pulled her down onto his chest.

"You're wonderful, Haley."

"You're pretty amazing too."

He cupped her head in a gentle, yet possessive gesture. "Mine," he mumbled. Seconds later, she recognized the long, slow breaths of peaceful sleep.

Crap. When the time comes to leave, will he let me?

"Jamir?"

Haley must have awakened in the darkness. He left his station in front of the temple and bounded over to her.

"Jesus!" she shrieked and crab-walked away as quickly as she could.

He shifted and rose on his two human feet. "I am here. You are safe."

Haley gripped her chest and took in several gasping breaths before she spoke. "Would you mind switching to your human form *before* you charge at me?"

"You sounded worried."

"Yeah, and your quick response had me just plain terrified."

He dropped down next to her. "I am sorry if I frightened you. I hope someday you will be as comfortable with my Tiger form as my human one."

Haley snorted. "Yeah, that'll happen."

He cocked his head and wondered why her words didn't seem to agree with her facial expression.

Her breathing slowed to a more normal pace. "Okay, well, now that you're here, I guess we should talk about sleeping arrangements. We probably should have discussed it before, but since I'm awake now, and it's already night..." She reached into her pocket and withdrew something metal on a short strap. It glowed. "Yikes, it's almost three in the morning."

He didn't understand everything she said and did, but he would in time. Their cultures were obviously different and patience would be required.

"You wanted to talk about sleeping arrangements?"

"Yes. I guess after all that good lovin' I just fell asleep right here in the grass, but that probably wasn't too smart. I should have some kind of shelter from the elements and—God forbid—predators."

"I will be happy to build you a shelter."

Haley's eyebrows rose. She pointed to the temple. "What about that big, strong-looking shelter right over there?"

Jamir reared back. "The temple? No! No one can enter the temple. Vishnu decreed it long ago. Our purpose all of these years has been to guard the temple from humans and animals alike."

"You can't be worried about little ol' me. I wouldn't do anything to harm it. I know how important it is to you."

"Haley. Please understand. No one except my brother and I are ever to enter the temple. It was decreed even before the sacred object was given to us."

"Sacred object? What sacred object?"

He glanced at the ground. "I have already said too much."

"Oh."

Thank the Gods she didn't push the matter. Jamir realized he probably should have built a shelter sooner, but he'd had no idea when or if she would actually come back to him. Huts didn't last, so he might have had to rebuild one dozens of times or more to be prepared before her arrival. Now that she was here, sleeping in the grass, he knew he probably should have kept one in good repair.

"Haley, Shahid is taking his turn to sleep and it is up to me to guard the temple, so if you will come with me, I will allow you to sleep on the steps."

"Wow, that sounds *way* comfortable."

Again her tone and expression did not match her words.

He rose and held a hand out to her. "Come. I need to return to my post."

Her eyes grew wary. "Do you need to return to tiger form?"

"No. I can stay human, but I will need to remain alert. We usually guard the temple in our feline bodies, because our senses are much sharper. We can hear and smell intruders coming sooner and do not have to shift to chase them off."

"That makes sense." Shaking her head, she added, "I don't know if I'll ever get used to you that way."

"What way? As a tiger?"

"Yes. The most ginormous feline on earth." Her eyes seemed larger. Or perhaps it was the moon illuminating them which made her look so anxious.

"Haley. I would feel much better, if you became at ease with our tiger forms—at least mine. Perhaps I can help you do that."

"How?"

"Come, let us sit on the temple steps, and I will tell you."

He extended his hand again, and this time she grasped it. He helped her rise and they strolled down the well-worn path to the stone structure.

"I suggest you sit on a step and I will lie at your feet. Then I will shift, but I will not move. I will retract my claws. You can touch me and I promise you, I still will not move."

She took a deep breath, but didn't sit. "What will that prove?"

"That you can trust me. That even as a tiger, I will not harm you." He took her chin in his hand. "I would never harm you, Haley." And then he kissed her.

Her lips were tentative at first, but when he let go of her chin and ran his fingers through her hair to cup the back of her head, she relaxed into him. Her body molded to his in a perfect fit. He slanted his head and when she opened to him, he deepened the kiss. Their tongues touched and explored each other.

When she leaned away, he broke the kiss and studied her face.

She smiled. "All right. I'll try it."

Relieved, he grinned. "Good. I will stay in my other form until you want me to shift back. Simply say the word, and I will change."

She nodded her agreement and sat on the third step—close enough, but not too close to where he would lay at her feet.

He crouched down and concentrated on his body as a tiger. Immediately, his form altered, and he lay on his side in his least intimidating posture.

Haley worried her lower lip between her teeth. All he had to do was keep his word and stay still. The rest was up to her.

She extended a hand, slowly. Eventually, she leaned closer and laid a finger on his fur.

Jamir barely breathed, hoping to still his side from rising and falling.

She leaned back, retracting her hand. He expected her to request he shift back, but she did not. Instead, she leaned over again and laid her whole hand on his side. Amazingly, she began to pat him.

"Your fur isn't as soft as I thought it would be. It's kind of wiry."

He responded in a low purr, but he was pleased she had touched him without recoiling. Perhaps someday he and his brother could proudly sit on either side of her. Maybe she would even throw her arms around their thick, furry backs. The image made him smile inside.

He lay still for several minutes, luxuriating in the feel of his lover stroking his fur. His eyelids grew heavy, and he caught himself a moment before they closed. He'd have to shift back to sit up and avoid falling asleep, yet he had promised he would wait until Haley asked him to. Perhaps he should take the risk of startling her instead of allowing the possibility of his falling asleep, leaving the temple unguarded. He just hoped this wouldn't be the last time Haley ran her sure fingers over his fur in a loving caress.

CHAPTER 10

"Jamir!" Shahid yelled.

Startled from a sound sleep, Jamir bolted to his paws and let out a roar.

Haley screamed and fled up the steps toward the temple opening, not knowing what to expect of a cranky tiger.

Shahid intercepted her, thankfully in his man form, and grabbed her waist. "Stop," he yelled. "You cannot go in there."

She tried to fight him, but he was too strong.

Jamir shifted and rushed to her side. "Release her!"

Shahid let go and Jamir dragged her into his embrace. "Where were you going? You know you cannot enter the temple."

Words refused to form, so Haley simply shook her head.

"You are shaking."

She didn't realize it until that moment, but as soon as the immediate danger had passed, the adrenaline left her quivering like a toy poodle.

A couple of deep breaths later, she managed to find her voice. "Guys, I think we need to talk."

Jamir's eyes widened. "Please do not tell me you want to

leave. I would not have harmed you, even if startled from a sound sleep."

Shahid crossed his arms over his broad chest and frowned. "You should not have fallen asleep, Jamir. You were supposed to be guarding the temple."

"I did not. I—I was simply resting my eyes."

Shahid raised his voice and practically shouted. "If you were not sleeping, I am a pregnant monkey."

The men glared at each other and their lips quivered on one side as they emitted a sound that could only be called a snarl.

"Guys!" Haley planted her hands on her hips. "Look, you can fight later. Right now I need to talk to Jamir."

"Boka Choda." Shahid pointed to Jamir. "This is not over. We must talk too."

Haley yanked Jamir's arm, but he was rooted to the spot. She pulled again. "Please come with me, Jamir. Please?"

He looked over at her and his stern expression softened. "I can deny you nothing, Haley."

At last, he took her hand and led her back to the spot where they'd made love. They lowered themselves to the grass and sat side by side. Haley stared past the river and focused on the horizon where the sky began to lighten with dawn.

"What is so important that you had to interrupt my brother and me?"

"Exactly that. I had to interrupt the two of you before you shifted and clawed each other's faces off."

Jamir's brows raised. "What makes you think we would do that?"

"You looked like you were about to."

He shook his head at the ground. "Haley, you do not know us. Obviously, we are not like other men. We never fight physically, because—you are right—we could seriously injure or even kill each other. The only time it looks as if we're fighting is in play. We don't even do that anymore since I got this." He pointed to the notch in his left ear.

"So, what keeps you from doing that?"

"Maturity. Mutual respect." His lips raised in a cocky smile. "Things that apparently the men of your time need to learn."

"You got *that* right," she muttered. "Okay, I'm sorry. I guess I misjudged the situation, but we do need to talk."

"What about?"

"About a safe place for me to go. A shelter."

"I said I would build you a shelter, and I will."

"Out of what? Sticks and mud?"

He shrugged. "Yes, plus some dried grass to hold the mud together."

"Yeah, that's what I was afraid of." She sighed. "I need someplace stronger than that. I need a place that can stand up to...to crocodiles, curious monkeys, or...whatever. In other words, more than a shack. Maybe I should try to find a place in the village and then visit..."

He bolted upright. "No. I want you here, with me. I cannot protect you in the village."

She didn't want to ask who would protect her from *him* and his brother, but that's what she was thinking.

"Look, where am I supposed to go if the shit hits the fan? Obviously, I'm not allowed inside the temple, but I can't for the life of me understand why not. It looks like the only safe structure around."

"I will protect you."

"You can't be there to protect me every minute. What if I had to outrun a really fast wild animal while you're hunting? I could never make it to the village in time."

"Shahid will protect you."

She wagged her head slowly. "I don't know, Jamir. Your

brother doesn't seem all that fond of me. It might be easier for him if I got eaten."

Jamir looked shocked. "He would never let that happen… and he *is* very fond of you. He told me so."

"Really?"

"Yes. Well, not in words, but…"

"Sheesh." *I feel* so *much better.* "Okay, let's say I don't have to worry about animal attacks. I understand you have some pretty crazy weather. Like rain I could drown in. Shouldn't I have shelter from the elements?"

Jamir stared at the grass. "Yes, I have been wondering what to do for you during our monsoon season." He didn't follow that up with any practical ideas, so she had to assume he hadn't come up with any.

"Doesn't it just make sense to let me hop into the temple in an emergency? I mean, come on. Let's be realistic." She pointed toward the red stone structure. "It obviously withstands floods since it's been here for about a hundred years."

"Three hundred."

"And how long have you been guarding it?"

"Three hundred years."

Her breath caught in her throat. "You're three hundred years old? Are you serious?"

Jamir tipped his head, appearing confused. "You are surprised? I thought you knew I was immortal. Did you not say so the second time we met?"

"Second time? Oh yeah, the reincarnation thing. I keep forgetting." *Yeah, I knew he was immortal, but I guess I hadn't realized* how *immortal.* As Haley thought about it, she felt pretty stupid. Immortal was immortal, right? He could have been born at any point in history.

"So, do you have trust issues or something? I promise, even if the most beautiful objects are in there, I wouldn't touch anything."

"There is only one object in there."

"Only one?" *What the heck could be so precious that two immortals would have to guard it for eternity?*

"The temple used to be empty. The sacred object fell from the sky only fifty years ago. We assumed the temple was built in anticipation of its arrival. Or perhaps we had to pass some test first to be sure the Gods could trust us with it."

"Wait a minute. Let me get this straight. You guarded an empty temple for two-hundred and fifty years, and now there's one measly thing in there that fell from the sky?"

"Yes. That is how we know it was sent by the Gods."

"Well, how big is it? Maybe we could put it in a safety deposit box, and you'd be free to come to New York with me."

Jamir reared back and stared at her, wide-eyed.

"What?" She turned her palms up and shrugged.

Jamir shook his head slowly. "Haley. We cannot know what the Gods may send in the future, and it matters not. Our purpose remains unchanged. We are to guard the temple from all intruders at all times."

"So you can't leave, and I can't stay."

Jamir's mouth opened to protest, but she held up her hand. "Don't say anything. I know what you're thinking." Haley took a deep breath. "My head hurts…I need to take a walk and think."

———

Shahid strolled over to his brother and laid a sympathetic hand on his shoulder. At least, Jamir *thought* it was sympathetic.

"I am glad you and Haley seem to be happy with each other again."

"Yes, I am relieved as well."

Shahid sat beside him. "I need to talk to you, brother. The subject may be difficult. I would ask your patience while I voice all my thoughts, uninterrupted."

Jamir glanced over at him and saw only sincerity in his eyes. "Whatever you have to say to me is better spoken than not. I will listen."

"Thank you. First, I want you to understand, I am glad for the addition of Haley to our lives. She has brought with her interesting new ideas and expressions. We badly needed this. We had little to break up our routine."

"Those are my thoughts too. I am glad we agree."

Shahid took a deep breath and forged on, speaking faster. "And as you know, we have sexual needs…"

Where is he going with this? Jamir squirmed, but he had agreed to listen.

Shahid continued. "You are enjoying Haley's body as well as her companionship."

"Yes…" Jamir responded, warily.

"Make no mistake—I have only happiness for you and I am not jealous, but perhaps a bit envious. They are two different things, are they not?"

"I understand the difference, yes." Now Jamir was becoming very uncomfortable. What was Shahid getting at?

"I would like to propose we share her body as well as the responsibility for her."

"You cannot mean what you are saying!" Jamir leapt to his feet.

Haley came running. "What happened? What's going on?"

Jamir bunched his fists and silenced Shahid with a glare. "Nothing. I just came to the realization that you would be better off living in the village after all.

"Really? What changed your mind?"

He focused on Shahid, but said, "You would be better off there. I will help you find a family to stay with."

"A family? I was hoping to find a place of my own."

Jamir straightened. "A young woman living alone? Unheard of."

"Not where I come from. I have my own apartment in New York."

"This is not New York," Shahid interjected. Jamir didn't know whether to be grateful to his brother for backing him up, or to remain angry with him.

Haley laughed. "Yeah, New York is more dangerous."

Apparently she hadn't noticed the tension in the air. Jamir felt it crackle up his spine. "Any place is dangerous for a woman without a protector."

Haley rolled her eyes. "I took self-defense classes. I can protect myself."

Jamir could only argue with her so much before she would decide to go back to New York—without him. If the Gods were listening, they would be sure no empty dwelling was available for her. If nothing else, she might be able to befriend the owners of the tea plantation. She had lived there as Helen. She would undoubtedly feel at home the moment she walked in.

"I have an idea," he said. "Come with me." He held his hand out to her. Shahid watched as he led her in the direction of the ridge, where they could look down over the fields of tea plants. Jamir glanced over his shoulder a couple of times. Shahid never moved, but his eyes continued to follow them.

Haley wondered where he was taking her. This was the one direction she hadn't explored—mostly because she remembered the unknown tiger scurrying off that way. "Where are you taking me?"

"You will see." He smiled as if he knew something she didn't. Well, of course he did. He could probably draw a map of the area with his eyes closed after three-hundred years here.

As they crested the ridge, a grand home and a smaller one next to it came into view. Rows and rows of plantings led to the buildings like a striped bedspread led to pillows. A feeling of *déjà vu* disoriented her for a few moments.

Jamir was studying her face. "Do you recognize it?"

"Uh, should I?"

His face fell.

"Actually," she hurried to add, "I have an odd sense of being here before. Even the scent of the air stirs up the feeling of a memory. But it's not real. It's called *déjà vu* in my language—well, not exactly. It's a French term, but English speakers use it."

"No. Your feeling *is* true, Haley. This is where you lived as Helen."

"Huh? Oh, you mean the past-life me."

"Yes, exactly."

She gazed out over the land and buildings and had to admit, the familiar feeling seemed to be more than déjà vu. *How weird is that? Maybe reincarnation does exist.*

Jamir motioned to the grass. "Sit. Meditate. Perhaps you will remember more."

Haley chuckled. "I'll sit, but don't count on my meditating." She lowered herself to the grass and got comfortable. "I can't twist myself into that pretzel position, and I have a hard time waiting for an appointment without a magazine."

"But meditation is what leads to enlightenment." Jamir sat beside her.

"So, if I close my eyes, you think I'll remember my past life here?"

"Perhaps. Why not try?"

"Okay. What do I do?"

"Try clearing your mind of all thoughts. Then repeat one word over and over. I would suggest 'Gita' for you."

"Okay." Haley closed her eyes, took a deep breath and began reciting, "Gita, Gita, Gita…" After a few minutes, she found herself saying, "ta-Gi, ta-Gi, ta Gi." She opened her eyes and saw Jamir grinning.

"I'm sorry. At some point I got it turned around."

Jamir grinned wider. "Do not be sorry. That was perfect. Ta-Gi means, one who has renounced everything for God."

"Really?"

He nodded emphatically.

"So, did you and Helen meditate together, or did you two —you know…" she elbowed him.

"What?"

"Roll around in the grass like we do."

He chuckled. "No. Times were different then. For Helen to get involved with me romantically was unheard of, and extremely brave of her. She took a terrible chance, just letting me kiss her. She was always afraid of being sent back to England. It must have been a terrible place. Mostly, we just talked."

"About what?"

"She was curious about my thoughts. As it happens, our beliefs were extremely different in some ways and remarkably similar in others."

"Huh? I guess I never thought much about it. In what ways are they similar?"

Jamir scratched his chin. "She taught me about the seven deadly sins. In a similar way, Gita says one should avoid *kama*, which is lust, *krodha*, which is anger, lobh, which is greed, moha, which is deep emotional attachment, mada or ahankar, which is arrogance, and matsarya, which is jealousy. These are negative characteristics which prevent man from attaining moksha, which is liberation from the birth and death cycle. Some call it Nirvana."

"So, how on earth did you and Shahid wind up liberated

from the birth and death cycle when you're full of that bad stuff?"

Jamir hung his head. "You are right in many ways, but we did not achieve moksha, which is the state man aspires to. We are committed to doing Vishnu's will on earth in our physical bodies for—as long as he wishes."

"Well, that doesn't seem fair. And speaking of unfair, what about that caste system? I noticed the village is divided up with some called untouchables off in their own no man's land."

"Life is not meant to be fair, and yet it is. All men may aspire to and reach nirvana. It is said: 'He who does work for God, he who looks upon God as his goal, he who worships God, free from attachment, who is free from enmity to all creatures, he goes to God.'"

"Yeah, everyone can go except you and Shahid, apparently."

"We know not what may happen. We must battle our own ego and serve God as everyone else does, only perhaps more so. We know our task and purpose on this earth. It is not ours to question it. Only to do it well with love in our hearts."

"I don't know if that sucks or rocks. You're either being punished or you two are the most selfless creatures on earth. Either way, I admire the heck out of you."

Jamir smiled again. "And yet, we must not do it to feed our ego."

Haley shook her head slowly. "Yeah, that part is way different from our culture. Did Helen understand this stuff?"

He laughed. "No, but she enjoyed talking about it. She said in her country, women weren't allowed to discuss such things. Only the men talked, and women were to do needlework."

"Times have changed, thank goodness. At least in Great Britain and America."

"Yes, I had gathered that the first time you stripped off the little bit of clothing you wore and bathed in front of me." He reached out and caressed her back. "And then what happened afterward, well, if I needed any more proof about how women were different now…" He leaned over and kissed her. And things progressed from there….

CHAPTER 11

Pitter patters of rain cooled Jamir's bare arms. He'd hoped the monsoons would hold off until he built Haley's shelter, but there was no hope for that now. He gazed out over the tea garden and faraway hills where the darkening sky loomed.

"Haley, I am afraid we must find you shelter sooner rather than later."

She extended her hand, palm up. "Yup. It's starting to rain. Don't worry. A little rain won't hurt me. In fact, it'll be a nice break from the heat."

"I do not think you understand. We are entering our monsoon season. It might rain for four of five days non-stop."

"Huh? I thought monsoon season wasn't until November! I remember specifically looking that up on the Internet and it said Northeast India has its monsoon season in November. I didn't think I'd be here that long, but even if I was, I just figured that was November Haley's problem.

Jamir did not know what the Internet was or why it would lie to her about their monsoon season. He mentally berated himself for not finding her a place to ride out the massive storms sooner. He had just been so caught up with her arrival and the joy her presence had brought…

"Haley, we need to get you to either the village or to your plantation home—now."

"Shit. You're serious. Monsoon season is right on top of us?"

"I am afraid so. You must decide quickly. Where do you wish to go?"

She glanced back over her shoulder toward the temple.

Oh no. She isn't going to ask to go into the temple again, is she? I cannot allow it. Shahid will bar her entrance in his Tiger form, no matter how much it scares her.

She heaved a sigh. "Let's run down this hill and see if the nice people in that sturdy looking house will let me in. I don't know what we'll do if they refuse."

"I will translate for you until they are convinced you have no other option, but I cannot stay."

"Holy crap. Okay. I guess I'll have to take my chances. Let's go." She took off running down the steep hill. At one point, she fell on her butt and slid several feet in the dirt. She stood and began to brush it off. "My backpack! I need—"

"There is no time for that. Perhaps they will have an extra saree you can wear."

"A saree? You think so?" As they sprinted toward the building she seemed to be smiling at the idea of wearing a saree. Relief washed over Jamir. He had seen the people who lived in the house from a distance, and they were no longer British. Chances are the Indian family would consider her current state of undress scandalous—she was almost naked, as was he. Haley's short shorts and tiny top certainly didn't bother him—or his brother, apparently, but he hoped this unfamiliar family did not close the door on them.

By the time they dashed up the stairs to the long covered

porch, the rain was pelting down and the dirt drive had started to turn to mud.

Jamir pounded on the door, probably a little harder than necessary. He had to reign in his panic or he could do Haley more harm than good.

A dark brown gentleman opened the door, took one look at them and moved as if he might close it. Jamir quickly babbled something in the beautiful language of the region. Whatever he said seemed to have made a difference. The stranger gestured for the two of them to enter.

He spoke to Jamir in hushed tones. Soon an older woman in a beautiful blue and gold saree joined them. Her eyes rounded and she said something sharply to the man. He held up one hand and spoke to her briefly, then turned back to Jamir.

Haley couldn't figure out how the conversation would play out. Everyone wore serious expressions, but no voices were raised in anger or disgust.

Finally, Jamir let out a long breath in a whoosh and turned to Haley.

"He said you can stay, but you will be expected to work. I told him you could educate his children in English."

"Terrific. Only one problem with that plan. I don't speak Bengalese."

"I can teach you some basics of Bengali when I come to visit. Meanwhile, you can point to things and teach them a few words."

She tried to join Jamir in his optimism. After all, she had little choice. The gentleman spoke to the woman and she hurried up the wooden staircase. Haley loved the sound of the language, but would it ever roll off her tongue like that?

"You may learn a few words from them too."

"I suppose. But please tell them I'm willing to do other things to earn my keep. I can cook, clean and help with laundry."

"I already told them, but they have a cook and a house-keeper. They live in the small building next door."

"I guess I'd be taking their jobs from them, and I don't want to do that."

"No, you do not. Just smile, treat them with respect, and you will be fine."

"In other words, change my personality."

"No. You can be very pleasant…when you want to be."

She snorted and laughed. "I guess I'll have to try." She turned to the gentleman and gave him her biggest, brightest smile. He reared back.

"I said pleasant, not idiotic."

Haley lost her grin immediately. "Excuse me? Are you saying I look idiotic when I turn on the charm?"

Jamir quickly said, "No! Maybe I used the wrong word."

Haley tried to squash her offense.

The woman who had dashed up the stairs now descended with her arms full of beautiful fabric. She pushed it toward Haley.

Jamir said something to the woman, and she imagined it must be thanks.

"Do you know how to wear a saree, Haley?"

"Nope. I haven't got a clue."

Jamir spoke to the woman again and she grasped Haley's wrist, tugging her toward the stairs.

"Aasun," she said.

Still talking to Jamir, Haley said, "I take it she's gonna help me get dressed?"

"Yes. This time. I am sure you will learn to dress yourself very soon."

I'd better. This lady looks none too happy.

Three days later, the rain abated enough for Jamir to make it back to the plantation house. He knocked, hoping Haley would still be there. What if she wasn't? It felt as if insects had been flapping around in his stomach ever since he had left her in less than ideal circumstances.

The door flew open and Haley stood there. His breath deserted him for a moment. The magenta and gold-trimmed silk saree draped her body in shimmering beauty.

She launched herself into his arms.

"Thank goodness you're here. I don't understand a friggin' word these people are saying...and I'm supposedly good with languages!"

He held her in his arms and stroked her back. "It is all right now. I am here."

She broke out of his embrace. "Hang on a minute."

She ducked into the house for a moment and returned with some white cotton clothing.

"Here, put this on. You really can't let the kiddies see you in just a loin cloth."

"Kiddies?" Another strange expression he didn't understand. Perhaps it was the family's surname.

"Yeah, you know...the children."

"Oh." He quickly hopped into the pants and tied the strings at his waist. Just as he donned the tunic, two children ran to Haley and hugged her thighs and waist.

"Haley! Haley!" they chanted.

In Bengali, Jamir said 'Hello' and introduced himself as Haley's friend. "Tumi kamon aacho?"

The children grinned and said simultaneously, "Aami bhalo aachi."

"What did you just say?" Haley asked.

Jamir patted the little ones on their heads. "I asked them how they were and each one said 'I am fine.'"

The kiddies seemed satisfied, grabbed his hands and led him inside.

"It seems as if they like me," he said, happy and relieved by their reaction.

"God knows why they like me. I've only been able to teach them a few words. They're probably happy to see you, because you can translate."

"It is a start." Perhaps he could teach Haley a few key phrases while he was here. Jamir focused on the children and asked them what they had learned.

The little girl pointed to herself and said, "I," then giggled.

"Yeah, Jamir. What's so funny about that?"

"In Bengali, *Aye* means, you come."

Haley bit her bottom lip. "Oh dear. Well, I can't imagine they know the double meaning of *that* in English."

"No, I am sure they do not. It is just funny that they are calling themselves, come here."

"I thought *aasan* meant, come. That's what their grandmother says right before she hauls me off somewhere."

"It does. There is more than one word for the same thing."

"Oh, marvelous. Just like English."

The little boy jumped up and down and chanted, "English, English."

Haley made a sound like *humph.* "At least they know what I'm teaching them one word at a time."

Jamir acknowledged that it must have been difficult and asked the children what else they had learned. The boy pointed at Jamir and said, "You."

Jamir nodded and smiled. He turned toward Haley and said, "In Bengali the words for you are Tui, tumi and aapni."

"Is it like French where one word is used for females, another for males and still another is the familiar slang?"

"Uh, yes and no. Do not worry about all the translations. You are very smart and I believe you will pick up the language in no time."

The little boy skipped around the room tapping pieces of furniture. "Chair. Table. Couch. Lamp."

Haley smiled. "At least they'll know how to decorate their homes, if they move to an English speaking country."

The little girl pointed to herself and her brother alternately. "I, you, I, you."

"Do not worry. Some words are easy. Jamir pointed to the boy and said, "He is Se." Then he pointed to the girl and said, "She is also Se."

Haley let out a deep breath. "Oh, thank goodness…at least one thing that's easy peasy."

Jamir cocked his head. "Peasy?"

"Forget it. That's not a word—just an expression."

Sometimes she confuses me more than I thought possible.

"Well, have a seat," she said.

He followed her to a chair made of thick woven reeds and made himself as comfortable as he could on the odd structure. He would have preferred a mat or the soft grass.

Jamir noticed the strong smell of food cooking—the kind of food the villagers prepared. He sniffed the air.

"It's almost time for lunch. I like to hang out in the kitchen and watch the cook when I can, but we should probably stay here in the living room until we're invited."

"You watch the cook?"

"I'm learning more about how to cook Indian food, but I'd use about half the amount of spices if it were up to me. Some of that stuff sets my mouth on fire."

Jamir pictured Haley breathing flames and assumed she was making a joke…or using another 'expression.' He hadn't eaten human food for three-hundred years, but he never needed a bucket of water to extinguish a blaze in his mouth.

The children were about to sit at their feet when they were called to lunch. They moaned and muttered under their breaths, wishing they could stay and learn more English.

At last, he was alone with Haley.

"I've missed you," he said.

"I've missed you too."

"I want you," he whispered. "Is there someplace we can go?"

Haley leaned toward him. "You mean to fuck?"

He nodded. Ordinarily he wouldn't ask, but he sensed Haley needed this as much as he did.

She glanced over her shoulder toward the rest of the house. There was no one in sight. "I guess we could go to my bedroom—if only I didn't scream so loud when you make me come…"

"How about outside on the porch? The sound of the rain could muffle your noise and it could be very sensuous— making love while the rain pours down around us."

She smiled. "That does sound romantic, but the kids… they could step outside at any point."

He hung his head.

She whispered in his ear. "Maybe we can get each other off without gearing down to our birthdays suits."

His brows knit. "Gearing down? Birthday suits? I don't think I have one of those."

"Trust me, you do. But what I mean is, maybe we can make each other feel good without getting undressed."

"Ah!" He grinned.

The two of them rushed to the front door and snuck out, latching the door quietly behind them.

Haley examined her saree. "It takes forever to unwind this

thing around and around, but at least I don't have any panties on under it."

Jamir grinned.

"Maybe you could just slip your fingers under the waistband and down—or under the hem and up. I can get into your pants through that handy gap below the draw strings. If we sit facing each other…"

He grinned. "Then no one would be the wiser if they should open the door and look over at us."

Jamir didn't need any help to get hard. He'd grown semi-erect just seeing her again. He loosened the string holding his pants up. Haley poked her hand through the opening and grasped his erection.

"Ohhh…" He shuddered with glorious sensations and couldn't help his grateful moan.

One more quick look around to be sure they were alone, then he plunged his hand down the front of her sari and under her petticoat. She gasped when he located her yani.

"Hurry," she whispered. "We shouldn't be discovered if we work fast."

He didn't need to be told twice. If they were discovered it would ruin Haley's reputation, as well as get her fired and tossed out into the mud.

He stifled all instincts to make noise and tried to concentrate on what he was doing to her. He slipped two fingers into her channel and moved his thumb across her sensitive bud.

He wanted Haley to come first. Finishing his own climax would take a split-second. He rubbed her nubbin faster and harder. She threw her head back and clamped her free hand over her mouth, obviously struggling to stay quiet. Her breathing grew more and more erratic, as did her pulls on his cock.

At last she vibrated with powerful contractions. Her

internal muscles squeezed his fingers and it killed him to think that his shaft was missing the fun. But as soon as she'd recovered, she clamped her hand around his staff and stroked him hard.

As expected, in no time he felt his balls tighten and his tension broke. He felt like a shooting star. A blaze of incredible pleasure rocked him as his consciousness left his body for a moment.

As soon as he could move, he retracted his hand and Haley did the same. They kissed and murmured endearments to each other. At last, he helped her off the porch and onto the steps. They giggled as they stood in the rain, letting nature bathe them.

CHAPTER 12

Almost six weeks later, the monsoons were finally over. Jamir had visited almost every day, and Haley had a rudimentary grasp of the Bengali language. Thanks to both her and Jamir, the Sengupta children were able to construct simple phrases in English.

One beautiful sunny morning Haley realized it was time to find her own place. These people had been wonderful to her. They had taken her in, fed her, given her clothes and kept her safe, but she didn't want to impose on the family any more.

She greeted the cook, had her breakfast and went in search of the family patriarch.

"Sri Kumar," she bowed slightly. "I want to thank you for your hospitality. She expressed the greatest thanks she knew. "*Ozasro Dhanyabad*. But it's time for me to leave." She motioned to herself, then she finger-walked her way toward the door. Sometimes when the words didn't make sense the sign language did.

He looked surprised. "*Tumi kothai jaai?*"

Haley was pretty sure he'd asked her where she would go. "To the village. I need to find my own house." She pointed in the direction of the village and tried to draw the shape of a house with her index fingers in the air.

"Aami tomar sathe aasbo."

She shook her head. "Thank you, but you don't need to come. I'm sure Jamir will want to go with me."

At that moment, Jamir knocked and opened the door simultaneously. The head of the household looked up and seemed relieved to see him. A lively discussion ensued. Haley tried to keep up, but they were speaking too fast.

At last, Jamir smiled at her. "The children will miss you greatly," he said. "But Sri Kumar, or as you would say, Mr. Sengupta understands. He knows how much we have missed each other. He appreciates your setting a fine example for his family."

"So he knows…"

"Knows what?" Jamir asked.

"If we're ever going to have sex again, I've got to move out."

Mr. Sepgupta's eyes widened and he looked as if he'd swallowed a bug.

"Great. He doesn't understand half of what I say, but *that* word he gets."

Jamir chuckled. "I will say it meant something else."

"No, don't. I'm not ashamed of our relationship."

"I am glad to hear you say that. More glad than you can know."

"Yes, but I'm still going to find a place to live in the village, as well as a job. I'll probably see you at the end of the workday, but that's it."

He grinned and winked. "We shall see."

Hmmm…odd. Jamir usually frowned and gave her a hard time whenever she expressed the desire to be independent. Now what did he have up his sleeve?

Jamir thanked Mr. Sepgupta for some suggestion and asked him something.

The man retrieved a business card from a desk drawer and handed it to Haley. She made out the name and title, which sounded like a Catholic nun, and beneath that was the name of an orphanage.

"Okay, so what is this for exactly?"

"It's his contact at the orphanage on the outskirts of the village. He thinks you can get a job there."

"Oh, thank goodness. I thought maybe he was trying to give me up for adoption."

Jamir squinted. "Is that another joke?"

"Yes," she said, pleased. "You're finally getting my sense of humor."

"I never said I thought it was funny." He waited for her look of outrage, then laughed.

"Oh, man. You got me. Not only are you learning what jokes are, but you're learning how to tease. I never should have taught you that."

"But why? It is so much fun."

She bumped him playfully with her elbow. "Yeah, when you're the one dishing it out. Now, will you be a dear and wait for me while I say goodbye to the rest of the family and get my things?"

"Of course."

Haley ran up the stairs and gathered the clothes she came with, plus the sari she wore when the one she was currently wearing had to be washed.

She followed the sound of the children's voices to the garden. Mrs. Sepgupta was with them. *Thank goodness. Now I only have to go through this once.* Saying goodbye to the kids wouldn't be easy.

"Tota. Pimpim." She called them by their nicknames. They ran to her and she squatted down to their eye level.

"This is difficult to say, so I will just say it. Goodbye. Aami Jaai."

"No!" they wailed.

Pimpim sniffled and asked, "Tumi ki amake bhalobasco?"

"In English," she reminded them.

The little one crossed her arms and shook her head, pouting.

"Well, then, I'll answer you in English. Of course I love you," Haley wiped the single tear away. "But it's time for me to go."

"Tumi kotha theke asecho?" Tota asked, then he seemed to remember himself and said, "Are you going home?"

Haley glanced up in time to see Jamir coming toward them. "I came from America. Far, far away. But I'm not going back there. I'm only going to the village."

They hugged her like they weren't about to let go.

Jamir told them he'd bring her back to visit, and they made him promise. Haley said her goodbyes to their mother and grandmother and asked if she could borrow the clothes she had been wearing a little longer.

"Ha nischoy," Mrs. Sepgupta said. Then she translated herself. "Yes." She patted the pile of fabric in Haley's arms and said, "Keep them."

"Thank you," Haley said, then in Bengali, "Dhanyabad."

With hugs all around, Jamir took her one free hand and led her to the road.

The village was a mile walk, but after only a quarter mile or so, he rerouted her toward the hills.

"Are you taking me to the temple first?" she asked.

"Yes. I hope you do not mind. I want to make love to you without layers of clothing between us."

"Sounds like a plan. A terrific plan—an awesome plan!" She grinned. "And it's not as if I have an appointment in town or anything. I can sleep in your arms tonight and go to the village tomorrow."

"That sounds like nirvana."

———

Jamir couldn't wait to see Haley's expression of surprise. He had spent his free time building her a shelter. It was not made of mud and sticks. He had found long, sturdy trees and poles, and dug deep to hold them in place. It sported the usual thatch of a village dwelling, but he wove it so tight and so thick that even monsoons couldn't penetrate it. The structure was strong and afforded protection from snakes, inclement weather, and probably everything except elephants.

"Oh, Jamir! You built this?" Her eyes widened.

"Yes, for you. For us."

"Show me."

He opened the flap and held it as she ducked inside.

She was shorter than he—not by much, but he knew she could stand up straight inside. He had placed her cooking utensils and the backpack she left behind in one area under a kind of pillow. Dried reeds rolled in fabric. A colorful blanket in the middle decorated the packed dirt floor.

"Do you like it?"

She threw her arms around him and exclaimed, "It's wonderful. I love it." She leaned back and gazed into his eyes. "I love you."

He enveloped her in an embrace that cradled her head and held her body firmly against his. "And I love you. I cannot wait to show you how much."

She sniffled. "You already did."

Stepping away so he could see her face, he noticed tears shimmering in her eyes. "Are you sad?"

"Oh no. Just the opposite. I'm deeply touched."

He smiled. Before, she had explained that when her facial expression and words didn't match, it was called sarcasm and generally meant the opposite, deflecting the real feeling with humor. This time, he didn't think it was an attempt at wit—so not sarcasm, but something else.

She leaned in and kissed him. He pulled her close again and let relief wash over him. He really didn't know how she would react to his building her a home here—not in the village. It seemed as if he had done the right thing.

They dropped to their knees, and quickly wound up horizontal on the blanket, a tangle of arms and legs. Haley yanked at her saree and tried to unwind it while lying down. It proved impossible. She finally straightened the fabric and rolled her body in the direction which freed her as Jamir watched and laughed.

He pulled the drawstring of his pants and allowed them to fall around his ankles while he removed the tunic. Soon they were lying naked in each other's arms.

"Haley, I missed you so much."

"I missed you too."

A more passionate kiss heated his blood. His animal nature wanted to take over, but she deserved more than a quick rut. Jamir took his time. He caressed her soft skin and murmured words of love in her ear. He moved to her breasts and sucked them thoroughly. He knew she liked that.

The whole time, Haley responded to every overture with grateful moans and gasps. When he sensed she was completely ready, he tested her wetness and found plenty to ease his way.

He tapped her inner thighs, and she separated her legs. As soon as he was between them, he stared into her eyes. "I love you, sweet Haley."

"I love you too," she said and sighed. He guided his lingham into her warmth. "Ohhh…that feels so good."

"Yes, it does. I have missed this."

"Me too—a lot."

Jamir began his rhythm steady and slow, relishing the warmth of her sheath. Their separation seemed so long, but they were together again, at last. He treasured every thrust, every moan, every stroke of her tight inner walls.

The mounting sensations blotted out all conscious thought. All he could do was feel and cherish this God-given expression of love. At last, he reached a fevered peak and let himself fly apart. Just as his seed spilled into her, she quivered, bucked, and let out a howl. She sounded as much like an animal as he was.

When they were both spent, he rolled off her. She was giggling.

"What are you thinking?"

"Just how lucky I am to have found you."

"How *did* you find me? You had no guide, no map."

"I followed my heart."

He picked up her hand and kissed it. "And now you are here—in mine." Staring into her eyes, he placed her palm over his chest.

CHAPTER 13

Back in New York, Barb had called Ronda and asked her to come over. Finally she heard a knock. Barb loved having a doorman who screened visitors, and she'd told him to let her friend Ronda come on up. He'd seen her so many times, she probably didn't need to tell him.

Letting her in, she said, "Thanks for coming over."

Ronda dropped her purse on Barb's credenza and said, "Sure. No problem. But what's so important you couldn't tell me over the phone?"

"Have you heard from Haley at all?"

"Not a word."

"It's been a few weeks, and I doubt the mail is that slow. She sent me one postcard soon after she arrived. Or, more accurately, she sent the card to Visa in care of me."

"Her cat?" Ronda laughed. "Sounds like her typical prank. So, did she say where she was or where she planned to go?"

"Sort of. The card was postmarked Kolkata. She said she planned to tour West Bengal with a group until she knew where to find the temple she was searching for."

"Oh. Well, that doesn't sound so bad. Maybe she's still on the tour."

"It gets worse. I think she never made the tour. I called all the tour agencies and no one knew who she was, Ronda. I'm worried."

"You think something has happened to her?"

"I'm afraid so. I just have a bad feeling."

"We need to call the American consulate in Kolkata."

"Did it. They haven't heard a thing."

"Call the local police, then."

"Did it. No help there either."

Ronda's jaw dropped. "Oh, crap! What the do we do now?"

"There's only one thing left to do, and I'm going to try it." Barb tipped her chin in the air, defying Ronda to talk her out of it.

"What?"

"I'm going to India. I'll take a recent picture with me and show it around until I find her."

"There's got to be something else we can do. How about hiring a private detective?"

"Do you know any PI's in India? Even if we found one, how would we know the person wouldn't just pocket the retainer and never look for her? No, it's got to be one of us."

"But..."

"But what?"

"What if something happens to *you?*"

Barb laughed. "You know I can take care of myself. Maura doesn't call me a bulldog for nothing."

"Oh, Barb..." Ronda wailed.

"Listen. There's one thing you can do to help."

"Anything. Name it."

Barb picked up Visa and shoved Haley's cat toward Ronda. "Take this damn slashing machine. And if you have any furniture you particularly like, slap some wide, clear packing tape on the corners and buy a scratching post."

Haley awoke in Jamir's arms. The night they had spent together had been absolutely perfect. Shahid offered to take Jamir's watch for him, so they could have more time together, but she sensed there was some kind of hidden agenda or deal they had struck.

Since they had all the time in the world, they took their lovemaking nice and slow—something they hadn't dare do at the plantation. In fact, there, they'd only sought relief a few times. Getting caught was not an option, so they held off as long as they possibly could. But burning for each other without some kind of sexual satisfaction proved impossible.

Today, Haley would speak to the Mother Superior about taking a job at the orphanage. She hoped they'd want an English teacher, not someone to change diapers, but when in Rome—or Rimbam...

Still lying next to each other, Jamir faced her. He brushed a strand of blond hair away from her eyes. "You do not need to find a home in the village anymore. I understand you want to work and earn some rupees to buy food, but I would love it if you would stay here with me and Shahid."

At least he asked and didn't demand. Haley thought about it for a few moments. It was true that she could live here. Homes in the village probably weren't much more luxurious. Some people even lived in tents. Sleeping with Jamir every night would be wonderful, but what would she tell the people at the orphanage if they asked where she lived? *Oh, I'm shacking up with a couple of tigers out by the old temple.* Yeah, that would go over big.

"Why don't I see about the job first? If they want to know where I live, I can say I'm staying with friends, temporarily."

He sat up. "Temporarily? Haley, please do not say you are leaving again."

She could tell he was trying hard not to overreact. *But why isn't he able to go with the flow—let things unfold however they're supposed to?* "I'm not saying anything." She let out a deep sigh. "I'm just worried about what they might think."

"About what?"

"About being unmarried and living with a man-tiger."

He chuckled and looked at her as if she were the loveable village idiot. "I didn't know you wanted to get married. Of course I'll marry you. But the villagers don't know my brother and I are the tigers they have seen."

"Whoa, tiger! I never said I wanted to get married right *now*. We have a few kinks to work out first."

His amused expression faded. "What are kinks?"

"Well, now, that can be answered a couple of different ways." *Having sex with a shapeshifting tiger might be considered kinky.*

She ran a finger through her hair. She found a few snarls that tugged her scalp, but working them out with a comb wouldn't hurt. "I should make myself presentable. Is my backpack around here somewhere?"

He lifted a corner of the blanket bunched up at the foot of their straw mat. In it he had tucked her meager belongings.

Haley was surprised by how little she really needed. When she had left New York, her pack was heavy and she thought she didn't have nearly enough. Now, reflecting on things, all she needed were a few items out of the pack, and the rest was just excess weight.

"Give me a couple of minutes to dress and brush my hair. Meet you at the campfire in a jiffy."

He nodded and left. There was no lock or hut door—just a flap. She'd have to try to make one and explain the concept of security to Jamir, but that could wait. Meanwhile, she donned the blue saree blouse and petticoat, and rewound the six beautiful yards of turquoise silk around her body. She loved this saree even more than the maroon one.

After running a quick brush through her hair, she was almost ready. She'd heat up some river water to wash up. It occurred to her that another thing had changed since she'd arrived. She was no longer terrified of getting sick. Her system must have adapted, because she hadn't had bottled water at the Sepgupta house. Other than a minor upset stomach in the beginning, she had been fine. Better than fine in fact. Surprised to realize it, she felt better than she had in her whole life. Still, she'd better not take foolish risks like drinking the river water. If only she'd thought to set out a few hundred rain barrels last month.

Haley stepped from the hut and stretched. The sun shone bright in a cloudless sky. Shahid mosied over to greet her.

"Jamir is getting water. Would you like me to make a fire for you?"

"You know what? It's so hot already, I might just prefer cool water to wash up."

"I thought you liked to cook."

"Oh, I do. But I have nothing to cook right now." Thinking he might volunteer a wild boar or something, she quickly added. "Don't worry. I can get by until I go to the village. I'll be leaving in a little while."

He nodded and retreated back to the temple steps. Something about him seemed different. As she stared at his retreating back, she noticed something beyond the temple on the opposite side. Something that hadn't been there before.

Strolling over toward him, sturdy bamboo and thatch entered her view.

"Shahid, are you building a hut?"

He nodded, but no explanation followed.

Always the strong, silent type. "That's wonderful. It looks like you're making the same structure Jamir built. I'm impressed."

He grinned. "I am glad you like it."

Uh-oh. Is he thinking what I think he's thinking? Does his brother suspect? Or—Oh, my God... Did Jamir agree to share me?

Haley didn't know what to think.

Well, when in doubt, ask. "Shahid, are you thinking of living here by yourself or are you preparing for company?"

He shrugged.

Damn. That doesn't help much.

Jamir returned from the river with a large basin of water.

She ran to him and threw her arms around him. "Thank you, thank you, my big, strong, handsome, *helpful* man."

He almost dropped the water in surprise, but managed to set the vessel down without spilling much of it. He pulled her into his arms and gave her a long, loving kiss. Taking a deep breath he announced, "I want to marry you Haley Hunnicutt. I have been thinking about it, and it is what I want more than anything in the world."

Shahid snorted. "Jamir. It is your turn to guard the temple." He spun on his heel and returned to work on his dwelling.

Haley figured she'd better change the subject. "I'll wash up, then go to the orphanage to ask about a job."

"But I want to go with you."

"I think it's better if you don't. How would it look if my boyfriend had to take me everywhere? I want them to know I'm not afraid to go and accomplish whatever they need me to do—alone."

Jamir looked as if he were about to protest, but then he gazed at the temple and shut his jaw so forcefully his teeth clicked.

So that's the secret. Be sure he's tied to the temple and freedom is yours, Haley. Was that the way she wanted to arrange her life? Around her possessive boyfriend's neurotic need to protect her every second? Jamir needed to hear that his hovering bothered her, but how do you tell a six-hundred pound tiger to cool it?

Haley's idea to teach English at the orphanage went over big —until they discussed the little matter of her salary. Apparently white skinned people were thought to possess plenty of money plus the time to volunteer their services as well. When Haley explained that wasn't always the case, Sister Mili suggested Haley visit the rice paddy. Many village women were employed there.

She left the school and followed the directions to the rice paddy—basically, take a right at the well, a few hundred yards away from the only road past the trees, there it would be. Not a hard thing to find in a village with about forty homes.

When she arrived, she found several men and women ankle-deep in a bog. Fortunately, one person spoke a little English. Between his heavy accent and her lousy Bengali, she managed to discover that the men were making one hundred rupees per day, but she would be making what the other women made—fifteen rupees.

Haley was so incensed, she marched back to the school to tell the nun exactly why she was needed there—and that she should be paid the same as any man doing the same job.

Sister Mili didn't seem upset. In fact, she seemed downright blasé about the whole thing.

When Haley pressed her for an answer, she said she had to think about it and get back to her.

Typical. I'm surprised she didn't say she had other candidates to interview and would be in touch.

"*Kar sathe ami jogajog korbo?*" Sister Mili asked.

"Whom should you contact? Well, if you'd like a reference, Kumar Sepgupta at the tea plantation can give you one. I taught his children." She hit her head with the heel of her hand. *Duh. Say it in Bengali, dummy.* "*Kumar Sepgupta, Banarhat tea garden. Etai uttor.*"

She knew her knowledge and pronunciation of Bengali still left a lot to be desired, but she'd do her best not to rely on Jamir.

Sister Mili nodded and Haley was relieved.

She found the Begali words to say, "I'll come back in two days, and you can tell me your decision, then."

When the sister shook her head, then shrugged, Haley decided to give her the quick answer. "*Shomba.*" Meaning, *See you Monday.*

Sister Mili quickly asked, "*Aap kahan se aa rahe ho?*"

Uh-oh. Haley knew she was asking about where she came from. Maybe she could deliberately misunderstand..."*Remun bonderi.*"

The sister frowned, then shrugged and nodded. Apparently the airport was a satisfactory answer.

CHAPTER 14

Shahid's muscles ached from stretching as high as he could to attach the roof of his hut. He had made his walls a little taller than Jamir's, hoping to create a grander feeling. If Haley was impressed with Jamir's…

"I don't understand why you want a house," Jamir said. "You never felt the need for one before."

"Do I need a reason, brother?"

Jamir studied him silently for a few moments. "You can't possibly expect me to change my mind about sharing her? She seems happy with me alone.'"

Shahid shrugged. "Perhaps I'll meet a woman someday, or maybe I want a hut for myself. The weather and vipers are not as easily survived outdoors."

"But we are immortal. We need not concern ourselves with survival—only the survival of others."

"Survive was not the correct word. Pass the time pleasantly instead of uncomfortably is what I meant."

"Hmmm…" A moment later, Jamir's face lit up. "Haley!" He rushed off in a direction Shahid couldn't see from where he stood. He had to assume she was returning from the village. When Shahid peeked around the side of his hut, he saw his brother kissing the woman they both wanted.

In time, he would broach the subject of sharing her again. Perhaps Jamir would grow tired of her, or maybe he could charm her into wanting him too.

Haley didn't know how she was going to tell Jamir her good news. Not about the job. He'd be fine with that. But Haley might have scored a place to live. It was more like a tent to escape to if she needed her space or if she didn't feel like listening to the brothers argue. A man was vacating the little tarp on poles and moving his things into a hut he had just finished building. He said she could use it if she wanted to. It would also give her the illusion of respectability in the eyes of the good Catholic missionaries.

Because she had overheard part of their conversation before Jamir spotted her returning, she was glad she'd decided to ask about it. It seemed as if Shahid might not be taking Jamir's *no* seriously. She'd never thought about a threesome, but did she really want one? With brothers? Was that incest? She was fairly sure they were both straight. Maybe they would take turns. Haley felt her cheeks heat, because of the naughty direction her thoughts were taking.

"How did it go?" he asked.

"Pretty well. I think I have the job. It's the pay that might suck."

"What do you mean?"

"At first they thought I wanted to volunteer—work for free. I insisted I needed at least enough to eat and pay rent."

"Rent? What is rent?"

"The money you pay to someone who lets you live in their building."

His eyes rounded in astonishment. Before he could protest, she placed her fingers against his mouth.

"Listen, I love you. I do. But I'm not ready to make a total commitment. I want a place of my own for a little while."

Jamir balled his fists and stared at the ground.

"I knew you wouldn't be happy about it, but I may not use it much. As long as you and Shahid are getting along, there shouldn't be a problem. But if you two start going at it, like I know you can, I want a place to retreat to. Besides, it gives me an address…even if it's 'third tent from the goat tied to the fence.'"

"It is only a tent?"

"Yes. Like I said, it's temporary."

"So as long as Shahid and I are not fighting, you will stay here with me?"

"Yes."

He nodded and seemed mollified for the time being.

"There's something else I want to talk to you about," she said.

"What is it?"

Haley took his arm and began to stroll toward their hut. "I need to learn more Bengali—and French, eventually. There's a French couple working at the orphanage, but all the French I know is *Frere Jacques* and *Merci.*

"We can continue your lessons. But the Sepgupta children learned quite well by copying your English."

"Yeah, speaking of copying… I'll also be teaching these kids to read and write. The only problem is I don't know how to translate written English into Sanskrit. It's a beautiful bunch of squiggles to me. Honestly, I mean—Vanna, can I buy an alphabet?"

He cocked his head at her.

"Yeah, I know, I know…cultural reference. I knew you

wouldn't understand it. But that's how I feel a good bunch of the time."

He ran a finger up and down her arm, making her shiver. "You will learn everything you want to know in time. Meanwhile, it is almost Shahid's turn to guard the temple."

"Ah, that's code for you're horny, isn't it?"

He grinned. "Can you blame me? I thought of nothing but you all morning. Now you are here and so beautiful."

She couldn't help but smile. "You're a charmer, all right."

"A charmer? No. I do not even have a cobra."

She chuckled. "Thank goodness for that."

Barb landed in Kolkata and showed Haley's picture around immediately. She began right at the airport. None of the customs officers on duty recognized her picture. Barb explained that her friend was missing and asked if she could leave a copy of her information for those off duty. She had made up two-hundred fliers with her satellite phone number on them in case anyone had seen her friend. About fifty were stuffed in her carry-on luggage. The rest were in her large rolling suitcase.

Barb was exhausted from jet-lag, so postponed her search until the next day. She had made a reservation before leaving home and purposely found one of the cheapest places, knowing that's where her thrifty friend would go.

If finding Haley required trekking through the country-side for weeks, Barb would kill her the minute she found her. No matter how paradoxical that would be.

By the following afternoon, it was clear that even though she was looking for a blond needle in a black-haired hay stack, there were just too many people trying to be helpful. In New York, most people would have barely glanced at the picture, shaken their heads and kept on walking.

Apparently in India, if a person had seen a Caucasian within the last fifty years, they were willing to tell you exactly where they'd seen them. As long as the helpful citizen spoke enough English to direct her, she might find a red-haired man or a brunette woman. Either all Caucasians looked alike, or the Indian people had the word 'no' permanently removed from the English-Bengali dictionary and replaced with the bobble head motion.

Unfortunately, there were more than fifteen million people in Kolkata, so talking to them all would take several lifetimes and way more patience than Barb possessed. She had to narrow her search. As much as she hated to think the worst, she began with the hospitals.

Barb knew nothing about Indian healthcare, but she imagined it ran the gamut. They probably had a few top notch teaching hospitals in the larger cities and some pretty bare-bones basic clinics in rural areas. Fortunately for her (not so lucky for the residents) general hospitals with emergency rooms were few and far between—even in the city.

She began with a bit of positive thinking and asked her cab driver to take her to the best hospital around. Her friend might be cheap as far as luxuries were concerned, but she'd never gamble with her health—Barb hoped.

The hospital was a large, modern facility, which made her feel better for a moment. They had no record of a Haley Hunnicutt having been admitted there. A quick search of all their data produced no one by that name ever being seen for anything—not a blood test nor a bandage. Barb breathed a sigh of relief.

Before she left, they helped her organize her search of other similar facilities. Her English speaking cab driver had waited for her and knew all the places on the list.

When she had covered all the possible hospitals and clinics, it was time to locate the police station. She had hoped to avoid this, having heard about corruption and knowing she couldn't afford a huge bribe.

Barb sent out a quick prayer for an honest cop, then found a place with wireless Internet and looked up police stations. *Oh, goody. Only forty-eight of them. Holy Hell. If Haley's not dead, I am so gonna kill one of my dearest friends when I find her.*

Fortunately, the first police station she chose had the capability to fax her flier to most of the others. They suggested she go have something to eat and check back later to see if anything popped up. Barb's empty stomach said that sounded like a good idea, so she set off to find a decent restaurant. Now, where to go?

Her trusty cab driver would know. First, she had to be sure they had bottled water. Next, food that was cooked thoroughly. A buffet would be nice. That way she could take a tiny bit of everything, and if one food set her tongue ablaze, she'd just move on to the next.

"So, Mr. Selva, where do American tourists eat around here?" *There. That was an innocuous question, right?* Haley would have been proud of her for using a word like 'innocuous', even in her brain.

The cabbie said, "Ah," knowingly. She got in and he whisked her off through the city until she was sure there must be only one restaurant Americans liked. At last he pulled up outside a familiar red and yellow color scheme with some golden arches. *Lovely. So much for a nice buffet.* She wasn't about to complain though. She'd vowed to be respectful, no matter how hard it might be. Barb passed up the burger in favor of chicken nuggets. Who knew what was in the burger? She was fairly sure it wasn't beef in a country that revered cows as sacred ancestors.

When she returned to the police station, they seemed more attentive and interested in her friend than before. Three of them crowded around her as she sat beside a desk.

"How do you know her?" the cop in charge asked.

"She's one of my best friends. She lives in the same building I do, in New York."

"And what was her business here?"

"She was looking for love."

The cops glanced at each other. Finally one of them said, "There are no men in New York?"

Barb smirked. "You might think so. None willing to have a serious relationship. It's hard to find a man for more than a one-night stand these days."

"And did Haley Hunnicutt know anyone in India?"

"Nope. No one."

"Your story sounds strange. Don't you agree?"

"Absolutely. I thought it was a weird plan from the get-go, but Haley seemed to think the right guy was here."

They all looked at each other and began conversing in another language. Barb didn't like their suspicious expressions.

Finally one returned his attention to her. "Did you know she ran from a hotel rather than pay the money she owed?"

Surprised, Barb couldn't help wondering if they had the right person. Behavior like that didn't sound like Haley.

"Are you sure it was her? I can't see her doing that."

"Quite sure." One of the cops held up a monitor showing a fuzzy picture of a blond woman rushing across a lobby with a large duffle bag slung across her back.

Barb had to admit, it looked like Haley.

"You must call us if you find her."

"Wait a minute. I thought *you* were going to find her. I

mean, don't you have more resources at your disposal than I do?"

"Yes, but it costs money to use those resources."

"How much?"

"It depends. How much do you want to spend?"

"Me? You want me to pay you to look for her?"

The cop raised himself up to his full height and crossed his arms, probably trying to look tough.

Barb rose to her full five feet ten inches and looked down into the cop's face. "Look Barney Fife, you need to do your fucking job. I assume you're already being paid by the city or state or something, right?"

The cop shrugged one shoulder.

"You have one hell of a nerve. I'd go to the commissioner, but he's probably just as crooked as you are."

She spun on her heel and marched out of the station. Her cab driver was parked nearby, patiently waiting for her. She threw herself into the back seat and slammed the door.

He looked in the rear-view mirror at her. "Where are you going now?"

"I have no fucking idea."

The cabbie seemed concerned. "Shall I take you back to the hotel?"

Barb thought a minute, then said. "No. Take me to the biggest shoe store you can find."

Jamir turned over temple guard duty to Shahid, then took his lover by the hand and led her to their hut. *Our home*, he thought. Haley would give up her silly notion of keeping a separate tent in the village soon enough. He would keep her safe and sexually satisfied, making her realize she'd be better off here than all alone.

"I treasure you, Haley," he said as soon as he'd pulled her inside and enveloped her in his arms. "I will provide you with anything you need to make you happy."

She kissed him gently at first, then returned his sentiments and kissed him again. Their passion ignited and Jamir crushed his lips to hers. She opened her mouth and they curved their tongues together. All the while, she fumbled with the knot of his loin cloth.

At last it came undone and fell to the mat. Undressing Haley was a bit more difficult, but as soon as Jamir was naked, Haley helped unwind the yards of blue silk covering her petticoat. She carefully folded the saree, then unhooked her blouse while he pulled the bow at her waist, which allowed her petticoat to fall. She stepped out of the fabric pooled at her feet and let him remove her blouse.

Even in the dim light of the hut, he could see and appreciate the contours of her beautiful body. Her breasts were full, and her waist nipped in nicely. She had hips built for childbearing, and Jamir wondered if someday the Gods would allow her to carry his child. Just the thought filled him with so much love, that he laid a hand on her abdomen and stroked it in small circles.

"Hey, are you rubbing my belly for luck or something? I'm not Buddha, you know."

Again, he didn't understand exactly what she was referring to. That didn't sound like the Buddha. As far as Jamir knew, he had never allowed his stomach to be rubbed for luck, but at the moment he didn't care enough to stop and discuss it. He took a step closer and his hand slid down to cup her yoni. She made an excited little sound and grasped his lingham, which was already rock hard.

"Lay down," Jamir said with an unexpected rasp in his voice.

Haley did as he asked, positioning herself on the blanket

where they slept. She lay still and allowed him to bow over her breasts and suck each of them thoroughly.

Jamir thought for a second he heard a female voice. He soon forgot about it as Haley cupped his head and moaned, gratefully. When she grasped his cock again, his animal nature kicked in. He growled and rolled her onto her stomach.

"Jamir, don't you want some—"

"No. I only want to be inside you. *Now.*" Perhaps he should apologize for his urgency…later.

He scooped an arm under her waist and hauled her up until she was on her hands and knees…right where he wanted her. Positioning himself behind her, he didn't even test her wetness. With a kiss to her neck, he drove home.

Haley gasped and arched.

He stilled. "Are you all right?"

She let out the deep breath and said, "Yes, I just wasn't expecting…"

Jamir had already started his thrusts and added a clit rub. She let out a low moan, then matched his rhythm.

They coupled like that for several strokes before Haley began to quiver.

"Oh, I'm already—"

She was unable to finish her thought, but she didn't have to. Her louder moans told him she was close.

A female voice coming from outside the hut called, "Haley?"

Jamir didn't want to stop until they had both reached satisfaction, so he moaned into Haley's ear, hoping she wouldn't hear the woman calling her name.

Fortunately, she began to buck and scream, letting loose what sounded like a major release. As her vaginal muscles clenched, Jamir's climax hit.

Shahid was arguing with someone right outside, and his voice sounded angry. Over Haley's shrieks of ecstasy, it was hard to make out his words. Hopefully, Shahid would be able to hold off whoever was out there.

Haley had stopped screaming but panted heavily. As if she recognized something about the unknown woman's voice and her conversation with Shahid, she said, "Shhh…" A moment later, she grabbed her saree and clutched it to her chest. Popping her head just outside the flap, she called, "Barb?"

A woman about Haley's age rushed into view. She had darker hair, but it was still too light to be Indian. Her clothing was different too. She wore shorts like Haley had been wearing when he first met her, plus a slightly immodest shirt—something Haley had called a t-shirt. Jamir was still on his knees.

The woman cried, "Haley! What the hell…" As soon as she spotted him, she whirled half way around and covered her eyes.

"I'll be right out, Barb. Give me a minute." Under her breath, she muttered, "What the hell brought Barb here? Did something happen at home?"

Haley quickly shut the flap and picked up her blouse. "Jamir, put on your loin cloth. I think my friend has seen a little too much already."

"Your friend? Why did you not tell me a friend would be coming to see you?"

"I didn't know. I still can't believe she's here." Haley had finished fastening the blouse and pulled up the petticoat, tying it around her waist.

"I do not think you are seeing things. I saw her too."

Haley smiled but didn't answer. She just folded and stuffed the saree material into the petticoat's waistband.

With another swirl of silk around her waist and the decorative end tossed over her left shoulder, she said, "Well, time to face the music."

CHAPTER 15

Barb stood with one hand on her hip and a smirk on her face. Haley knew she was in for the ribbing of a lifetime, but didn't care. Sex with Jamir was worth whatever teasing Barb could dish out.

"Barb, what are you doing here?"

"Interrupting your little tryst, apparently, Hunnicunt."

"Yeah, thanks for the nickname. And that much I already knew. Maybe I should have asked, *why* are you here?"

Barb's mouth thinned and her complexion deepened. *Uh oh.* Haley knew that look. She called it *Ballistic Barb.*

"Because everyone thought you'd dropped off the face of the earth! No phone call. No email. Not even a fucking post card! Did you think your friends wouldn't miss you? Did you think about *us* for one single minute? Because if you did, you wouldn't have let us panic like this."

Haley held up both hands. "I'm sorry you got upset, but I *did* send postcards, one to each of you, shortly after I got here."

"Did you forget to mail them?"

"Of course not, I—" Suddenly a sick feeling invaded

Haley's stomach. She retreated into the hut, fished through her backpack and—yup, there were the postcards. *Damn.*

"Don't leave while I'm yelling at you," Barb said to her back.

Haley turned around, producing the cards. "I—I'm sorry. I don't know what to say. I must have gotten distracted..."

Barb let out a snort. "Ya think? While you were over here shagging your ass off, we were all waiting for some kind of word. We tried calling the U.S. consulate, the police, anyone we could think of, and no one knew *anything.* Finally I had to come over to this oven of a country and look for you myself. Did you know indoor plumbing is as rare as purple cats outside the cities?"

Haley pictured Barb encountering her first *squat toilet*— basically a hole in the floor and that's it. Toilet paper, sinks, and paper towels were nowhere to be found. Usually a bucket of water sufficed in public restrooms.

She groaned. "Barb, I'm sorry you came all this way. It was really sweet of you to worry, but—"

"No. No buts. My butt is still angry with you. You don't get out of this just by saying you're sorry."

"So, what do you want? A pound of flesh? Because I hear lipo isn't all it's cracked up to be."

Barb let out a long sigh. "Well, I'm glad you're alive. You look fantastic, by the way. You must have lost about twenty pounds."

"Yeah, backpacking across West Bengal with almost no food will do that to a person."

Jamir stood by, looking confused.

"By the way, Barb. This is my immortal lover, Jamir."

Barb's eyes grew wide.

"It worked, Barb," Haley said. "The spell worked."

Her expression darkened again. "Well, I'm glad it worked for *one* of us."

"You mean no one else has met their immortal yet?"

"Not that I know of—but I've been a little busy looking for one of my best ex-friends."

"Really? I wonder why it worked for me, but not for the rest of you. Did you visualize your lover like Maura said to do?"

"I visualized the shit out of him. Maura said all of the original four woman found their immortals, but not at the same time. Different factors figured into the timing, I guess."

Haley could only sympathize. It didn't seem fair. *Wait! Maybe Barb had to go in search of her immortal too. Maybe she was meant to come here. Maybe Shahid...*

Haley focused on Shahid, sitting on the temple steps. She wondered what could be going through his head. Three hundred years with only his brother and then for a short time, his brother's girlfriend...make that plural if you're not into reincarnation...to talk to, and you'd think he'd be all over a single woman showing up out of nowhere.

Haley stepped close to Barb and whispered in her ear. "What do you think of Jamir's brother? He's immortal too."

Barb stepped away and raised her eyebrows. "You mean the Neanderthal who was about to wrestle me to the ground rather than let me get near you?"

"Shahid is a little overprotective of the temple, but not me, per se. He may have thought you wanted to get into the temple. You never want to do that, by the way."

Barb's eyes narrowed. "Why not?"

"I don't know, exactly. They've been guarding the temple for three-hundred years. About fifty years ago something fell out of the sky—something holy or sacred. They believe it was sent by their Gods for them to protect, so they put it in the temple, and now no one can get near it without—oh, did I mention they turn into big-ass Bengal tigers?"

"Shit!" Barb's eyes popped open and she searched the landscape, as if wanting an escape route.

"Relax. They can control it. They're really just big pussycats."

Barb let out a nervous sounding, "Ha!"

"Seriously, Barb. Think about it."

"What I'm thinking about is getting back to Fifth Avenue and taking advantage of the big end of season sale."

"Come on. You have to admit, there are good things about being here. Like no co-eds ready to take our guys. And I doubt I could lose Jamir if I tried. He seems to think I'm his one and only destined mate for all time."

"But what if you're not?"

"Bite your tongue, woman! Look, it's weird, I know, but there's stuff I haven't told you."

"Like what?"

"I had visions before I left New York. I saw Jamir in my dirty dishwater."

"How romantic. Look, I hate to stop you, but I need to water a bush—and I'm guessing that's exactly what you have to offer."

"Uh, yeah. I kind of wander over there." Haley pointed to the tall brush near the river.

"Figures," Barb muttered.

As she trudged off toward the small clump of privacy, Haley yelled, "Watch out for the cobras!"

Barb shrieked and jumped about a foot in the air. Haley held her stomach and doubled over, laughing. Meanwhile Jamir and Shahid rushed over.

"What happened?" Jamir asked.

"Nothing. I was just messing with Barb."

"Why would you do that?" he asked.

Barb gave Haley the finger and stomped off behind the bushes.

Haley tilted her head. "It's just something friends do to each other where I'm from."

Shahid shook his head. "If that is true, I am glad I am here and have no friends."

"Oh, Shahid...*I'm* your friend," she said, and she meant it. He gave her a sad smile. Shahid might want more from her, but friendship was all he was going to get. She would *not* be the cause of a tiger fight to the death. Could immortals kill each other? She imagined a severed head would do it.

If only Barb would consider staying long enough to fall in love with Shahid. But somehow, Haley couldn't picture it. They were both too...bossy. Yeah, that was the word. Barb was a take-charge woman and wouldn't play by anyone's rules other than her own. All Shahid would have to say is "You can't," and she would! *Oh, jeez, I hope he doesn't demand she stay out of the temple. That's like issuing an invitation.* Haley would have to warn him about that, but before she could, Barb reappeared.

"I wish I had known to bring my own TP," she grumbled. "Leaves and grass just aren't working. And where the hell do you bathe around here?"

"Uh, the river, but you might want to have one of the guys check it out for you first."

"Why are there snakes in the river too?"

Haley simply gave her an apologetic grin and shrugged.

"Oh, terrific. That's just fan-fucking-tastic."

"Or you can haul some water out of the river and take a sponge bath. I have a bucket..."

Barb held up one hand. "Never mind. We won't be here that long. I can wait for a hotel shower."

Jamir straightened and glared at Haley. "What does she mean when she says 'we' won't be here?"

"Nothing. We haven't talked about our plans yet."

Barb raised her eyebrows. "Haley, you can't possibly be thinking of staying here."

"It's...complicated."

"Oh, my friggin' God."

Shahid stepped closer and growled.

Barb, never one to back down from a challenge, jammed her hands on her hips. "Yeah, tiger-boy? What do you have to say about it? Are you her jailor or something?"

"Barb, no," Haley warned. "Whether I stay or go, it's *my* decision. No one is forcing me to do anything."

"Jesus. You might actually *choose* to stay here?"

"I might."

Barb threw her hands in the air. "Well, at least I'll get a couple of snarky greeting cards out of this."

Haley loved her friend's creative Hallsnark cards. "Like?"

"Like, roses are red. Violets are blue. This road trip sucks and so do you."

Haley folded her arms. "Oh come on. You can do better than that."

"Fine. I'll give it some thought on my way back to civilization. Meanwhile, I'm starving. You got anything besides monkey brains for dinner?"

"Yes. I'm learning to cook some of the local dishes, and I'm getting quite good at it as a matter of fact. Tonight we're having Macher Jhol. Literally translated it means fish in gravy."

Barb stuck out her tongue and inserted her index finger as if to say, "Gag me."

"Oh come on, you'll love it. I should start cooking the rice and shaak."

"What's shaak?"

"Don't worry, it's only veggies cooked in mustard oil. You'll like it. After that, we'll have dal and after that I made some mango chutney."

"Sounds like a lot of trouble."

"Oh, it is. I mean, if you have a cook, he or she might prepare a five course main meal every day."

"I thought people over here were starving."

"Not if they have jobs. I still have to get one. I'm running out of money."

"Oh for pity's sake. You have a perfectly good job at home. The semester is starting soon, right?"

Jamir slipped a protective arm around Haley's waist. "She is happy here."

Haley patted Jamir's cheek. "Maybe you guys should go back to the temple. I'll talk to Barb while I prepare dinner."

Both men looked hesitant.

"Hey, the temple is unprotected. You really should go," Barb added.

Shahid's upper lip quivered like he was about to let out a low growl.

"Only one of us needs to watch the entrance to the temple," Jamir said.

Haley gave him a tiny shove toward his brother. "I've got this. Now go. Let me talk to my friend."

Shahid said, "She does not treat you with respect, brother." He wasn't lowering his voice, so he wanted her to hear it.

Haley jammed her hands on her hips. "Shahid, it goes both ways."

Shahid frowned. "What does?"

"Respect. You two should respect my need to speak to my friend *alone*."

Jamir grabbed Shahid's arm. "Come on, brother."

As they were walking away, Barb pulled Haley in the opposite direction. "I thought they'd never leave. Now, before another minute goes by, I'm getting out my satellite phone, and you're *going to* call our friends back in New York. Everyone's worried sick about you."

"Really?"

"Of course, idiot."

Barb rummaged through her knapsack and fished out her phone. "Here."

Haley took the bulky phone from her. "It's so big."

"Yeah, and it wasn't cheap, so don't drop the damn thing."

Haley sighed. "So who should I call? It must be the middle of the night back home. Maybe I should wait…"

"Call!"

"Okay, okay." It was late over there. Haley figured she could always call their places of work and leave a message to avoid waking anyone. At least she could let them know she was okay. She couldn't remember Ronda's job's contact info, so she decided to try Maura's uncle's tavern.

After learning the country code for the U.S. and dialing *O'Malley's,* an operator had to intervene anyway. At last she got through.

"Hello, O'Malley's," said a heavily Irish accented male voice.

"Mr. O'Malley?"

"T'is."

"Oh. Hi. I thought the bar would be closed, and I'd have to leave a message."

"Weel, now. Would ya like me to hang up then?"

"No!" Haley chuckled. "No, I just wasn't expecting…I'm in India. Is Maura there?"

"India? You must be Barb then. Did you find that idiot friend of yours?"

"Ah…this is Haley—the idiot."

"Isn't that nice. So she found ya, did she?"

"Yes, she did. And if I woke you, I'm terribly sorry. I just wanted to let Maura know I'm all right."

"No, I was awake. I'm doin' inventory. The bar won't stock itself."

"No, I guess not."

"So, what on earth did you go to India for?"

"A man."

"Ah. It's a good thing I'm a romantic, or I'd never understand that."

"Well, I'm glad you do."

"Oh, my yes. For every old stocking, there's an old boot."

"Excuse me? I'm not *that* old."

"Sorry. It's just an expression. So, does his boot fit your stocking?"

Haley covered her mouth with her hand and tried not to laugh. When she thought she could speak without snickering, she said, "Yes, we seem to be soul mates."

"Then it's good you went. When will you, he and Barb be comin' back?"

"Um…I don't know."

"Well, it's a good friend you have there. She'll make the road shorter."

"Pardon? Uh, never mind. Is Maura around by any chance?"

A long sigh on the other end gave her pause.

At last, Mr. O'Malley said, "Weel, that's the thing. Maura's still on her extended shopping expedition and Ronda isn't here right now, either. Your friend Ronda won a trip for two to Europe, and since she's always wanted to go to France, she up and went. Didn't care about leavin' her old friend's Da to wait tables. Even dropped off a damn cat for me to feed."

"A cat? What does the cat look like?" Haley glanced over at Barb who quickly looked up at the sky and began whistling.

"It's orange and white—and it looks like a cat."

"Is its name Visa?"

"Eh? I suppose it could be. He's everywhere I want to be. I never learned the bugger's name."

"Yup, I think that's my cat you wound up with, Mr. O'Malley. I gave him to Barb to watch for me."

Barb crossed her arms. "And I gave him to Ronda. What was I supposed to do? I couldn't take your friggin' cat on an airplane for eighteen hours."

Haley narrowed her eyes and slapped a hand over the phone's mouthpiece. "You never liked my cat."

Barb laughed. "I never liked *any* cat, and if you cared about it so much you wouldn't have palmed it off on me."

She couldn't argue with that, but she did feel bad for Visa.

"I'm sorry you wound up caring for Visa, Mr. O'Malley, but I really appreciate it. He's a good cat."

"Ah, don't worry about it. Maybe he can earn his keep by catching mice in the storeroom."

"I hope so. Well, I should go. I'm sure this call is going to cost a small fortune."

"Nice to talk to ya, Haley. I'll be lettin' the girls know you're all right, if they're home before you are."

"Thanks, I'd really appreciate that."

"Good bye, now."

"Bye." Haley handed the phone back to Barb. "Maura and Ronda are so worried about me, they went to Europe."

"Huh? That doesn't make any sense."

"Apparently Ronda won a trip. He said something about Maura being on an extended shopping trip."

"Really? Wow—must be nice. I'll bet they have mattresses and sheets and a shower and everything!"

"Oh, quit complaining. I never asked you to come here."

"Did you honestly think we'd just forget about you?"

"Well, I did say I had no idea when I'd be back."

"In the postcards you never sent?"

"Yeah. I guess so."

CHAPTER 16

That evening, Haley retired to her hut. Shahid had given his mostly finished hut to Barb, and he was prepared to sleep outside while Jamir kept watch.

"Life has suddenly become quite complicated, brother," Shahid said.

"I have faith in Haley. She will make the right decision."

Shahid shook his head. "I am not so sure of that. The new woman seems determined to cause trouble."

Jamir sighed. "Yes, I wish she had not come. Haley was ready to find a job in the village. I think she had decided to stay."

Shahid clapped him on the shoulder. "We have not lost her yet, brother. If her love for you is as strong as you say, she will stay."

Jamir remained quiet for a few minutes. At last, restlessness overtook him. "Perhaps, since we are both awake and the women are out of sight, one of us should shift and hunt," Jamir said. "I will volunteer if you watch the temple. I need a little time and space to think."

"You never used to have to 'think,' Jamir. All you did was dream."

Jamir smiled at him. "I had nothing to think about—and my dreams have suddenly come true." Becoming serious, he said, "It has been too long since I prayed. I would like some time alone in the temple first."

With that Shahid motioned for him to go ahead.

Jamir entered the temple, reverently. At the altar, he closed his eyes and took some deep pranic breaths to connect to the universal consciousness. When he felt ready, he spoke in a normal tone. "Vishnu, I come before you with the highest respect and thanks for all you do to keep the universe even and balanced.

"Oh controller of all things—you are the well-wisher of all the souls. There is no limit to your glories. Nothing can go on without you, and yet you are separate. From you the Vedas have come.

"You are time and in the course of time, you will destroy all things. You are the cause of creation, maintenance, and destruction of all the manifested universes, and you are Paramatma in everyone's heart, directing their actions.

"You are the object of meditation of great yogis, the guru of the whole universe, and the goal of all devotees.

"Oh Lotus-eyed One, please accept my obeisance again and again. Your glories are unlimited. As part of your design, we are able to choose how we live our lives. I chose to honor you and love those around me. Thank you for sending Haley back to me. I will honor you by loving her and caring for her, always."

After a long meditation, Jamir opened his eyes, pulled the string of his loin cloth, and shifted to his tiger form.

On his way down the steps, he nodded to Shahid. *"Thank you. I should be back soon. Maybe I'll get lucky and bring down an elephant."*

"Please don't," Shahid said. "We cannot possibly eat all the meat, even with guests, and it will spoil. Find a nice deer or goat."

"I will try," and off he bounded toward the forest.

His heart soared. He had so much to be grateful for. Vishnu would find a way to keep Haley with him.

Jamir had been silently creeping through the trees when a net dropped over him. He struggled and tried to run but only got more caught up in the net. A group of men with rifles surrounded him. His heart pounded and he roared.

Despite his panic, he knew better than to lunge at them. It didn't seem to matter. One tall man took aim and fired. A dart hit Jamir's leg. He tried to bite the end so he could pull it out, but he couldn't move his head enough. Before he realized what was happening, he couldn't move at all. The last thing he heard was a man saying, "We'll get top dollar for this beauty."

Haley emerged from her hut the next morning, tossing the end of her saree over her shoulder. She had expected Jamir to be there when she woke up, but her bed was empty and cold. Usually he spent part of the night guarding the temple and the rest of the hours sleeping, curled up next to her. A sick feeling invaded her gut.

Shahid stood behind the temple, shading his eyes as if searching the ridge and beyond. Haley approached him.

"Do you know where Jamir is, Shahid?"

The look he gave her was something akin to sympathy. In any case, it did nothing to ease her concern.

"I have not seen him for hours. He went to hunt but has never been gone this long."

Haley's mouth went dry. "Are you sure? I mean, maybe he had to go farther off to find enough rabbits for all of us."

"He was not hunting rabbits. He was going to find a deer or goat. Something plentiful in these parts that would feed us all."

"Well, maybe he's not having much luck."

Shahid bit his lower lip as if there was more he could say but didn't know if he should.

"What is it, Shahid? What are you thinking?"

"I am thinking I should look for him, but I cannot leave the temple."

"Barb and I can guard the temple..." When she saw his dubious look, she quickly added, "or we can look for him."

"It is dangerous, and Jamir would be very upset if anything happened to you."

"Well, what are we supposed to do then? Just sit here? Hasn't this ever happened to you before?"

"No. He has never been gone this long."

"Never? In three-hundred years?"

"Never."

Haley's knees weakened and she sunk to the grass. In a whisper, she asked, "Do you think something's happened to him?"

Shahid gazed off in the distance and nodded.

Tears stung the back of her eyes and threatened to spill. She told herself crying wouldn't do Jamir any good. She had to either get Shahid to go look for him, or go herself. He could be hurt or in trouble.

"Shahid. Jamir needs our help. Either you or I have to look for him. If you can follow his scent, you'd find him more quickly than I could, but I understand your concern for the temple. If I give you my word to stay out of it, and keep anyone else who might wander by from entering it, would you go look for him? Please?"

Shahid glanced between the temple and the ridge, obviously torn.

"Please!" Haley begged.

"I do not trust your friend."

"I'll explain the importance to her. She won't disrespect your beliefs." *At least not in front of your face.*

At last he nodded. "I will go, but first you must explain our rule to your friend, and she must swear to respect it."

"Fine. I'll get her." Haley strolled over to Shahid's nearly finished hut. "Barb?"

She heard a yawn. A couple of minutes later, Barb opened the door and stepped out, wearing the same shorts and t-shirt as the day before.

"What time is it?"

Haley shrugged. "I stopped wearing my watch a couple of weeks ago."

Barb scratched her scalp. "Whatever. So, why did you get me up? Is it time for fried monkey meat?"

"Cut it out. We have a serious situation. Jamir is missing."

"What do you mean, missing? Maybe he just went for a walk or something."

"No, he's been gone half the night. Shahid wants to go look for him, but he wouldn't believe me when I said you'd stay out of the temple while he was gone."

Barb reacted exactly as Haley had hoped she would. She straightened her back and indignantly exclaimed, "Why? Does he think I can't be trusted?"

"Look, all I know is that he wants you to promise to stay out of there before he'll leave."

Barb rolled her eyes. "Fine." She strolled over to the temple steps where Shahid was pacing, relentlessly.

"I promise."

He stopped and looked hopeful. "You do?"

"Yes. You don't have to worry. Now, go look for your brother."

She didn't have to tell him twice. He ripped off his loin

cloth, letting it fall to the dirt, shifted into a magnificent Bengal tiger and rushed off toward the thicket of trees before Barb could react. When she did, her ass hit the dirt.

Shahid had no trouble following Jamir's scent for about half a kilometer. Then it abruptly stopped in the woods. Shahid noted signs of a scuffle. Many human odors mixed with his brother's feline panic. The forest floor had been stomped down and swept from side to side, all in one spot. He sniffed around for more clues. A faint hint of petrol remained in the air. A few meters away he found tire tracks.

Boka Choda! He has been taken by hunters. Shahid tried to think of where his brother might be now—with whom, and why. Jamir knew not to engage that many humans in a fight. He must have been taken by surprise and overpowered somehow. He must have had no time to flee. That did not bode well. The only ray of hope Shahid could glean from the situation was a lack of blood. Jamir had not been shot—probably not.

Shahid had to get back to the temple. The troublesome woman may have promised to stay out of it, but he still didn't trust her.

"Back already?" Barb said to the giant tiger lumbering into their midst.

He didn't answer. Just stopped and stared at her.

Haley who had been sitting on the steps jumped up and rounded the corner of the red stone structure. "He's back?"

The tiger still had nothing to say.

"Shahid, will you please shift? I may be getting used to your tiger form, but Barb isn't."

"He doesn't scare me," Barb said, puffing out her chest. "Like you said, he's just a big pussycat." Barb rose and the tiger's upper lip began to quiver. A low growl emanated from his throat. She stopped moving, but she wasn't about to give him the satisfaction of a fearful reaction.

"Um, Barb. You might not want to tease him. These guys can be awfully touchy."

Barb folded her arms. "What's the matter big boy? No sense of humor?"

Just then, another tiger strolled into view.

"That must be Jamir, right?" Barb asked.

"Uh, no. I recognize Jamir by the little chink in his left ear. He got it in a fight with a sloth bear a couple of decades ago."

"Wait a minute…if that's not Jamir and this is not Shahid…" Barb's throat went dry and she felt as if something hard lodged in there, preventing her from speaking or even breathing. At last she managed to squeak out a couple of words.

"Oh, shit." She whirled on her heel and took off running for the front of the temple. Suddenly a third tiger roared and sprang into the fray.

Haley ran after her friend. "No, Barb! Not the temple."

"Are you out of your friggin' mind? There's a real-ass tiger out there!" Barb managed to reach the temple door and take one step inside before a huge tiger fell on her. Haley screamed.

As Barb prayed and prepared to die, the tiger's sharp teeth gripped her t-shirt hem and dragged her back outside.

Shahid shifted, then stood over her. "Where did you think you were going?"

Barb pushed herself up to a sitting position, but with her

legs like jelly, she didn't think she could stand. "I was running to the closest, tiny bit of protection I could find. I don't know if you realize this, but two shapeshifters plus one more tiger equals at least one real-friggin tiger!"

He extended his hand. "Come."

Barb wasn't sure why he was suddenly calm. She wouldn't have let him help her up except she didn't think she could stand any other way. After he hauled her to her feet, he grasped her arm and escorted her down the steps. That was no surprise, but when he continued to drag her around toward the back of the temple, she tried to dig in her heels.

"Wait. Where are you taking me?"

"I need to show you something."

"Yeah, sure. I'll bet that's what you say to all the humans you throw to hungry tigers."

He shook his head at the ground. Then lifted and carried her. She couldn't resist his strength. Wherever he wanted to take her, it looked like she would be going.

When they rounded the corner, she saw her friend talking calmly to two naked men.

"What's going on?" Barb asked.

Haley turned to her and said, "They say Vishnu created and sent these two new shapeshifters to guard the temple."

Shahid smiled. "Our prayers have been answered."

Haley looked at him askance. "You prayed for more shifters?"

"I did not presume to tell Vishnu how to help us. I only thought I would need his help if Jamir left me—for you."

"So...you didn't find Jamir?" Haley asked, nervously.

Shahid hung his head. "No. I followed his tracks to a place where many scents and signs pointed to humans. I think they somehow trapped and took him. "

"But couldn't he shift back and explain to them he wasn't a regular tiger? He was actually a man?"

"No, Haley. Once we're seen in one form, we cannot risk shifting to another. Our true nature must be hidden. Man is too curious. They would never let it go."

"You got that right," Barb mumbled under her breath. "But, if he didn't shift, he's probably a rug by now."

Haley burst into tears. Barb rushed to her side and wrapped an arm around her. "I'm sorry. I didn't mean for you to hear that."

"Hear what?"

Thank god she didn't hear me and just burst into tears on her own.

Shahid's expression turned dark. He was clenching and unclenching his fists as if barely able to keep himself under control.

Oops. I forgot about that superior tiger hearing.

"Come on, Haley, let me take you to your hut where you can lie down."

"No. I want to know what happened to Jamir." She faced the three naked men. "Can one of you ask Vishnu where he is? He's a God, right? He must know."

"Vishnu knows everything, but he doesn't share all his knowledge with us. We would not be equipped to comprehend that much."

Haley's face reddened. "I don't want to know everything...just where Jamir is!"

"Come on, hon. This can't be good for your blood pressure. Let's get you—"

"No! I don't need to lie down. I need to find Jamir!"

CHAPTER 17

Jamir came to, groggily. At first he didn't know where he was and had no memory of what had happened, then slowly his memory returned. He had been hunting. He came to the edge of the forest and suddenly, he was the one being hunted—and captured.

He raised his heavy head and gazed at his surroundings in the dark. Thick black bars surrounded him. He lay on straw over a hard wooden floor. A wood ceiling over his head would limit his ability to stand. He was in a cage. If only he could shift and try the door…but he knew he was trapped.

The world seemed unstable. A slight tug to the left was followed by a tug to the right. It was as if he were floating—or more accurately, the room in which he found himself was floating and bobbing.

Now that his eyes had adjusted, he peered beyond his cage. Other cages held other dangerous predators. Snakes, a sleeping lion, a sloth bear. None of them shifters, he surmised.

If he were to shift, the animals would see his two forms, but they weren't human and could not report it to anyone. However, if any human who put him in this place as a tiger were to see him as a man in the cage, he would be violating the number one edict of shifters everywhere. Never let anyone know you exist. People would demand to know how he got in there.

He peered around the bars of his cage door. The padlock was affixed to the hinge and it was closed tight. Just to be sure, he head-butted the door. The wall of bars moved only slightly. He was well and truly caught.

Haley and Barb said goodbye to Shahid and gave him their contact information in New York—just in case Jamir returned. He'd promised to keep it safe and find someone in the village to help him make a telephone call. Now that they'd done everything they could think of, they hiked to the village with all of their belongings.

Haley had insisted that before she left India, Barb allow her to contact the various tiger preserves and ask if anyone had discovered a tiger with a small piece missing from the edge of his left ear. Barb said her battery was low, but Haley wouldn't compromise. The village was on a daily bus stop, and if they had to, they could be on their way to a larger village or city at a moment's notice.

"I wonder if anyone has electricity or a land line here." Barb asked. "My battery is getting *really* low."

"Oh, crap," Haley whined.

"Relax. If no one has a land line and I can't recharge the battery, we'll take the bus to a bigger town."

"Thanks Barb." Haley knew on one level, Barb wanted to help, but she suspected it was only to get her over the hump of acceptance and once hope was lost, Barb would work on her to go home.

Haley didn't remember seeing any power lines in the

village and had pretty much resigned herself to getting on the next bus out of the area. They wouldn't have to go all the way to Kolkata. She remembered an Ashram with white people not too far away. Certainly no American in their right mind would go without the ability to communicate with the outside world—no one except her, but apparently she wasn't in her right mind when she came here.

At last they trudged into the village. "We can start at the orphanage and school," Haley suggested. "I'd think if anyone knows about a link with the outside world it would be them."

"Okay. Let's go."

A few minutes later, Haley ascended the steps to the school and asked a little girl if she could see Sister Mimi.

"Aye," said the youngster and motioned for them to follow.

Out back, Sister Mimi was hanging some wet, clean clothes.

"Take out your sat phone, Barb. I don't know the right word for it in Bengali."

"You think she'll even know what it is?"

"It's worth a try. Twenty-first century India is a confusing mix of modern knowledge and ancient ways."

"Okay, Hale. Let's give it a try." Barb dug the phone out of her backpack. Both items she'd had to buy as soon as she knew she was leaving the city. Haley felt guilty when she'd told her she'd had to sell her expensive suitcase, but apparently a Brit with an eye for fashionable luggage was willing to give her three-thousand rupees for it. That was about sixty-five bucks. Haley owed her a new suitcase when they got back to New York. There was no way she could reimburse her for the sat phone—even if it was an older model.

Haley gestured to the phone and explained to the best of her ability that they needed a power supply.

At first, Sister Mimi seemed confused, then light dawned

in her eyes. "Ah." She spoke excitedly, but the only thing Haley understood was, *"She came by something yesterday."*

"Who came yesterday?" Haley translated.

"Ha," the good sister said. Then she took Haley's arm and led her into the orphanage.

A Caucasian woman Haley hadn't seen before was feeding a baby.

"Lorraine ," Sister Mimi said when she addressed the woman, then she proceeded to speak quickly. Haley lost the thread but saw the woman nodding, appearing to understand.

She and Haley shook hands, then in an unbelievably welcome American accent, the woman said, "I have a sat phone and a laptop."

In a shriek of excitement Barb exclaimed, "A computer? Get out."

"How do you get power to it?" Haley asked, encouraged to hear this but trying not to get her hopes too high.

"It runs on a car battery."

"Un-friggin-believable," Barb said.

"Can I use it to find the phone numbers of some...um, wildlife preserves?" Haley said. She didn't want to push her luck and ask for a ride until and unless she found a promising lead.

"Sure."

Haley was more hopeful than she had been since Jamir's capture. As she and Barb followed Lorraine to the far side of the building, Barb asked, "So what are you doing here?"

Lorraine smiled. "A little of this and a little of that."

"Are you getting paid?" Haley asked.

"Ha!" Lorraine chuckled to herself as if Haley's question figured into some private joke.

Okay, I guess I know where the idea of Americans working for free comes from.

Rounding the corner of the building they came upon Lorraine's Toyota. She pulled out her keys and unlocked it. As far as Haley knew, it was the only car in the village. No wonder she kept it locked and somewhat hidden. The curiosity factor alone would have kids climbing all over it.

Haley and Lorraine sat in the front and Barb sat in the back. There were some converter boxes and things Haley wouldn't understand without a degree in electronic engineering.

At first Haley didn't know if Lorraine would help her translate. Maybe she'd want to stay and watch her stuff...or if she trusted them, she might return to taking care of the kids. It didn't matter. She knew enough Bengali to ask about a tiger that was a beloved pet. That didn't seem too ridiculous, did it?

She powered up and waited for a connection. When it happened, she almost cried. Feeding the question into a search engine, she found her answer. There were forty eight tiger preserves in India. *Damn. Forty-eight!*

It didn't matter. She'd call as many as she could before Lorraine decided she wasn't willing to share her toys any more.

Jamir's stomach growled. Or was that another animal snoring in its sleep? At the next rumble, he affirmed it was his hunger making itself known. *I hope they intend to feed us. Why go to the trouble of capturing us alive only to let us die of starvation?*

As if he had been heard, two men opened a door into their cargo hold. Jamir smelled meat. Delicious, raw meat. He got to his feet and wished he could pace.

"So how do we feed them without getting bit?" one guy asked the other.

"Slip the steak between the bars. When the animal grabs it, let go."

"What about water?"

"What about it?"

"You've got to give them water. They'll die in days without it and the trip to New York takes almost a month."

New York? Jamir's ears perked up.

"Look, we'll think of something. Maybe if we toss an open bottle of water to them, they'll lick up what spills."

"That doesn't seem very efficient."

"Okay, fine. *You* can reach in and fill their water dishes."

"I'll ask the captain. He does this all the time, so he must know."

Jamir almost roared in joy, but he contained himself. This was one time he wanted to cooperate fully with the humans. They were heading to New York. He remembered Haley saying that's where she lived. Surely she'd go back there.

She might be on her way now. She has no reason to stay in India with me gone—unless Shahid... No. His brother would not hold her there, no matter how much he might want her. Haley had her own mind and she had wanted to go home. For once he was glad of that.

The meat was inserted between his bars and he accepted it carefully. He did not want to get anywhere close to the fingers that fed him. As soon as he had it to himself, he fell on it, ravenously.

Haley had called all the tiger reserves on Lorraine 's phone. She had given each of them Barb's satellite phone number in case Jamir was found later, but something told her she'd never receive a call.

Hanging up after talking to the last possibility, Haley slumped down in the passenger's seat.

"No luck, huh?" Lorraine asked.

"No, I'm afraid not."

"Who did you say owned the tiger?"

"Oh—a friend of ours." She glanced at Barb in the back seat, who shrugged, so Haley figured she had no better ideas.

"I don't think they're supposed to be kept as pets."

"Yeah, well…"

Barb piped up. "He was born in captivity. Doesn't know how to care for himself in the wild."

That was about as far from the truth as it gets, but Haley couldn't complain, especially when that explanation seemed to satisfy Lorraine .

She nodded. "Well, I'm sorry he's missing. If I hear anything, I'll give you a call."

"Thank you. I'll write down the number for you."

Lorraine chuckled. "You've given it out so many times, I have it memorized."

Haley nodded. "I'm really grateful for your help. The use of your computer and phone and…everything."

"Don't mention it. You'd do it for someone else, I'm sure."

The women got out of the car and Lorraine locked the doors.

Barb stretched. "Where to now, Hale?"

"I guess it's time to wait for the bus," she said sadly.

"Unless you want to stay for lunch," Lorraine offered. "Or longer…we can really use the help."

Haley glanced at Barb. She knew her friend wouldn't consider a stay at the orphanage, no matter how much they were needed. "I'm not hungry, but if you are…"

Barb laid a hand on Haley's shoulder. "It'll be all right. Someone will call."

Haley just couldn't be brave any longer. She sank to the dirt and began to cry.

Lorraine tried to comfort her with a hug, but once the tears had started Haley didn't think she could stop them.

"Oh, Haley…" Barb threw her hands in the air. "Okay, we'll stay a little longer."

Haley jumped up, whooped, and threw her arms around Barb's neck. "Thank you!" She sniffed. "You're a true friend."

"I'm a true moron who'll probably regret this, but a couple more weeks won't kill us—I hope. We can probably stay with the Ti—I mean, the guys if there's no room here."

Barb was actually relieved when they agreed not to take up precious space at the orphanage and instead, decided to return to the temple. Her reaction kind of surprised her, but she could think of two reasons to return.

First, she kind of liked Shahid. Yes, he was an obvious alpha, but to be honest, that turned her on. Her second reason was to get another look inside that temple. She only got a glimpse of what was inside, but if it was what she thought it was, the guys ought to know. Either they had no idea what the object was, or their Gods were playing a cruel joke on them—or both.

Strolling up to the temple, they found the other two men, still naked, sitting on the steps. Shahid was finishing his hut and wearing his loin cloth, unfortunately. Barb wanted a peek behind the leather.

He stopped working. "You are back."

Haley heaved a sigh. "I can't leave yet. Barb kindly agreed to stay another couple of weeks, in case Jamir returns."

Shahid smiled at Barb. "I think she finally realizes the depth of your love for my brother."

Barb threw her hands up. "What can I say? I'm just a big mushy romantic under all my bluster."

Haley giggled and Shahid grinned.

"Wow, I think that's the first time I've seen you smile," Shahid.

Shahid strolled over to her. "You entertain me, Barb. Is that the right word?"

"Sure, that'll work." She winked. "I could entertain you in another way as soon as you finish that hut, if you're nice to me."

His eyebrows shot up.

Haley gasped. "Are you saying you want to have sex with Shahid?"

Barb shrugged. "It occurred to me." She quickly turned to Shahid. "It's not like I'm in love with you or would even consider staying like my friend here." She gestured at Haley with her thumb. "It would just be for a little fun."

Shahid chuckled. "I like fun." He returned to working on his hut with more speed than before.

Haley faced Barb with her arms crossed. "I thought you weren't interested in Shahid."

"I'm not interested in a long-term relationship, especially because he's kind of a tyrant, but he turns me on. What can I say?"

Haley laughed. "You don't have to say anything. Enjoy him while you can. If nothing else, it'll give you some interesting memories and maybe another Hallsnark card."

"Hopefully not. I have cards for one-night-stands, but this fling better not fit one of those. They're nasty."

"Like?"

"Like; *Violets are blue, roses are red, don't call again, 'cause you're lousy in bed.*"

Haley doubled over, laughing. "Please tell me you don't sell a lot of those."

"Not as many as some of the others, like the break-up cards. Those go like hotcakes."

"Give me an example of your best seller." Barb tapped her chin, trying to think—it seemed as if her business were a million miles away. "Okay, I think the one we sell the most of is actually a wedding card. It says, *Wishing you good luck, on this your wedding day,* and on the inside it says, *Grateful for my luck that you're the one that got away.*

Haley burst out laughing, but stopped when Shahid strode over, picked up Barb and threw her over his shoulder, then carried her off to his finished hut.

"Whoa. Slow down, caveman."

Shahid stood over Barb where he laid her on the straw. "I thought this is what you wanted."

"It is…I'm just—well…" She began disrobing as she talked. "You understand the concept of foreplay, don't you?"

"Of course. All creatures use some type of foreplay. They may display bright feathers, or growl, or dance…"

"Yeah, but I like it to last longer than three seconds."

"Is that what you thought?" He untied his loin cloth and let it fall to the straw floor. He was already erect. "By telling you to roll onto your hands and knees that I did not intend to give you foreplay?"

Her breath hitched. "Well, yeah. What *did* you intend?" She tossed her t-shirt, shorts and panties off to the side, heedless of where they landed.

He looked as if he might drool. "Never mind that now. Tell me what you want and I will give it to you."

Barb sighed. *I suppose I can't hold it against him. He probably doesn't get many willing women walking into his midst, and if they did he's contractually obligated to run them off.* "Okay, this is what I like...lay down next to me."

Shahid only hesitated a moment, then did as she asked. Apparently it wasn't worth arguing as long as he got laid in the end.

"Now, kiss me." She hoped he knew how to kiss.

He swooped in and delivered the most toe-curling kiss she'd ever experienced.

Good God. I guess I didn't need to worry about that.

Her thoughts dissipated like vapor. She lost track of time and space, everything except the sensations exploding in her own body and the strong, hard, man in her arms.

When, at last, rational thought returned, she grasped his cock and squeezed gently. He moaned into her mouth. She cupped his chin with her other hand and guided him down to her breast. "I like to be suckled."

"But I am not a child."

She snorted. "You can say that again."

"If you wish, I will do it."

"It'll get me hot and wet for you. That's kind of the whole point of foreplay."

"I understand."

And he must have, because he sucked her nipples hard enough and long enough to cause ripples of bliss to shoot straight to her womb. She stroked his penis and he occasionally emitted a growl from deep in his throat.

At last he let her breast pop out of his mouth. "What is next?"

She chuckled. "It's not a formula. You should simply follow what your instincts are telling you from moment to moment."

"My instinct is telling me to fuck you. Now."

Barb smiled. "In that case..." She rolled onto her hands and knees and presented her backside to him.

He groaned but positioned himself behind her. "You have a most beautiful *yoni.*"

"A what?"

He fingered her slit and she grabbed his hand. She placed the pad of his big finger on her clit and said, "Rub that spot, right there. It'll drive me wild."

He emitted a low growl. She wasn't sure how to interpret it, but she figured he might be frustrated. "You can do it while we fuck. In fact, I prefer it that way."

"Good."

He didn't say any more, he simply thrust into her and rubbed her clit while he found his rhythm. She moaned. Powerful sensations overwhelmed her all at once and she found herself quivering right away. Her moans increased in volume and frequency. Before she knew it, she was screaming. Her orgasm burst out of her like never before. It was as if a damn broke. She shook and cried out her climax as he jerked and grunted.

When she finally reached her last aftershock, she batted his hand away from her clit. "No more. I can't take it. Stick a fork in me, I'm done!"

"Afork? What is afork?"

Barb burst out laughing. He withdrew and watched her as she collapsed and rolled back and forth chuckling.

"Are you making fun of me?"

She shook her head and wiped tears from her eyes. "No. Not at all. It's just that...ah, hell. I feel great. Thank you. I needed that."

He eyed her strangely, then shrugged. "I enjoyed it too. If you want more, I am agreeable."

"Oh, you sure are. I'll definitely take you up on that later."

CHAPTER 18

Jamir thought some of the other animals weren't looking very well, but all had been fed daily. Ice fed through the bars into their dishes was supposed to keep them hydrated. The only problem was some of the animals didn't know what to do. The lion didn't wait for it to melt. He'd take a bite in the middle and large pieces would explode onto the straw. He'd paw at it and eventually, he might bite it again, or just break it into little bits that melted faster. The snakes slithered around it, or tried to choke it. If lucky, they'd swallow it whole.

The one thing Jamir had been given that made all the difference was hope. That alone kept him going during the long voyage.

He'd had a lot of time to think about what he would do as soon as he got to New York. He had to be let out of this cage at some point. It was too small and getting foul, since there had been no attempts to clean it.

As soon as he saw an opportunity, he'd escape. If he could find something to hide behind, it would only take a moment to shift. Finding clothes would be the next challenge, but he'd figure that out later. For now, all he planned to do was get out in the open and run.

This ship seemed to have stopped. Yes, he eventually learned that he was on a ship. A few days ago they'd sailed around something called The Cape of Good Hope. It confirmed Jamir's belief that this was a change he did not want to resist.

At last the door to the cargo hold opened. Several men entered. More than Jamir had seen before.

"I want to get a good look first. No sense in buying a dead animal," the man in the dark clothing said. He strolled by the lion and stopped. "He looks kind of skinny."

"You can fatten him up when you get him to wherever you're taking him. Where are you taking the big cats anyway?" the one they called the captain asked.

"Does it matter?" the first muttered, dismissively.

"Nope. It might even be better if I don't know. So, are you satisfied?"

The guy took a quick glance in Jamir's direction and said, "Sure. Put 'em in my trailer."

"Do you want them together?"

"Why not? Do you think they'll fight?"

"They don't get along in the wild, but they've actually mated in captivity. Ever heard of a liger?"

"You're kidding me."

"Nope. Look it up. There's also a tigon. A liger is bigger. Depends on if the lion or tiger is the daddy."

"Do you think these two—?"

The captain burst out laughing. "Not unless you've got a female back at the ranch. These are both males."

"Damn. I'll bet I could get a small fortune for a liger."

"I imagine so, meanwhile you still owe me a small fortune for these two. Pay up. We won't off load them until you do."

The guy pulled a piece of paper and scribbled some words on it. Handing it to the captain, he said, "Put the lion in first. I have a steak and trough of water in there for him. As soon as he's there, we'll close the barrier between compartments, then put the tiger in. This bad boy doesn't look quite as hungry as the other guy. If they're busy eating, they'll be less interested in fighting. Right?"

"Whatever you say." The captain barked out some orders to his men and they shoved rolling carts beneath the cage. As they heaved the lion to the doorway, the big cat protested with a weak roar.

It sounds as if I'll be missing a good meal when I make my escape.

Barb and Haley were having dinner in a Kolkata restaurant before returning to their hotel. Haley had tried to convince Barb to wait a few days longer in case there was any news of Jamir while they were in the city, but then Barb told her the Kolkata cops were looking for her.

"For skipping out on a hotel bill? I was only a few hours late checking out."

Barb winced. "I may have accidentally identified you. I made a slew of pictures and showed them to everyone when I was trying to find you. The cops must have showed it to the hotels. They figured out who you were and offered to help me—for a price."

"Are you kidding me? They wanted a bribe?"

"Don't worry. I didn't pay the bastards."

"I'll bet you told them what you thought of them too."

"You know me well."

"Think you can make a card for that?"

"Honey, I can make a Hallsnark card for any and every occasion. How about; *Your blackmail attempt hit a glitch. Next time try it with someone who's rich.* Yeah, that one needs work. I'll think about it on the plane."

"I wish I could laugh, but I'm afraid I'm just not in a humorous mood right now."

"I understand. You found a real hottie. Jamir is the love of your life... Maybe you can come back over at Christmas and see if he made it back."

"Yeah." She sighed. "Meanwhile I'll be going crazy, wondering where he is—what he's going through."

"Chances are, he'll be fine. He's immortal, after all."

"Yeah, but I can't stop worrying anyway. Who took him and for what purpose? Is he hungry? Is he stuck in a cage and unable to get out?"

"Worrying won't help. Besides, he's probably more at peace with his circumstances than you are. Isn't he some kind of acidic?"

"I think you mean, *ascetic.*"

"Yeah, that. He's probably praying or meditating or something. Transcending the whole mess. You should probably try that too. It couldn't hurt."

"Believe me, I've been praying. To my God, to his Gods and Goddesses, to anyone who can tap into to my heart and soul... I really wish I could stick around longer to see if anyone is listening."

"We've already waited too long as it is. Just get yourself back to New York and try to lose yourself in your work or something—while you still have a job."

"Ugh. Do you know how hard it is to teach when your mind is elsewhere?"

"Sorry, no. Look, you can have the sat phone. If anyone calls, you'll know what happened right away."

"Thanks, Barb." It was little consolation. Jamir might be immortal, but she was fairly certain there were things even he couldn't survive.

Barb moved on to the next question. "So, should we try to book a flight, or just show up at the airport in case the cops put out an APB or whatever they call it here?"

"Let's call the airlines. At this point, I don't care if I get arrested. At least I'll have a bed and three square meals a day."

"In a Calcutta jail? Don't count on it."

Haley mulled over the possibilities and said, "Yeah, you're right. Let's just show up and see if we can get out of the country. I doubt the Indian government will extradite me for a hundred and fifty dollars."

"Sounds like a plan."

After a few moments of quiet reflection, Haley asked, "Barb?"

"Yeah?"

"What will I do when I get back to New York and no one calls?"

"You can't think like that. You have to stay positive—even if it's a long shot."

"I guess you're right. It's just that as each day goes by…"

"I know. Well, to answer your original question about what you're going to do, you'll just return to work and continue to wait, I guess."

"That's not what I mean. What about when I'm not at work. I can't continue to go out with you, Maura, and Ronda, trying to meet ordinary men. I just can't do the dating thing anymore."

Barb paused, like she was thinking it over. "I'm not sure what to tell you, Haley. I guess you'll go through the loss and mourn him like anyone would in your situation—not that anyone has been in your situation, but you know what I mean. Then, who knows? Someday, you might find someone else you're just as crazy about."

"Doubt it." A lump formed in her throat and unshed tears burned her eyes.

Barb reached across the table and grasped her hand. "Look, I'm no good at this, but I want to be supportive. I'll help you get through it."

Haley couldn't hold in the tears any longer.

Barb rounded the table and gave her friend a hug. "Will you do me one favor?"

"If I can…" she expected it had something to do with bucking up.

"Will you go shopping with me? I'll never have another chance to pick up the gorgeous fabrics and jewelry they have here at their ridiculously low prices. Besides, you owe me a suitcase."

Haley chuckled through the tears. "Sure. Retail therapy sounds like a great idea."

Jamir calculated his timing precisely. As soon as they had wheeled his cage to the loading dock and come close enough to the trailer so they could usher him from one to the other, they opened his door. Instead of walking into the enclosure holding the meat and water he so badly wanted, he made a sudden sharp turn, leaped off the platform, and hit the ground, running.

"Hey!"

"Fuck!"

"What the hell?"

Their voices faded as he dodged his way through the maze of shipping containers and emerged in a busy metropolis. Wide, hard streets were filled with moving vehicles. The sidewalks were clogged with people. At least the humans had the good sense to be afraid of him and shrink out of the way.

Shrieks followed him wherever he went. He had to find a

place to shift in private, but people were everywhere. They scattered before him so he could keep moving, but eventually he had to slow to a walk. Without proper food and exercise, he tired quickly.

At last, he found a space between buildings where he could see no people. A large metal structure would hide him from view for a few moments. He hoped it would be enough.

He charged down the alley and hid behind the foul smelling bin. In a split second, he shifted. Standing up from his crouched position, he could just see over the top of his hiding place. A couple of faces peered in his direction while leaning into the gap between the buildings.

"Hey! Did you see a tiger in there?" one of the men called.

What could he say? If he said, "no," they'd realize he was lying. Then they'd probably bring him to the police for interrogation.

"He ran right past me," he answered.

"Jesus." The other one said. "My kid's school is in that direction."

"I will look for him," Jamir called back to them.

"Hell, no. I'll call animal control and the police." He was fishing something out of his jacket as he spoke.

A woman peeked around the corner and said, "Can you believe it? A tiger in the city! I wonder where he came from."

As the onlookers discussed their opinions on the matter, Jamir realized his nakedness was a problem. He couldn't step away from the dumpster without covering up somehow. He spied a pile of folded papers tied with a string. While he was still hidden, he untied the string and used the paper to fashion a loin cloth. It was easy since they were already folded, and just draping the folded paper over the string made about the right size garment to cover his private parts. One flap in the front, one in the back. Perfect.

He tied the string around his waist and nodded, satisfied

with his resourcefulness. At some point, he'd have to find clothing like the people here wore. Perhaps he could appeal to the people standing on the hard walkway.

Strolling toward them, he asked, "Can you please help me find some clothing?"

The woman gasped and the two guys started laughing. The woman shook one of the guys and said, "Don't laugh. He's obviously homeless."

"Hey buddy," one of them said, "Did you get rolled, or did you give someone the shirt off your back?"

"And your pants..." the woman added.

Jamir didn't know what to say. Rolled didn't make sense to him, but giving his clothes made him sound noble, so he'd go with that. "I gave them away."

One guy elbowed the other and mumbled something that sounded like, "Nutbag" under his breath.

Instead of someone answering his request for clothes, the people walked off, leaving him in no better condition than before. Perhaps they had gone somewhere to get him clothing and food. Or perhaps they were treating him as most beggars were treated in his country—as if he wasn't even there.

He strolled to the opening and saw more people walking by at a fast pace.

"Excuse me," he said to the first few faces he saw. They glanced at him, then faced forward and kept walking. No one spoke to him. At last, someone tossed a rectangular piece of green paper with someone's face on it at him. What it was for, he had no idea.

Barb and Haley had gone through the exhaustive check-in procedure, made it through security, and boarded the plane for London. Afraid she'd lose the tenuous control she had over her tears, Haley had been quiet throughout. Barb seemed to realize she needed emotional space and didn't press her to talk.

As soon as they settled into their coach seats, Barb pulled a book out of her carry-on.

"Where did you have room to stash a book?" Haley asked.

"Huh? Oh, you mean among all the gorgeous souvenirs I picked up?"

"Yeah. What did you get, by the way?"

"At last count, two sarees with matching blouses and petticoats, three kurtis, and four pashminas. The jewelry is in the front pocket, and I think you were with me when I bought all of that."

"Not a bad haul for half a day of shopping."

"Hey, when the price is so right and I know I'm never going to return..." Barb glanced at Haley with an anxious expression. "I'm sorry. I didn't mean to upset you."

"It's all right, Barb. I realize it's a long shot. But if Jamir makes it back, *I'm* going to return to India. I know you didn't like it, but I was starting to adapt."

"You sure were. If you had told me a couple of months ago that Haley Hunnicutt would leave her cute Manhattan condo to sleep in a thatch-roofed hut in the wilds of India, I'd have peed myself laughing."

Haley smiled. Barb had a way of pulling her up and out of herself when she needed it most. Sadness returned quickly, however. All she had to do was think about going back to her old life—alone, and everything she'd lost came crashing down again.

Barb must have noticed. She shoved the book in the carryon and pulled out the bag of jewelry from the front pocket.

"Help me decide which piece to give to Ronda. I know she

can make almost anything, since jewelry design is her hobby, but I might find something she could take apart and redo however she likes, or something she wouldn't think to make for herself."

It didn't take a genius to realize she was offering Haley a brief distraction. As Barb laid out her treasures on the fold-down tray table, Haley thanked her lucky stars for such caring friends. She knew they were wonderful, smart, giving women, but to actually go after her, half a world away...

"Barb?"

"Yeah?"

"I don't know if I ever thanked you."

"For what?"

"Being my friend."

Barb snorted. "Don't get mushy, okay? I just did what any friend would do."

"No, you did more than most close friends would do. *Much* more."

"You didn't think we'd just forget about you, did you?"

"No. I thought..." *What did I think?* "I guess, I just thought you were all off meeting your own immortals and too busy to be worried or concerned about me. Oh, and I *had* thought I mailed those post cards. If things had worked out, I'd have sent you all invitations to my big, fat Indian wedding."

Barb chuckled. "I guess it hasn't been a total waste. I got all this loot." She swept her hand over the jewels on the tray table. "And you had one hell of an Indian experience. How many people can claim to have fallen in love with a Bengal tiger in West Bengal?"

Haley smiled slightly. Yes, she had quite a story for her memoires, but is that all it would ever be? A chapter in her life's history? What about Jamir? Is that all it would be to him? Would his belief in reincarnation help him move on?

Did she want him to just forget her and wait for the next version of Haley? Or Helen? Helen .3?

Barb broke into her reverie. "What do you think? The ruby ring?"

"What about it?"

"For Ronda."

"Oh, yeah. I'm sure she'd love it."

"The scroll-work seems like something she'd never have the patience to do. I'm betting she'll appreciate the time it took to get it right."

"Probably. Good choice."

"Okay, now what do you think Maura would wear?"

Haley had to admit, gazing at shiny baubles was a nice distraction from her sad thoughts. "I like this one." She pointed to a silver necklace with a pendant gem that might have been an emerald, but darker and more opaque than expected.

"Green is a great color on her. Okay, so the jade is for Maura."

"So that's a jade?"

"Yup. A beauty too. It's natural, not manufactured like the ruby."

"How can you tell?"

"I had quite a nice conversation with the shop keeper while you were buying shoes. Do you think Ronda would rather have a natural stone?"

"No. Don't second guess yourself. I think you had it right the first time."

"Probably. So, how about you? Which one would you like?"

"You got one for me?"

"Of course. You were too depressed to shop for fun stuff. All you got was what you needed to wear home."

Haley sighed. "You're such a good friend."

"Hey, what did I tell you about the mushy stuff?"

"Okay, okay." Haley took a long look at the remaining jewelry. There were a pair of pearl earrings…no, too pure for how she was feeling right now. A yellow gem…again, too sunny. "What's this brown stone?"

"Ah, of course," Barb said, like it was the perfect choice. "Tiger eye."

She picked up the gold necklace and fastened it around Haley's neck.

"Are you sure you don't mind? I mean, this is gold. It was probably very expensive."

"You'd be surprised how ridiculously cheap these were compared to what they'd cost at home. Thank goodness I have a high limit on my credit card."

Haley put her hand over the tiger eye pendant between her collarbones. Barb was right. It was the perfect stone to remember her "Indian experience" or whatever it would turn out to be.

CHAPTER 19

"You poor man," a gentleman exclaimed.

He rushed over to Jamir and took off his jacket.

Since Jamir didn't know what to do with it, the gentleman draped it around his waist and tied it. "What are you doing here, and with no clothes on?"

"I am not sure. I was kidnapped. When I got away, I ran. This is as far as I got."

"Oh, my goodness! You must have been scared to death. Are you hungry?"

"I am, yes."

The man may have been in his fifties. He had straight, gray hair cut short. His black pants matched the top he gave away.

"Let me take you someplace that can help you."

"That would be most kind."

"My name is Bruce. What's your name?"

"Jamir."

"All right, Jamir. First order of business. We need to get you some clothes. Then I'll buy you dinner and call some homeless shelters."

"Thank you," Jamir said. "I knew a city of this size would have a few kind people willing to help me."

Bruce took Jamir's arm and strode off into the city. "How did you find yourself in this state?"

"What state? New York?"

"Well, yes, that too, but I actually meant this state of undress."

"Oh. I was naked when I was kidnapped."

"By whom?"

"I don't know."

"Oh, silly me. Of course you don't know, or you'd have gone to the police. Right?"

"Yes, right."

Bruce shook his head and made a tsk, tsk noise. "How long were you there on that corner?"

"I don't know. Several minutes?"

"Do you know if they demanded ransom?"

"From whom?" Jamir felt he had used the word correctly. If only Haley were here. He would ask her—or she would offer the right word without his asking. He liked how she did that. He sighed, quietly. Finding Haley would have to wait until he was able to walk through every inch of the city and look for her. Right now, he needed the help he'd been offered.

It gave him comfort to know Vishnu was with him everywhere he went. Just as the Gods watched over him in India, they also kept Jamir safe here. He hadn't learned much about Haley's religion. Was she Christian, like Helen? It didn't matter to him, but he hoped whatever her spiritual beliefs were she had strong faith that would sustain her while they were separated.

Bruce interrupted his thoughts. "I have a friend who works at Barney's, but I can't bring you in there like this.

There's an inexpensive department store on Cortland St. That's where I'm taking you."

Inexpensive sounded good to Jamir. He didn't want to cost this gentleman a day's pay just to cover his nakedness.

"The employees tend to be surly though, so let me do the talking."

"As you wish," Jamir said.

Soon Bruce found the store he was looking for. They walked in the front door and a security guard stopped them.

"Hey, you can't come in here like that. You're half naked." He pointed to Jamir's strangely dressed body.

"Why do you think we're here?" Bruce asked. "Certainly not for *my* wardrobe."

"Look, I don't care how much you spend on clothes, this guy can't come in."

By now other employees had spotted them and were whispering to each other. One of them picked up a telephone and made a frantic sounding call.

The argument continued until finally, a well-dressed man approached the trio.

"I'm the manager. What's going on?"

"This guy isn't dressed. He can't come in here." The guard crossed his arms.

Bruce puffed himself up. "Excuse me, but does this establishment sell clothing?"

"Of course we do."

"And I assume you've seen the movie, Pretty Woman?"

The manager smiled. "Are you saying you're prepared to spend an obscene amount of money on this gentlemen's clothes?"

"No," Jamir had to speak up. "Please don't."

Bruce held up one hand. "Let me do the talking, Jamir."

As much as he needed the help Bruce was offering him, he didn't want to cause a scene or get the man in trouble, and he certainly couldn't pay him back for a lot of clothing he didn't need.

The manager turned and waved them to follow. "Come with me. I'll have someone attend to you, personally."

"That's more like it," Bruce said.

The security guard scowled as they strode off to the men's department.

The manager found a reasonably polite employee and said, "Fritz, take good care of this gentleman and his friend. Find a dressing room for him right away, and bring him what he needs."

"Yes, sir." Fritz said. Then he gave Jamir the once-over, appraising him from head to toe. "Follow me."

"I'll pick out his clothes," Bruce said.

"Thank you," Jamir said to the manager before he departed. "Thank you," he echoed to Bruce. He said one more thank you to the man called Fritz and allowed himself to be escorted to the edge of the showroom floor, then closeted in a small room. At least it was larger than the cage in which he was kept for over a month.

Haley dropped her duffle bag in the middle of her seven hundred square foot, one bedroom condo. She tried to picture Jamir here. *What was I thinking?* The place was tiny. It had no view—or more accurately she had a view of a brick wall. It was the best she could afford with her inheritance in a decent Manhattan neighborhood, and living in Manhattan where her friends were was worth the sacrifice of space and greenery.

Plus Haley could walk to the college where she taught, or take public transportation during inclement weather. She owned her place, outright, and only had to pay the maintenance costs. That gave her plenty for clothes and shoes—things that used to be important. Things she was ready to give up completely for love.

Barb sublet the place down the hall and it wasn't cheap, but her greeting card business had taken off and was doing well. Barb had the life, according to a lot of people. Worked from home doing something she loved, and had family help for the grunt work. Her brother owned a print shop where the cards were made, dirt cheap, and yet another brother ran a warehouse and handled the distribution for her. Her little sister was a talented artist and wanted to help make the cards too.

No wonder Barb was anxious to return home. All Haley had was her stuff and her little cat, and she'd bet even Visa was missing his old life. She had to get to O'Malley's soon and take Visa off Mr. O'Malley's hands.

Barb knocked on Haley's open door.

"Can I come in?"

"Sure. You didn't get your fill of me on an all-day, all-night commute?"

"Oh, I'm gonna crash in a minute. But before I do, I just wanted to say welcome home."

Haley's eyes began to tear up again.

"Oh, crap," Barb muttered. She strode into the living room and hugged Haley.

"I'm sorry," she sniffled. "I'm just so conflicted about being here. I feel guilty for leaving him, even though I don't know where he is."

"I understand. Get some rest. I'll call the girls tonight and see if they're back and ready to go out."

"No, don't bother. I have to call O'Malley's anyway. Got to pick up Visa. Maura's 'Da' will tell me."

"Right. Well, maybe we can all meet there. You know how he loves us to bring a little class to his bar."

"Yeah, very little." She chuckled.

"That's the Haley I know. Keep that sense of humor going. I'll see you tonight. Now go sleep off that jet lag."

"Will do."

Haley knew sleep would come hard, if at all. Every time she closed her eyes, she saw a brown-skinned man with black hair and love in his eyes.

Jamir had to extricate himself from Bruce, but after the man had been so kind to him, he didn't know how. Vishnu was merciful enough to lead Jamir to Haley's city. That was not an accident. He worried about Shahid but knew that Vishnu would not let him starve or leave the temple unprotected. As they had pledged their loyalty to Vishnu, he had promised to keep them safe and well for eternity.

"I need to look for my friend. Thank you for helping me. You have been most kind. Now that I am dressed appropriately, I can try to locate her." Jamir scratched at the itchy textile covering his legs. *Why do men limit their motion and suffocate their skin in such a fabric?* The shirt material was light weight, but Jamir couldn't bring himself to take the jacket Bruce wanted to buy for him, never mind the blue noose! He politely declined the items repeatedly until Bruce and the salesman gave up.

"What's your friend's name?" Bruce asked.

"It's Haley. She is a beautiful woman with light hair and skin," he said, wistfully.

"Oh." Bruce sounded let down. "Well, what's her last name?" He pulled a shiny black item out of his inner jacket pocket.

"I do not know. All she said was 'Haley.'"

Bruce stared at him. "That's it? No last name?"

Jamir thought hard, trying to remember any additional name, then shook his head.

"Where did you meet her? Some bar?"

"No. She came to me in West Bengal." Jamir thought again about his home. How was he to return? Would he ever see his brother again?

"Christ. And you're sure she's somewhere in New York?"

Jamir nodded. "She has a job here. Her friend Barb came to get her and bring her back. She seemed concerned about how much time was left before she had to return to her job."

"Okay. Do you know the friend's last name?"

"No." *If only I could get away from him, I am sure Vishnu would lead me to her.* Jamir's love might be tested, but he would not give up.

"Do you have a picture of either of them?"

"No. I wish I had a picture of Haley, but I do not."

"Great. No last name and no photo. Does she have any individuating characteristics? Like tattoos or birth marks?"

"No. She is unmarked." Glancing at the dozens of people walking by, and remembering the crowded streets he'd already seen, Jamir realized he might have a hard time locating her with so little to go on.

"Oh boy," Bruce muttered. "I don't suppose you know where she lives."

Jamir sighed. "Sadly, no."

"Did she mention a borough? Anything about her neighborhood?"

"All she said was New York."

Bruce placed a hand on Jamir's shoulder. "I'm sorry, friend. I'm afraid there's no way you'll ever find her."

"I cannot accept that. Fate will find a way."

"Good luck with that." Bruce strolled off in another direction, leaving Jamir to find his lover without any help.

It is as it should be. I will find her on my own.

A few seconds and steps later, Bruce halted. "I can't do it." He strode back to Jamir. "I can't leave you here, knowing you'll probably get taken in by con artists. There are people in this city who'll eat you alive."

Jamir smirked. "I doubt that will happen, but thank you for assisting me. Your good karma will repay you, even though I cannot."

"Yeah, yeah. I'm sure."

Haley and Barb strolled into O'Malley's bar. Ronda hadn't arrived yet. Maura's cousin Molly was flirting with a guy by the pool table, so they ambled up to the bar. The TV overhead droned the local news.

A light of recognition sparkled in Mr. O'Malley's bright blue eyes when he turned around. "Ah! It's Barb and Haley back from adventures on t'other side of the world," he said in his Irish brogue. "What can I get for you ladies?"

"A glass of the house white wine for me," Barb said.

"I'll have the same. Thanks again for watching Visa, Mr. O'Malley." Haley placed a statue of Ganesh on the bar. "This is for you. It's supposed to bring luck."

"We can all use a little good luck. The gift is lovely and the thought much appreciated." He opened the refrigerator and grasped a bottle. "Just don't forget to take the cat with you when you leave."

"Don't worry. I won't," Haley said.

Molly spotted Maura's friends and excused herself from the guy playing pool. She rushed over and hugged Haley. "Thank God you're home! We were so worried about you."

"Weren't you worried about me?" Barb asked.

"Ha. India should have been worried about you. But thank you for going after Haley."

Mr. O'Malley placed their drinks in front of them and said, "Did you hear about the big tiger from India that escaped somewhere near the docks?"

Haley and Barb stared at each other. "No. What happened?"

"It's been all over the news. Apparently a ship carrying some dangerous animals to be sold illegally lost a tiger. They caught the ship's captain, but not the animal. It was spotted in the financial district and caused an understandable panic. The damn thing's still got to be roaming around the city somewhere. Can you imagine taking out the trash and finding a six hundred pound tiger in the alley?"

Molly chimed in, "I'm just piling up the trash in the back room until they shoot it. Even the boys are behaving themselves, so Da won't toss them out in the alley to settle their differences."

Haley's stomach twisted and her head began to spin.

Mr. O'Malley cocked his head. "You don't look so good, Haley. You're as pale as a ghost."

Barb grasped her elbow and led her to an empty table. Molly rushed ahead and pulled out a chair.

Ronda waltzed in. "Hey, sorry I'm late, but the cab…Jesus, Hale—what did India do to you?"

"Nothing. I'm fine."

"You look like you contracted the worst case of dysentery in history."

Barb shoved Haley's neck down until she was bent over with her head between her knees. "Breathe."

"I'm all right, dammit," Haley yelled at the floor.

Barb let go of Haley's neck and took a step back. "Well, forgive me for helping you not faint."

Mr. O'Malley appeared with a few damp napkins in his hand. "Here. Put these on your forehead, lass."

"I'm fine—really, but thank you."

"If I'd known you'd react to the tiger story like that…well, I probably would have told you anyway. Better you pass out here with people around than at home where you're all alone."

Haley *so* didn't need to be reminded that she lived alone.

Barb squeezed her shoulder in a comforting gesture. "Let's find a more private table."

Did Barb want her to tell the others about her immortal? *I suppose they should know the spell worked…at least for one of us.*

CHAPTER 20

"So that's the story," Haley finished, and leaned back in her chair.

Ronda and Molly stared at her with their jaws hanging open.

Barb snapped her fingers in front of their shocked faces. "Hello...aren't you two going to say anything?"

"I, uh..." Ronda seemed lost for words—a rarity.

Molly cleared her throat and frowned. "Okay. If you and Barb are playing some kind of joke on us, so help me, I'll pour a pitcher of beer over both of you."

"It's not a joke," Haley said.

Ronda finally found her voice and blurted, "That's the craziest story I've ever heard. How can he change like that? I mean, the very physics of it..."

Barb threw her hands in the air. "I knew they'd never believe it. Look, I might not have believed it either, but I saw it with my own eyes."

Haley crossed her arms. "It's not like the werewolves you see in movies. They don't grind and howl and break and pop as they come back together."

"Thank God," Barb added.

"It's some kind of ability bestowed upon them by their God Vishnu back when they were mortal men, so they could better guard his temple. They're more like X-men or something."

"Look, it's a lot to take in," Molly said. "Don't give Ronnie a hard time for expressing her disbelief."

"I didn't say I disbelieved it." Ronda ran her finger over the condensation on her beer mug. "Gee, I missed cold beer while we were in England."

"Huh?" *Random Ronda strikes again.* "What's that got to do with the price of loving a tiger?"

"Nothing. But what did you want us to say? It's a sad, weird, terrifying story. Kind of hard to comment, you know?"

Haley exhaled a deep breath. "Yeah, I guess it is. But I swear on my grandparents' graves, it's one hundred percent true. My parents were cremated and scattered in the ocean, otherwise I'd have sworn on their graves. That's how much I mean what I'm saying."

Ronda nodded. "I get it."

"I should check on my customers," Molly said as she rose from the wooden chair.

"Wait." Barb grasped her arm. "You're just going to get up and go back to work after hearing the biggest news of our lives?"

"I have a job to do. It's probably a miracle my Da isn't giving me a hard time for sitting down with you."

"It's more of a miracle that Haley found her immortal," Ronda said. "I'm still trying to wrap my head around it."

"Oh my God. Look." Molly pointed to the TV and chewed her lip.

"...and in other news, there's still no sign of the escaped tiger. The police are baffled and don't know why a full grown Bengal tiger seems to have disappeared into thin air after a traipse

through Manhattan's financial district. One person snapped this picture..."

Haley bolted out of her chair and got as close to the TV as she could. The image was slightly blurred, but she could have sworn it looked like Jamir. Unfortunately she couldn't see the animal's left ear. That was her only way to be sure.

The story ended with no more information other than a zoo vet stating the tiger was a male and about six-hundred pounds. He said the local police would be carrying tranquilizer darts. Haley didn't know whether to cheer or cry.

Barb sidled up next to her and rested a hand on her shoulder. "You don't really think that he...you know, was captured and sold to a U.S. collector."

Haley had no answer for her. Could Jamir have been taken by hunters and sold on the black market? While researching online, she had learned there were more tigers in the U.S. than in any other country—including India. It was a thin thread of hope, but she grasped it. She knew she was desperately searching for anything to keep her hope alive, but she wouldn't apologize for it either.

Jamir held onto the metal pole until his knuckles turned white. The underground train sped forward. He had never encountered or even dreamed of such a conveyance. Bruce said the contraption was called a subway, and it was taking him to the Bowery. Bruce told him to be careful who he trusted.

In his other hand, he clutched the crude map meant to direct him to a shelter. He thought he would just sleep in the patch of grass called Battery Park, but Bruce said that was not allowed. So he would investigate the shelter.

He wondered why Bruce didn't want to accompany him

but figured he must have been busy. Besides, the man had done so much for him already, he'd never be able to repay him. His last act of generosity had been to give him a green piece of paper, which he explained could be exchanged for things like bus and train fare when he looked for a job.

Jamir didn't have to stay on the subway very long, thank goodness. Bowery was the next stop. Perhaps he should have walked, but Bruce said it would be good for him to get used to taking public transportation. He tried to strike up a conversation with an old Asian woman seated near him, but she turned away. Perhaps she was deaf.

At last Jamir made his way up the stairs to the street. The map indicated the station with an X, and showed him which way to go to get to the other X.

Fortunately it was a day meant for walking—cooler than India, but the sky was blue and clear. Many other people must have decided to enjoy the comfortable weather as well. Dodging them as he traveled along the sidewalks presented a challenge, but he was up for it. He was in Haley's home town, after all—a place he intended to enjoy or at least get used to.

At last he arrived at the place that matched the numbers on his map. The building looked quite old and the windows could use a good washing. Perhaps he could offer to do that for them, thus repaying their kindness.

He entered the building with a smile. Row upon row of empty beds looked promising. Then he followed the sound of voices to a nearby office.

"Hello. My name is Jamir, and I am here for shelter."

The man and woman behind the desk frowned.

"I'm afraid we're full up," said the man.

"Oh. But I saw many empty cots."

"Everyone is out looking for work, or…whatever," said the woman.

"I was told if I came here, you would have food and

shelter until I got on my feet." He pointed to his new shoes. "Thanks to a kind man named Bruce I am on my feet, but I still have no shelter or food." His stomach growled to demonstrate the point.

The woman gave him a pitying look. "The soup kitchen is across the street." She glanced at a device on her wrist. "They'll be open in about an hour. I suggest you get in line now, meanwhile I'll call around and see if I can find a bed for you somewhere."

The man whispered behind his hand, but Jamir heard him say, "You don't have to do that. Just give him the list and let him go."

The woman considered his comment, then turned back to Jamir. "Can you read or write?"

"Sadly, not well. Haley was teaching me when we got separated. I am still looking for her." *Bruce may not have known her, but perhaps these people do.* Hopefully, he asked, "Do you know Haley?"

"What's her last name," the woman asked.

"I do not know. I am aware there could be many Haleys in the city of New York, but she is uniquely beautiful with light hair and skin."

"Sorry," the man said. "There are over eight million people in New York City. Lots of them are beautiful, considering it's home to fashion models. Is she a model?"

"No. She is a teacher."

"That doesn't narrow it down much. There are a lot of schools too," he said.

Jamir's smile, as well as his hope, faded.

The woman cleared her throat. "Go get something to eat, and I'll try to find you a bed somewhere. Stop back after dinner."

"You are most kind. Thank you. Vishnu will shine his light on you."

She smiled, but the man rolled his eyes.

On his way out, he heard the man mutter, "Damned Hari Krishnas. He probably gave them everything he had."

It bothered Jamir to think anyone could be so angry with Krishna, but he sensed it would be wise to avoid talking to the gentleman about it. Bruce had cautioned Jamir to be careful not to trust everyone in this area. Perhaps a difference of opinion could not be discussed here.

With a complete lack of grass or trees, plus the filthy air, how could anyone celebrate life or their place in the world? How could they even think straight? No wonder so many seemed angry. His intuition told him Bruce was right. He would keep his opinions to himself.

Haley and Barb shared a cab to their building. During the silent ride Haley had a chance to run all the possibilities through her head. She didn't know how long a ship from India would take to get to U.S. shores, but she guessed he could have made it here by now. She had spent the rest of the summer—almost a month working in the orphanage and waiting for word from one of the tiger preserves or Shahid, who said he would find her, before finally coming home to rescue her job.

Shahid… She wondered how he was doing. With the other shapeshifters to help him, he was probably doing the same thing he always had—just with a little more help. *Vishnu should have created three shapeshifters from the get-go. Maybe Jamir and I could have found a little time to vacation together. Cripes, I went all the way to India and never saw the Taj Mahal.*

Upon arriving back at their building Barb paid for the cab, and Haley didn't argue with her about splitting it. Her bank account was still smarting from her sabbatical. The doorman greeted them as he always did, but they were both too preoccupied to say much more than, "Hi."

As soon as they were safely ensconced in the elevator, alone, Barb broke the silence.

"Maura would have believed us, since it was her idea in the first place, but do you think Molly and Ronda did?"

"I think so." Haley hit the button for their floor. "It was a good thing you were there though. No one would have believed me if you hadn't backed me up."

"Can't say I'd blame them. It's a pretty fantastic story."

"I know. I lived it and everything's still a little unreal. I didn't hallucinate the whole thing did I? I mean, a tornado didn't pick up something heavy and knock me out, right?"

"Highly unlikely, unless I had the same hallucination at the same time."

The elevator stopped on the second floor and the doors swished open.

"Do you want to come in for a nightcap?" Barb dug her keys out of her purse.

Haley smiled. "Are you coming on to me?"

"Hell, no. I just thought you might want to talk about it some more."

Haley let out a long sigh. "I don't think talking will help. Besides, I have to prepare for tomorrow."

"Isn't the first day of school just for orientation?"

"Not really. I mean, yes, the freshmen got their orientation today, but my first classes start tomorrow. I hope I can concentrate enough to learn their names."

"You're usually pretty good at that. What do you do, use a demonic device or something?"

Haley laughed. "It's called a mnemonic device."

Barb grinned. "I know. I just wanted to hear you laugh again."

"I guess I haven't been much fun to be around lately. I'm sorry."

"Don't be sorry. Just try to get back to normal soon. I plan to meet my immortal someday, and I want you to be happy for me—not jealous."

"I won't be jealous. I'll be thrilled for you." Then she winked. "Besides, who says you haven't already met him?"

Barb smirked but didn't respond as she slipped her key in her lock. "Well…I guess I'll call it a night. Get some sleep and have a good day tomorrow."

Haley's smile faded. "I'll try."

Jamir found a vast array of people waiting for the soup kitchen to open. Men, women and children of different colors and dispositions. He made small talk with the only person who would talk to him at all. A young man of about twenty years. Jamir wondered how someone so young could have fallen on hard times already.

"I'm tryin' to find a job," the young man said. "But I get beat out by the guys with experience. So, I just get in line with the rest of 'em, tryin' to get the temporary stuff. It's usually hard physical labor, but at least it pays the bills." He laughed.

"What are bills?" Jamir asked.

The kid raised his eyebrows. "Boy, you really are right off the banana boat, aren't ya?"

The door finally opened, and hungry people filed in. Jamir followed the person in front of him and ignored the young man's question. How could he tell him he had indeed come over on a boat, but it was full of wild animals and reptiles, not bananas?

"Grab a tray," the kid directed. "By the way, what's your name?"

"Oh. Forgive my rudeness. I am Jamir. What are you called?"

"The name's Jim."

Good. Short, simple. Easy to remember. Jamir followed the rest of the line through to the end where he was handed a plate of food. It smelled good, but he wished it contained more meat. Perhaps deer or even monkey.

Jim took his plate and proceeded to a table with empty chairs. Jamir sat across from him, hoping to continue their conversation.

"Can you tell me what this is called?" He pointed to the brown slice of something on his plate.

"That's meatloaf."

Jamir grinned. *Meat! No wonder it smelled so good.*

Jim then pointed to the pile of white stuff. "That's mashed potato." Then he pointed to the orange vegetables. "Those are carrots."

"Ah. I remember carrots. Haley cooked them for me." He took a bite and chewed. "It tastes different, but similar."

"Who's Haley? Your girlfriend?"

"Yes. I am looking for her. Do you know a beautiful woman with light skin and hair named Haley?"

Jim looked thoughtful for a moment. "Nope. I can't say I know anyone like that. And I'd remember. I like women. Someday I hope to find a sugar-mama."

"Sugar mama?"

"A cool lady who has money and spends it on you."

"Oh. I guess Haley was my sugar mama. She had some rupees and bought food, which she shared with me."

"Yeah? You're lucky. You said you're lookin' for her. Why don't you know where she is?"

Jamir hung his head. "I do not know her last name, or her

address. All I know is that she is a teacher and lives somewhere in New York."

"Oh. I guess you didn't know her that well, then."

"But I did. I knew her very well—when she lived with me in India."

"Wow. You were livin' together in India? I guess she left you, and you decided to follow her, then."

"Not exactly, but it does not matter how we got separated. I must concentrate on finding her now. I wish I could find a place to sleep outdoors."

"If you're not stayin' at the shelter, you should check out Central Park. You can probably find a private spot to crash there."

"Excellent. I will look for this Central Park." Jamir took a bite of the meatloaf. "This is good. Do you know what kind of meat it is?"

"Hamburger."

"I have not heard of that kind of meat. From which animal does it come?"

"Cows."

Jamir shot out of his chair and it tipped over, making a racket. All eyes were on him.

"Hey, Dude. What's the matter?"

"You said we are eating cows."

Jim scratched his head. "But why...Oh, Christ. Now I remember. Cows are sacred in India, right?"

Feeling sick, Jamir just nodded. *I am so hungry. Why did they have to slaughter a cow?*

One of the cooks strode over to them.

"Is there a problem here?"

Jamir pleaded with his eyes, hoping for an alternative. "I cannot eat cows."

"Well, too bad. That's what we're serving today." He

walked away muttering under his breath. Jamir heard the words "Ungrateful bastard."

"Jamir, sit down and finish the other stuff," Jim said. "You won't get anything else until breakfast."

He stared at the carrots and remembered how good they tasted when Haley cooked them. These were a poor substitute. *Maybe the potatoes will be better.*

He picked up his chair and sat in front of his meal again. The dead cow bothered him, but he would just have to eat around it. He took a mouthful of the mashed potato and choked it down. It was even more flavorless than the carrots.

"Hey, I'm sorry, dude," Jim said. "I don't think they get many Indians here. Maybe they'll have chicken tomorrow."

"I hope so."

But Jamir didn't intend to visit this kitchen often. Maybe he could trade some of the green paper for food instead of transportation and walk wherever he had to go. He'd just step up his search for Haley, and as soon as he found her, life would be wonderful again.

"Thank you for your friendship, Jim. I may not see you again. I will look for Haley when I leave here."

"Hey, good luck, man. If she's a teacher, you might check the schools. But don't hang around outside waiting for her. They'll think you're a perv."

"Perv? What is a perv?"

Jim cast his eyes to the ceiling. "Crap. How can I explain this?"

CHAPTER 21

Haley had been called to the dean's office. That was never good, but this time she expected the worst. While teaching, her mind had been wandering so badly, she'd actually answered some of the student's questions incorrectly. Other times, she'd barely heard when asked for clarification and just affirmed whatever nonsense they said to her.

"Do you want to tell me what's going on with you?" the woman asked.

Haley sighed. "Can I sit down?"

The dean lifted her eyebrows, but nodded.

Haley dropped into the uncomfortable wooden chair in front of the dean's desk. "I'm afraid I've been a little distracted lately."

"A little? I was told you said a synonym for drek was Big-Mart."

Haley smirked then tried to quickly hide it.

"I hope you're taking your responsibilities seriously, Haley. You always have before." The dean's face softened. "Something must be going on. What's changed?"

Haley bit her lower lip and tried to think of an explanation that wouldn't sound ridiculous. That left out the truth, for sure.

"I—um...I'm afraid it's well..."

"Spit it out."

"My boyfriend is missing."

"Missing? Like he just went out for a pack of cigarettes and never came back?"

"Sort of...but no. Jamir was absolutely devoted to me. I just know something awful has happened to him."

"Jamir? Is that why you went to India? To meet his family or something?"

"Yes, I met his family."

"And how did that go?"

"Fine."

"Are you sure? Maybe they're more traditional than you think and he was pressured into..."

"No. He only has one brother, and he likes me. That's not the problem."

"Well, I'm clearly not aware of the details, so I can't offer any help. I can, however, encourage you to snap out of it as quickly as possible. Your job depends on it."

A gasp lodged in Haley's throat. "My—job?"

"Yes, your job. You're not tenured, so you *actually do* have to teach these kids."

"I—I... I will."

"Well, thank you for being honest with me about your personal problem. I want to be honest with you too. If I get any more reports about your head being in the clouds, the next step is a written warning. One more after that, and you'll be let go."

Jamir was exhausted by the time he'd found Central Park. He

must have walked four or five miles and the sun had set. If only he was able to use his tiger strength and speed. But it would be impossible to avoid detection with so many people clogging the streets and sidewalks.

Central Park did look promising as far as finding a bit of privacy. It was much larger than Battery Park, and contained woods and hills, rocks and ponds.

It was time to find enough meat to hold him until the following day. He saw several squirrels in the trees and detected many birds, although most had quieted for the night. He did not know what kind of wild animals might live here, but he hoped for something large enough to provide a decent meal.

If he shifted, he could see in the dark, smell his prey and run faster in order to catch and hold his dinner. Perhaps hiding behind a large rock would afford him enough privacy to change for a minute or two. That's all it would take.

I have to try it.

Jamir strayed from the path and eventually spotted a large, secluded rock that would hide him, both in man and tiger form. He raced behind it and stripped off his clothing. With a sense of urgency, he shifted and sniffed the air.

I think—yes! I smell an animal. He followed the scent out from behind the rock and into the woods. He cringed as his footsteps gave him away. In the grass, he could hunt silently, but under the trees a layer of deciduous leaves crunched each time he set down one of his big paws. He hoped the animal might freeze in fear long enough for him to pounce.

At last he spotted the creature. It was like nothing he'd ever seen. It was a medium sized mammal, which resembled a cat, but with a black mask across its eyes and white eyebrows. The rest of its body was covered in dense black and brown fur. He hoped they were not distantly related.

Apparently the animal became aware of him too. It tried

to scurry away, but Jamir used his superior speed and strength and pounced.

"Jesus!"

Jamir whipped his head in the direction of the shocked voice.

Barb and Ronda had dragged Haley out for a shopping trip, but she wasn't in the mood to socialize. Instead, she pretended to be exceedingly interested in the rack of ready-made dresses while she swept them across the bar, one at a time.

Ronda came up beside her and bumped her arm. "Why are you so mopey, honey? I mean, other than the usual. You seem extra moody today."

Haley let out a long sigh. Ordinarily she wouldn't burden people with her problems, but these were her best friends, and she could use the sympathy. "My boss told me my job is in danger."

"Aw, crap. Is the school downsizing?" Ronda asked.

"No." Haley remained silent for a few moments. The girls stared at her and she knew they'd get an explanation out of her one way or another. "I've been distracted lately."

Barb straightened her spine. "They can't fire you for that. Hell, lots of people go through emotional stuff and get a little distracted from time to time. Besides, don't you have tenure?"

"No. Unfortunately when I changed from teaching public high school to a private community college, I had to give that up and start over. Even if I had tenure, I could still be fired if I totally screwed up."

Ronda shook her head in disbelief. "Christ, it's not like

you have Alzheimer's or anything. You'll get over your loss and get back to normal soon. Right?"

Haley shrugged. "I'm not sure I want to teach anymore."

Barb gasped. "I thought you loved teaching. You get to correct people all day long, and they don't get ticked at you for it."

Haley rolled her eyes. "Yeah, there's that."

"What would you do instead?" Ronda asked in a soft, sympathetic tone of voice.

Should I tell them? What the hell...they'll find out sooner or later. "You know how I used to do dog grooming on the side sometimes?"

Ronda smiled. "Oh yeah. I forgot all about that. Do you want to do that full time?"

"Either that or… I've been thinking of becoming a veterinary technician."

Barb narrowed her eyes. "Why? So you can keep an eye out for a certain tiger?"

Haley chewed her lower lip and finally came out with it. "I've been searching the animal hospitals and shelters—you know, just in case. Anyway, whether I find him or not, I want to help those poor, frightened animals."

Ronda placed a hand on her hip. "Leave it to you to want to rescue the underdog."

Barb looked as if she were about to point out the obvious pun, but Haley held up her hand. "It doesn't mean I can't go back to teaching someday. But for now, I think it might be better to hang out with animals. They don't need my help conjugating difficult verbs and explaining the use of the past perfect tense—and they don't rat on you for making mistakes."

"No, they pee and barf on you instead. You could even get bitten."

Haley picked up a cute tailored black dress. "Look at this.

It's perfect for about a million occasions." *Not that I want to go anywhere at the moment.*

"Don't try to distract us," Ronda said. "We're not the ones with an attention deficit."

I really don't feel like defending my choices right now. Maybe the best defense is looking offended. She jammed a fist on her hip. "How I handle my life is my business."

Barb lifted her hands, as if to say, *don't shoot.* "We're not trying to take over your life. We just care about you and want you to be happy. If working with animals will do that, go for it. We'll support you no matter what you decide."

"Thanks." Haley *did* feel a little better getting that out in the open. Just knowing she had friends to love her unconditionally helped more than anything. "I'm going to try this on," she said and held up the classic, simple dress.

"That-a-girl," Ronda said. "You deserve something pretty."

That evening, Haley begged off going out to the clubs and settled on her sofa for a little television time. She had just switched on the power and was about to check what had recorded in her absence when she saw a picture of a Bengal Tiger in the upper right corner in a graphic box. An anchor woman stood in front of the Merchant's Gate entrance to Central Park.

Haley turned up the volume.

"...another tiger sighting, only this time in Central Park." The reporter tipped the microphone toward a middle aged man in a park uniform. "Do you think this could be the same tiger that escaped from a ship last weekend?"

"It's hard to believe it could be the same tiger that escaped on Sunday and was last seen in the financial district. I can't imagine that a giant Bengal tiger could have made it that many miles through the city without being spotted—even at night."

"It does seem ludicrous, in the city that never sleeps" the reporter said. "What about the Central Park Zoo? Are there any missing tigers?"

"The zoo's animals are all accounted for. I'm beginning to wonder if the eye witness account may have been unreliable. No one has been able to verify what the jogger said he saw last night. The police and animal control officers have scoured the park with no visual evidence of a tiger."

"So it may have been one person's imagination or his eyes playing tricks on him."

"It seems likely."

"Let's hope so. Thank you, and now back to the newsroom."

Haley grinned. She turned off the TV and danced around her tiny apartment. There was absolutely no way a tiger could be spotted at opposite ends of the city with no one seeing it travel from one place to the other—unless the tiger could blend in—like if he turned into a man. Knowing her lover, he'd want to be out in nature, thus the park and not the concrete jungle.

"It has to be Jamir!" She said to herself, triumphantly. "It just has to be, and now I know where to look!"

The encounter with the human had been unnerving, but Jamir still felt his best chance of survival was to stay in the park at night and look for Haley during the day. He was no longer as hungry as he was with just the soup kitchen's vegetables. The park provided plenty of small wildlife that he could be sure were not cows.

He sat on a bench with his eyes closed, taking a moment

to commune with nature and Vishnu and the Universe before setting off.

Someone sat on the other side of the bench but didn't interrupt his thoughts. When he opened his eyes, he looked over at his quiet companion.

His eyes grew wide and he gasped. It could not be... "Haley?"

She grinned, then just threw herself into his arms. "Jamir!"

"By the Gods! Please tell me I am not dreaming."

She laughed and squeezed him harder. "You're not dreaming. I was afraid *I* was seeing things."

"Oh, Haley. My love. How I have missed you!"

"I've missed you too—more than you could imagine. I thought I was going to be alone the rest of my life, because you've ruined me for all mortal men."

She pulled away and they grinned at each other like idiots.

Finally, she stood and held out her hand. "Let's go home."

"Home," he repeated. He rose and took her hand, having no idea where she was taking him, but he'd follow her to the ends of the earth and back again without complaint.

They walked hand in hand, talking about the past several weeks and what had happened since his capture. From time to time, he just watched her mouth move, remembered every detail of her beautiful face, and caught the sun sparkling in her golden hair.

How fortunate we are not only to have found each other again, but also to have found each other in the first place.

Jamir halted.

She stopped walking and talking and smiled at him. "What?"

He pulled her into his arms. "I wish to make you my mate.

Will you stay with me for—well, for as long as Vishnu allows it?"

"I will," she said.

He couldn't imagine a happier man on the earth. He lifted her off her feet, hugging her at the same time. She giggled until he set her down, then they kissed so long people around them began to comment. He didn't hear what they were saying, nor did he care. All he cared about was her.

Haley had taken him to a tall building she called home. He couldn't imagine living here with no trees or grass, but wherever she was would be home to him.

She introduced him to someone she called her doorman. That seemed to be his entire job. Opening the door. Perhaps he could get a job like that in another building. It did not seem too difficult. But there was plenty of time for that.

Right now, all he wanted to do was make love to his mate. She led him into a small room with doors that closed by themselves and then moved! When the doors slid out of the way, they stepped out of the room and into a hallway. She led him past other closed doors, but pointed to one along the way.

"That's where Barb lives."

"Behind that door?"

"Yes. Her place is a rental, but I own mine."

"Ah. Like you were going to pay rent to someone in the village to use his tent."

"Exactly."

She seemed pleased that he remembered. He remembered everything. Every moment of their time together. He had lived on those memories as if they were food and water.

When they reached the last door at the end of the hall, she put a metal object into a slot and turned it. It clicked.

"Here it is. Be it ever so humble…"

She swung open the door and he stepped inside. It did not seem humble at all. It was filled with belongings. The house at the tea garden was much larger, but she seemed to own as many or more things. They were all crowded together.

"You have so much. Is this why you did not want to stay in India? Did you miss all these items?"

Haley shook her head. "Amazingly, no. I could have walked away from all of this. It's just stuff." She turned to him and placed her hands against his chest. "Given the choice between you and all my worldly goods, I'd pick *you* every time."

Her words gladdened him, yet he was still confused. "Why then did you want to come back here so badly?"

She chuckled. "Can you imagine asking someone to get rid of all this stuff and sell my place for me? That would have been more than I could ask of anyone. This place is my responsibility, whether I stayed or not."

"I understand. I also understand why freedom from possessions is a prized spiritual ideal among my people."

She glanced around the room. "You have a point." A sly smile spread across her face. "If you think I have a lot of stuff in here, you should see my bedroom."

Ah, we're finally getting to the lovemaking. "I'd like that very much."

She led him to a smaller room with large furniture. Clutter seemed to fill every surface. He tossed several pillows onto the floor and pealed back three coverlets layering the large bed.

"I want you naked on this."

"Your wish is my command," she said.

He liked the sound of that. As she stripped off her pants and top, he unbuttoned his shirt. It took much too long. *I will have to find one of those shirts I can simply pull over my head like she did.*

"Last one in is a rotten egg," she called out as she bounced onto the soft surface.

Rotten egg? It must be another expression he had to get used to—in time. Right now all he wanted to do was make love to his beautiful Haley. Her nude body stretched before him ready and willing, and his mouth watered.

As he crawled over her, he said, "I may be a rotten egg, but I hope you want my company anyway."

"Oh, yes. I want you, all right."

She reached for him and he dove into her arms. His lips met hers. He wanted to devour every inch of her. Their legs tangled as they rolled back and forth, kissing and groping each other.

As he kissed his way down the column of her neck, he murmured, "I missed you so much, Haley."

"I missed you too," she whispered. "So much."

She arched to meet him when he reached her breast. He sucked hard and she moaned louder than she used to.

"You have been unsatisfied for a while," he said, knowing it was true. His Haley would not have taken solace in another man's arms.

"Yes." She reached beneath him and grabbed his lingham.

Welcome sensations promised an end to his sexual hunger—or at least momentary satisfaction. He leaned over and captured her other nipple. She moaned gratefully as he suckled her.

"I love you, Jamir. Even more than I realized."

Joy filled him as he moved down to her yoni. "And to think, we will be making love to each other like this for the rest of your life."

She suddenly cupped his chin and gazed down at him. "I'll get old and wrinkled. Won't that bother you?"

"Not in the least."

She smiled and lay back, allowing him to feast on her most sensitive spot. She grasped the thin fabric beneath her and cried out in bliss over and over. At last, her legs vibrated and she begged, "No more. I can't take any more."

Jamir raised his head, grinning, and wiped his face with the back of his hand.

"I can't move," she said weakly. "Come up here. Kneel over me and stick your cock in my mouth."

It sounded as if she really wanted to suck him too, yet he had exhausted her. Well, helping her out was the least he could do—right? He smiled and walked up on his knees, eventually straddling her face.

She grasped his lingham and guided him into her mouth.

The most powerful phenomenon rolled over and through him as she sucked him. He would never last. "Stop, Haley, or I will spill my seed in your mouth."

She mumbled, "Uh-uh," and went right on sucking.

"You want that?" he asked.

"Um-hm."

Tingling at the base of his spine warned he was close. Any moment... "Gods!" His orgasm hit hard. She swallowed his liquid as he spurted into her mouth. He shuddered and bucked, losing all control. Never had he felt anything so powerful.

At last he withdrew and collapsed beside her.

"Haley..." was all he could articulate.

She propped her head on her elbow and grinned. "Liked that, did you?"

He chuckled, then his laugh grew and grew until a cathartic guffaw loosened and rid him of all the tension from the weeks since his capture.

CHAPTER 22

Jamir paced back and forth in front of the windows. Something wasn't right, and she didn't have an inkling what it might be.

"Jamir? Is there something you need to tell me?"

He halted and turned toward her. That powerful, tan, naked body almost made her drool. "I am worried about Shahid."

She slapped her forehead. "Damn, I should have told you sooner. He's okay. Two more shapeshifters showed up to help him guard the temple."

Jamir's eyebrows rose. "Vishnu sent two more?"

"Yes. Two more tigers."

Jamir closed his eyes. He placed his palms together and said, "Praise the Gods!"

Haley chuckled. "I thought Barb was going to jump out of her skin when she realized three tigers meant one of them was not you or Shahid."

"But they shifted so she would know they were not dangerous?"

"Not right away. She raced for the temple, but only set

one foot inside the door before Shahid fell on her, grabbed her shirt with his teeth and dragged her out."

Jamir's jaw dropped. "She set a foot inside the temple?"

Haley nodded. "Why? What's so awful about that?"

"I should have been there. I am faster than Shahid."

"I'm sure now that there are three of them, the temple is quite safe."

Jamir resumed his pacing. "Shahid does not know I am all right. He will wonder and worry. I do not wish to make him suffer."

Haley let out a resigned sigh. "Go ahead. Say it."

He paused again. "Say what?"

"You want to go back to India, don't you?"

He joined her on the sofa. "Haley, it is natural to miss my home and my brother. Besides, I do not know how you live without a view of earth or sky." He swept his hand to indicate the brick wall view outside her windows.

Visa jumped onto the couch. Jamir scooped him up and scratched under his chin while he purred. "I'll bet your little cat would like to lie in the cool grass as much as your big cat does."

She thought about making a joke about having a couple of cool cats, but it wasn't the time. Haley placed her hand over his. "I know it's not much, but it was the best I could afford. We can always go to the park or the river to make you feel more at home here."

He shook his head. "It is not only that. This box you live in…it is so small. I almost feel as if I am in a cage again."

"Oh. Is that why you've been pacing?"

He stared at the floor. "Yes. I am sorry. I know that is not what you wanted to hear."

She kneaded his shoulders. "I understand. But one of us has to compromise if we're going to be together."

He smiled weakly. "I know. But it is not a compromise when one has to give up everything for the other."

Haley thought about that for a moment. "You're right. It shouldn't have to be that way. Let's look for a new place. Somewhere with a view of grass and trees."

His expression brightened immediately. "You would do that?"

"I can try. It might not be easy to find a place like that on my salary alone. I hate the thought of leaving my friends, but your happiness is important. I can do some more dog grooming on the side."

"What is this salary?"

"Oh, it's the amount of money I make."

"The green paper?"

"Yes, exactly."

"I was told that my labor could be traded for green paper too."

"You think you could get a job?"

He frowned. "Why not? Do you think I would let you provide everything for me while I do nothing?"

"No, of course not, it's just that…"

He waited.

Nuts. How can I put this that won't insult him? "It's just that over here, you need experience to get a good job."

"I have experience. I can guard a building. I protected a temple for three hundred years. Can anyone else say they have more experience than that?" He crossed his arms, looking defensive.

"Well…" *Of course! He could be a security guard…maybe. With a little imaginative background creation.* "You know what? I might be able to talk to a couple of friends about getting you a job guarding something we consider very important over here."

"Really? You have temples?"

"Not exactly. I mean, not spiritual temples. Over here, we worship money. Our temples of money are called banks."

"Oh. The green paper is sacred?"

"It is to a lot of people."

"That is why Bruce wanted me to hide it, and not let anyone take it from me."

"Probably." She wasn't crazy about how warped her explanation was, but it was the best she could do to impress him with the importance of a job in security. *But what if he has to handle a firearm? He has no experience with that, and he can't very well shift into tiger-mode.*

"I like the idea of that job, but it seems strange. If I guard the green paper, and they give me some of it, will they not run out, eventually?"

"They make more of it all the time. But, now that I think of it, there might be other places you could use your experience. Like at something called a museum and that would be more what you're used to. You'd be guarding sacred objects."

"Ah! That sounds much more satisfying."

And much less dangerous. Whew! "Let me make a few telephone calls. Meanwhile, I can teach you to read and write English as well as you speak it. That will give you a much better chance of beating the competition."

"I must beat other people to get this job?"

"Not physically!" *Dear Lord. I have to teach him a shit-load of expressions too.* "You simply need to convince the right people that you're the best man for the job."

"That is all? I am confident I can do that. I am fast and strong."

Haley squeezed his bicep. "You certainly are." Her thoughts turned naughty again. "Want to go back into the bedroom and show me how strong you are?"

His eyes lit up. "How?"

"I like it when you hold yourself up on one hand and play with what you call my yoni with the other."

"What do you call it?"

"There are lots of names, but vagina is the proper one. I'll teach you the other expressions sometime."

"I would like that, but not right now." He scooped her up and carried her to the bedroom. "We have more important things to do."

Haley and Jamir made love well into the afternoon. About the time Haley was getting a little sore, someone knocked at her door.

Whew! An excuse to rest. She smiled as she threw on her robe, realizing she'd never needed a rest from sex before. Life had certainly taken an interesting turn after Maura's summoning spell.

She threw open the door. Barb stood there, holding a paper bag.

"Hey, Barb. What's up?"

"I wanted to know if—"

Suddenly, Barb's jaw dropped and she stared at something over Haley's shoulder. "Jamir?"

Haley glanced behind her, hoping Jamir had put on some clothes. Only pants, but thank goodness he'd done that much.

"Hello, Barb. I had hoped I would see you again."

"Well, I'll be damned." Her large brown eyes opened wider than Haley had ever seen them.

"Why are you damned?" Jamir asked, seriously.

"I'm not...I'm just—surprised. How did you get here?"

"It is a long story."

Haley stepped aside to let Barb in. "He was captured, sold on the black market, and sent to New York on a cargo ship."

Visa rubbed up against Jamir's leg and he picked him up by the scuff of his neck like a parent tiger would lift a cub. Then he cradled him and scratched behind his ear while Visa purred.

"I heard on the news last night that he had been spotted in Central Park," Haley continued. "As soon as it was light enough to see, I went out looking for him."

Jamir set Visa down, smiled and slipped his arm around Haley's waist. "She found me sitting on a bench. I had just been meditating and asking Vishnu to help me find her. I opened my eyes and there she was."

Barb placed her hand over her heart and sighed. "Someday I hope to find what you guys have."

"You will," Haley said, grinning at Jamir. "And we'll have a huge party when you do."

Barb pointed to him. "So, *you* were the tiger that escaped from a boat and ran around terrorizing New York."

He reared back. "I did not terrorize anyone. I merely needed a private place to shift when I got away. It is not easy to find privacy in a city of this size. And speaking of that, Haley, I need to relieve myself. Where do you do that privately in a city like this?"

"We have a special room for that. It's called a bathroom and it's the pocket door on the right." Haley pointed back toward the bedroom. "Aim for the water and I'll show you how to flush it later."

Jamir left to use the little tiger's room, and Barb smirked.

Haley crossed her arms. "Don't say it."

Barb feigned innocence. "Say what?"

"Whatever you're thinking."

A moment later Jamir rushed back toward them looking

awestruck. "Haley! You—you have a sacred object in your bathing room."

Confused, she glanced from Jamir to Barb and back again.

Suddenly Barb's eyes rounded. "The throne." She burst out laughing. "Oh God, Haley. It *was* a toilet seat I saw in the temple."

The light of recognition dawned slowly. *Shit.* "Jamir and Shahid have never seen a toilet before. It must have dropped out of some plane since he said it fell from the sky." Haley cleared her throat. "Jamir and I have a few practical things to take care of."

"I guess you do. Holy crap." Barb almost doubled over, laughing.

"Hardy har, Barb. Look, he needs to learn a lot about our culture quickly. If you can pull yourself together, I'd appreciate it."

Jamir's stunned expression turned to confusion.

Barb wiped the tears that were forming in the corners of her eyes and straightened up. "Sorry Jamir. I guess Haley's right. You have a lot to adjust to."

Quick, change the subject. "Yeah. Sometime soon he'll need a job and I was thinking of museum security. Do you know anyone?"

"Hmmm…security is a great job for him, but I don't know about museums. Won't he have to be paid under the table? It's not like he has a birth certificate or a social security number."

Haley's face fell. "This is true."

"Hey," Barb snapped her fingers. "Maybe he can be a bouncer."

Haley nodded, absently. "Yeah, that might work out. Do you know anyone with a club?"

"As a matter of fact, I do. That's what made me think of it. My friend Ralphie and his brother are always looking for help. I'll bet they can use another bouncer. Let me give him a call."

"Ah, brothers…" Jamir said, wistfully. "I wish there was a way to contact Shahid and let him know I am all right."

"Do you still have my sat phone, Haley?" Barb asked.

"Yes, and it's all recharged. Let's call the orphanage and see if Lorraine is working."

"Even if she isn't, Jamir can talk to the nuns in Bengalese," Barb said.

Haley rolled her eyes. "It's Bengali, Barb."

Jamir bumped Haley with his elbow. "I remember when you called it Bengalese."

Barb's eyes brightened. "Ha! The languages expert isn't so perfect after all."

"Yeah, yeah. It was bound to happen at some point." She ran to her kitchen and grabbed the sat phone off the counter. "So, let's give the orphanage a call."

Jamir scratched his head. "But how will the people at the orphanage tell Shahid? The villagers stay away from the temple because they know tigers roam there."

"We asked Shahid to go to the village from time to time. He said he would ask for any news from us at the orphanage."

Jamir smiled broadly. "That is wonderful! Please call the orphanage right away."

Haley was already dialing.

Haley and Barb had invited Ronda over to meet Jamir. She looked both excited and terrified when she offered him a warm handshake. He'd have tried to make her feel less awkward, but he didn't know how. Thank the Gods, Haley stepped in.

"You should probably close your mouth before you start to drool, Ronnie."

Rhonda laughed. "I'm sorry. It's just that…" Her cheek color changed to pink.

Jamir had seen Haley turn that color occasionally, but no one else.

"I know," Haley said, smiling. "He's gorgeous, isn't he?"

Ronda giggled and backed away. *So she is embarrassed because she thinks I am attractive?* He hadn't expected that—but it pleased him.

"I'll get dinner on," Haley said. "Rhonda, will you help?"

"Of course."

As Haley and Rhonda returned to the kitchen, Barb said, "I called my friend Ralphie, Jamir. He said you can meet him at his club tomorrow at seven p.m. Here's the club's address and phone number."

Jamir stared at the card she handed to him. It was red on black and the print gave it a certain mood. Sensuous was the only word he could think of to describe it.

"What type of club is it?"

Barb shrugged. "A nightclub. Just a place where people go to drink and dance. Singles go to meet other singles, groups hang out, and couples go there on dates sometimes."

"And what would my job entail?"

"You'd better ask him. I'm sure he has certain criteria for letting people in or turning them away."

Jamir was used to frightening people away, but without morphing into his tiger form to intimidate mortals, he wasn't sure how to deal with that. "What if someone is very determined to enter?"

She told him not to worry about 'the daily grind' tonight. He and Haley had found each other again. Shahid now knew they were safe. Everything else could wait.

He nodded and knew she was right, but the way she

described work as grinding did not sound pleasant. This city held a lot to get used to. He began to long for his simpler life with Haley in India.

"Come and get it," Haley called.

Ronda and Haley set steaming bowls on the small table, which he had helped make larger by pulling it apart and inserting a plank that Haley called a leaf. Even with the extra room, the table was crowded by dishes, bowls, candles, and a large platter of something that smelled delicious.

Everyone took their places around the table and Jamir followed their leads by placing a square of linen on his lap.

"Usually when four of us are together at this table it's Maura who sits there," Barb said to Jamir.

"I haven't told him much about Maura yet." Haley lifted a plate and served up some of the meat from the platter. "Just that she was the one who knew about the summoning ceremony." She passed the plate to Ronda and asked, "Has anyone heard from her? Is she okay? Last I heard she was going to Romania."

"Yes, she sent us postcards from Bali—her latest stop on an around the world tour with her new immortal honey, Adrian—unlike some forgetful friends of ours," Ronda said, shooting her a pointed look.

"Sorry—*again.* How many times do I have to apologize for that anyway?"

"Not too many more," Ronda said as she set a plate in front of Jamir.

"Speak for yourself," Barb interjected. "She'll be apologizing to me until my bank account recovers. I'm the one who had to go after her."

Jamir could see Haley getting frustrated and figured he'd change the subject. "What is this dish that smells so delicious?"

"It's Coq au Vin," Haley said.

Jamir leapt to his feet. "We are eating cocks?"

The girls' mouths dropped open for a moment, and then they all burst out laughing. The giggles continued for some time, but he didn't think eating a man's sex organ was funny at all.

Haley recovered first. "No, Jamir. It's French for chicken in wine."

He felt foolish. But how was he to know Americans just randomly shifted into speaking French? Didn't Haley tell him she didn't know any French words? He lowered himself back down to his folding chair. "I thought you did not speak French."

"I don't. The French invented this dish, so everyone calls it by their name."

"Oh." He poked at the meat. The consistency and color might mimic a Caucasian man's member well enough. The size was a little off though. He certainly hoped the meat tasted like chicken.

Barb spoke behind her hand to the others. "Why is it men get so wigged out over their penises?"

No one answered her. They just giggled.

When everyone was served and they had all passed the other bowls and helped themselves, he waited for one of the others to take a bite of the meat first.

Haley closed her eyes and said, "Mmm…" as she chewed the Coq au Vin. "Not bad, if I say so myself."

Barb mumbled, "It's very good."

"Do you like Haley's cooking, Jamir?" Ronda asked.

"Yes, I do. Very much."

"Then why aren't you eating?"

He hadn't realized he was still waiting and watching everyone else as they enjoyed their meal. "No reason."

He took a bite and the tangy taste resembled chicken enough, but there were more ingredients mingling with it. A heady fragrance rose from it too. *At least I didn't have to hunt it down and kill it.*

After the meal, Ronda asked what his and Haley's plans for the future were.

They glanced at each other.

"We still have stuff to talk about."

"Really? What have you been doing all da—" Rhonda slapped her forehead. "Never mind. Stupid question."

"No question is stupid." Jamir echoed what he'd been told by Jim at the soup kitchen. It had made him feel better at the time.

It made the girls laugh. Clearly he had a lot more to learn about Haley's culture. *Did she feel this out of place in my country?*

Barb rose. "Speaking of dessert..."

Jamir was confused again. No one had been speaking of dessert. She strode to the kitchen and returned with a large plate and more food.

He could eat more, but he didn't need to. "My hunger is quite satisfied. People here consume much more than necessary."

Barb had a knife in her hand and was about to hand it to Haley. She stopped abruptly. "Them's fighting words, Jamir."

Perhaps he should have waited until Haley had possession of the knife.

"I do not want to fight you. I am saying that you can have it all. I do not need any more food right now."

Barb laid the knife down and jammed her hands on her hips. "Look, I baked a cake for your reunion. If you don't choke down a piece, my feelings will be hurt."

Haley set a steadying hand on Barb's arm. "It's okay, Barb. He doesn't have to eat if he doesn't want to."

Barb sighed and dropped into her chair. "Yeah, sorry. That was my Italian mother's voice you just heard."

"No, I am the one who is sorry. I did not know it was rude to refuse. I will gladly eat your cake."

"You don't have to. Really. It's okay," Barb said, but she still seemed sad.

"I would be honored to eat what you made for us, Barb."

She brightened. "We'll compromise. I'll give you a small piece."

That word again. *Compromise.* He was beginning to understand that concept—but where was the compromise between New York and India?

After dessert, Ronda asked if he'd mind demonstrating his shifter form.

He glanced at Haley.

Her eyebrows rose. "Are you sure you want to see a big-ass tiger in my living room, Ronnie?"

"If he knows who we are and won't eat us, then yes."

"I know who you are in my tiger form, and I'm too full to eat anything right now."

The girls laughed.

He glanced at Barb. She seemed comfortable, so perhaps she got used to seeing Shahid transform.

Haley took his hand. "I guess if you don't mind performing for my friend, it would go a long way toward showing her the truth of what you are."

He squeezed her hand and smiled. There was nothing she could ask of him that he wouldn't try to do. "I do not mind. Perhaps I could use your bedroom and she could stand in the doorway. In that way, you could close me in if she becomes frightened."

Haley cupped his face. "That's my tiger. Always thinking of others."

Jamir captured her hand and kissed her palm. He could not wait to be alone with her again. Just her touch aroused him.

"Come on you two," Barb groused. "We know you're in love. You don't have to rub it in."

Haley grinned. "I can't wait until you find your immortal. I am so gonna to give you the business."

Business? I thought Barb already had a business. He sighed. Just one more thing he didn't understand.

"So will you do your tiger thing for me, Jamir?" Ronda asked.

He dropped Haley's hand and strolled to her bedroom. There wasn't much room anywhere in this apartment, but the bed was one expanse on which he could sprawl.

He removed most of his clothing, then crawled onto the bed on his hands and knees, turned so he faced the foot of the bed and concentrated on his alternate form. In a shimmer he became what he knew was an impressive sight. Ronda gasped.

The bed dipped under his enormous weight and something began to crack. Visa came rushing out from under the bed with a yowl.

"Shift back, Jamir. Quick. The bed is going to break," Haley begged.

He did so, but his head spun. He dropped onto his side and closed his eyes until he got his bearings.

"Holy shit," Ronda muttered.

"Pretty amazing, isn't it?" Barb asked.

"Unbelievable."

When he opened his eyes, Haley looked at him with concern. "Are you all right, love?"

"Yes. I am just not used to shifting twice so quickly.

"I'm sorry. I won't ask you to do that again unless you're on a solid surface."

"Yeah, like concrete," Barb added.

CHAPTER 23

Haley had to work the next day and Jamir had nothing to do until the evening. Learning about the sacred object he and Shahid had been protecting disappointed him, but at least he was free of the responsibility for it. Now he could concentrate on other things—mainly how to convince Haley to return to India with him. She adjusted to life their far easier than he was adjusting to life here.

He didn't like the idea that he would have to work every evening if he got the job as a 'bouncer'. Haley had to work during the day. When would he ever see her? He did not like this arrangement. Why would any couple do this?

He went to the park to think. He would prefer the job Haley mentioned before. The one where he would guard the sacred items inside something called a museum. It sounded like a wonderful place the way she described it. He would like to see this place.

He stopped a young man on a bicycle. "Excuse me, where is the museum?"

"The Met?" he asked.

Jamir had no idea what the name of the museum was, so he just said, "Yes."

The man gave him directions and happily it was nearby. Jamir turned to follow his instructions when he almost tripped over a small dog. The dog growled, then cowered and whimpered. It was attached to a line held by a human male about Jamir's size. He also controlled a number of other dogs the same way. All the dogs strained at the lines that held them.

"Hey, watch where you're going."

Before he could respond, the man and dogs scurried away. Yet another strange sight to ask Haley about later.

He walked to the museum and strode up the steps. The building resembled an immense and elaborate temple. Inside many people lined up in one spot and waited to go into a large opening. There was another opening that was empty, so Jamir began to stroll through that one.

A man wearing dark pants and a white shirt rushed after him. "You can't go in this way."

Jamir asked why not, and the gentleman said, "This is the exit. You need to buy a ticket and go in the entrance."

"Oh. I need the green paper to get in?"

The man squinted for a moment, then seemed to understand. "Yes. You need money to get in."

Frustrated Jamir asked, "Is there anything in this city a person can do without money?"

The guy laughed. "Not a heck of a lot. You can take a walk in the park or window shop, but that's about it."

"I need a job to get more green paper. Do you think I could get a job here?"

The man looked him up and down. "I doubt it."

I must convince Haley to return to India with me. This is not working.

"I am sorry, Haley. I cannot go to the interview."

She had just stepped through the door and hadn't even taken her sweater off yet. "Why not?"

"I would never see you. As much as I would like the green paper, I will not sacrifice my only reason to be here at all."

She was tired. It had been a strange day. She'd had to back track to get her snotty, entitled, ungrateful students up to speed *and* grovel for her job—a job she wasn't sure she wanted any more.

"Look, Jamir. If you don't want the bouncer job, that's fine. You can find a different job. I don't care if you work or not, frankly."

She dropped her purse on the coffee table and flopped onto the couch. Closing her eyes, she leaned back and took a few moments to relax before she focused on yet another problem.

"Are you all right, Haley?"

She took a deep breath, then sat up. "It was just a trying day."

"What were you trying?"

She chuckled. "I was trying to remember why I wanted to be a teacher."

"Oh!" His expression brightened. "Then perhaps you are willing to make a change?"

Uh oh. What is he thinking? "Perhaps," she said warily. "It's not that easy to change a profession. You usually have to give up money or benefits or both."

"Hmm…"

His pensive look was unsettling. He definitely had something on his mind, and she didn't think she was going to like it. Maybe it was time to change the subject.

"If you're not going to the interview, you should call Emilio and tell him. Otherwise he'll be waiting for you when he might be able to do something else."

"Call him? Is he near?"

"No, you'd have to use the phone to make a phone call."

"I see. Can you show me how to use the sat phone?"

"The *sat phone?*" Oh boy. He didn't know the difference between land lines, cell phones and satellite phones. This would take a bit of an explanation. "Why don't I just call him and I'll show you later."

"Haley, I need to learn."

But I don't need to teach. I don't want to teach another human being another thing until tomorrow...and maybe even then.

"Look, Jamir. I'm sorry. The fact that you want to learn is admirable. I wish the kids in my classes were as eager as you. Unfortunately, no one goes to a community college to be an English major. A four year degree school gets the serious students. But my course is required, so they have to come to my classroom, bad attitudes and all."

He straightened. "They are ungrateful for the knowledge you give them?"

Haley snorted. "You could say that."

"Why do you continue to do this?"

"I have bills that continue to need to be paid."

"Ah, the green money." He turned his back and paced. "Perhaps I should go to the interview after all. If I have a job, you can stop teaching and we can be together during the day."

"I'm sorry, Jamir. It's more complicated than that."

He halted. "I do not understand."

"I know that. I need insurance, for one thing…"

His pacing resumed and she could tell his frustration was mounting. He wanted to help her, but everything was so complex he couldn't possibly understand it and she didn't have the patience to explain it all right now.

"Jamir." She rose and held out her arms to him. He entered her embrace and looked directly into her eyes as if trying to see all the way into her brain. *If only that were possible. It would cut out a lot of pesky learning time.*

"We'll iron out all the details later. But right now, all I want is to do is relax and love you."

He smiled and kissed her. Jamir's kiss thrilled her from the ends of her hair to the tips of her toes. Suddenly she was floating. It took a moment to realize he had lifted her into his arms and was carrying her to the bedroom.

When he gently placed her on the bed, she opened her eyes. His intense gaze devoured her and he crawled over her in a predatory swagger.

"I love you, Jamir," she whispered. "I'd do anything for you."

He grinned. Rather than say he loved her too, he carefully unbuttoned her blouse and slid his hand inside her bra, cupping and massaging her breast as she moaned.

She hastily unbuttoned his shirt and helped him shrug out of it. They fought off the rest of their clothes as if they couldn't wait to be free of the layers between them. At last they lay naked and in each other's arms.

"Haley, you don't know how happy I am right now."

"Why don't you show me?" She winked.

He dove for her mouth and devoured her with passionate kisses. She found his cock and stroked it's hard length. He growled into her mouth, then broke the kiss to latch onto her nipple and suck.

She arched and moaned. The visceral sensations rippled straight to her clenching core. "Oh God, don't stop."

He only paused long enough to switch sides and suckle her other breast just as thoroughly. Her pussy dampened and craved fulfillment. Eventually, she couldn't stand the exquisite torture another second. She pushed him onto his back and he chuckled.

Haley shut him up as soon as she took his cock into her

mouth and sucked. He threw back his head and groaned. After only a few deep pulls, he grasped her hair and stilled her.

"No more, Haley. I do not wish to spill into your mouth."

"But—"

"Hush. I want to make love to you."

He rolled her onto her back and stuffed the pillows under her ass. Kneeling before her, with her opening at the right height, he sunk his cock inside and immediately began his rhythm.

"Oh, God, Jamir…"

He kept right on thrusting and added a clit rub.

Haley gasped and clutched the sheets. Strong ripples of pleasure built up and up on top of one another until she was spiraling out of control. At last, her orgasm exploded. She flew apart and screamed out her release. She bucked and vibrated uncontrollably as every nerve ending in her body jolted.

Jamir jerked and grunted as she experienced every after-shock. At last, he collapsed on top of her and they lay together joined. The two of them panted until their breathing returned to normal. Tears threatened to spill. Haley had just had a mind-blowing orgasm, so why did she want to cry?

Jamir must have noticed because he pulled back and searched her face.

"Are you all right my love?"

She let the tears shimmer, but smiled. "Yes. I'm perfect."

He swiped his finger across her cheek. "You certainly are."

A few minutes later, Jamir held her close and asked, "Did you mean it?"

"Did I mean what?"

"You said you would do anything for me."

She hesitated, but eventually said, "Yes, I meant it."

He rubbed her arm, slowly. "I am happy to hear you say that. I would also sacrifice for you, but I am afraid the amount of change I must accomplish to fit into your world is almost beyond my capability."

"What are you saying?"

"I am saying it is much more difficult for me here than I expected. I would gladly guard your sacred objects—even your sacred money temples, but I do not possess the necessary numbers."

"Numbers? What are you talking about?"

"I spoke to a man at the museum this morning. He said everyone here gets a number at birth. That number is necessary in order to work."

"Oh. He was talking about a social security number."

"Yes. Apparently it is something I would need to be hired for any job."

"Yes, that's true…"

"Yet I do not have one." He waited. It seemed as if she had more to say but stopped for some reason. When she didn't continue, he launched into his speech and hoped for the best outcome.

"I think we would be happier in India. We would not need to worry about so many regulations. You could easily find fulfilling work as a teacher of English. I can hunt, fish, build, or learn a trade. I will keep you safe, fed and happy there. We can live in a village or even a city if you wish. However, here, it seems I cannot do anything to help you."

He waited. She said nothing and he couldn't see her face. After what seemed like an eternity, he heard her sniffle. He grasped her chin and tipped up her head until he saw her eyes, shimmering.

"Why are you sad?"

"Well, I—I understand what you're saying, and I can't fault you for feeling that way. "It's just…"

Her words trailed off and even though he waited anxiously, she didn't pick up where she'd left off.

"What are you feeling, Haley? You must tell me."

"Well…I guess I've been realizing some of that too. I'd just hoped…"

He waited through another long pause. Soon he would feel like he was pulling teeth if he understood the expression correctly.

She sighed. "Part of me agrees with you. Another part of me thinks we just need to get more creative. I don't want to give up my friends and my comforts. There are other options."

"I am willing to discuss options. What are they?"

She threw her hand in the air. "Damned if I know, but there must be something."

She threw back the covers and climbed out of bed. Opening a door, she retrieved a robe and slipped it on. A single tie, knotted in the front held it closed. "I'm going to look something up on the Internet."

Jamir got out of bed and followed her. He didn't bother putting on anything. She had seen him naked more than she'd seen him clothed.

She sat at a small desk and opened a lid on a black rectangular object. She touched some squares that made clicking noises. Jamir noticed words forming on a screen above at the same time.

"What are you doing?"

"Looking up laws on working without a visa."

He waited and watched as the screen filled with words in small print. She moved the words down the page as she read.

He tried to read over her shoulder, but he was not well versed in written English. He had never had to use it.

Eventually she heaved a huge sigh.

"What is wrong?"

"I'm afraid the only job you can get without a work visa is boyfriend."

"I don't understand."

"It means you can't hold a paying job—at all—of any kind. It's illegal and you could be sent back to India if you got caught."

The harsh reality slammed into Jamir. He could do nothing? Nothing at all?

"Haley, this cannot be right. I have seen many people from all over the world here."

"If they're making money, they applied for and received Visas."

Jamir leveled his palm over the floor at about domestic cat height. "Visas?"

"No—that just a name. He could be called Tigger or Kitty. A visa is a piece of paper you apply for in your country of origin in order to be given permission to work in another country."

Jamir groaned. "More paper."

"You said it."

Jamir scratched his head and began to pace. "So, as a citizen of this country, and because we are here now, is it possible for you to get a visa for India?"

Haley's gaze dropped to her lap. "I—uh…I already have one."

Jamir couldn't believe his luck. Now the answer was obvious! *But why did she not mention it before?*

He walked up behind her and rubbed her shoulders. "My love, you could have told me this sooner."

"I know."

She seemed pensive. It was hard to be patient while she put the pieces together but he knew it would be better if she reached the right conclusion by herself. He waited and waited.

At last she hung her head. "Shit."

She got it.

CHAPTER 24

"Are you out of your friggin' mind? You want me to be your maid of honor at your big, fat Indian wedding—*in India.*" Barb crossed her arms and glared at Haley.

"All I can tell you is it's the one thing that makes sense." Haley strolled over to Barb's couch and sat. "And it feels right."

"Right for who? You or Jamir?"

"Whom, and it's right for both of us. Barb, my job has been unfulfilling and stale here in New York. I needed an adventure when I went to India the first time and teaching English there was the right kind of challenge for me. I loved it. You saw me in action at the orphanage. I enjoyed what I was doing. Even though I was worried sick about Jamir, my work helped me take my nose out of my bellybutton."

Barb's expression softened. She took the streamlined armchair. "You're my best friend, and naturally I want you to be happy. Selfishly, I want you to stay, because I know I'll miss you like crazy."

"I'll miss you too. But you have to admit, if you found the love of your life and he could only get a job in another country, you'd probably make the sacrifice. Wouldn't you?"

"Oh, honey, I'd pack up and leave you so fast, your head would spin."

Haley grinned. "That's the Barb I know and love."

"But I'm not so sure about going to India again—even for your wedding. Can you have it in a fancy hotel with indoor plumbing?"

"We were actually thinking of asking the Sepgupta's if we could have it at the tea garden and invite the whole village."

"Do they have a western toilet?"

"Yes, darling. They do."

"I'll think about it. Are you going to invite Maura and Ronda?"

"Of course."

"Anyone else?"

Haley read between the lines and smiled. "Like Shahid? Yes, I'm sure he'll be there. Jamir wants him to be his best man, and now that there are other tigers to guard the temple, he has no reason not to attend."

Barb shrugged. "I suppose it might not suck."

"Gee thanks. Is that a yes?"

"It's still a maybe. Give me a day or two to adjust to the idea and look at my bank balance."

"Take a week or two. I have to finish out the semester, plus sell my place and most of my possessions. Then I can probably help you with the finances."

"Holy crap. Are you going to live in the hut again?"

Haley laughed. "No. I'll try to get a paying job in a small city or town...and Jamir agreed to live in a house—with indoor plumbing."

"Why wouldn't he? He thinks a toilet seat is sacred."

"Don't you dare tease him about that, and don't say anything to Shahid. The only reason Jamir's faith wasn't shattered was because he had me to soften the blow."

"How did you manage to do that?"

"I told him it was a simple misunderstanding. Anyone can make a mistake, right?"

"Yep. That's a lesson we all have to learn at some point."

Haley softened her voice. "So can you see how it would be a mistake if I let Jamir go or insisted he stay here and be miserable?"

Barb sighed. "Yeah. But it won't be the same without you."

"If it's any consolation, I have the feeling you're next."

"Next? For what?"

"For finding your immortal. Maura and I have both found ours. Now it's your turn."

"Me and Ronda."

"Exactly. And I can't wait to hear all about him."

"Then you'd better keep the sat phone."

"Or get a land line. Don't worry. I'll be sure we can stay in touch."

"Promise?"

Haley laid her hand over her heart. "I swear on my toilet seat."

Both women burst out laughing.

Haley recovered first. "I'm probably going to Hell for that."

"Oh, definitely. Or at least you won't be reborn into the upper class."

"That's okay. As long as Jamir is waiting for me, and we find each other again—as he swears we will, I don't care how rich or poor I am."

Barb smiled. "Let's hope India continues to grow more civilized so by the time your next life rolls around, you won't need to worry too much about casts—or plumbing."

"Here, here. And I hope to contribute something toward that goal."

Barb left her chair and sat next to Haley so she could hug her. "You're an inspiration."

Haley hugged her back. "So are you."

———

Jamir had no need for a wedding, but Haley seemed to want one—badly. She had researched the laws, which had said there were certain stipulations that would be tricky, but not impossible.

Because the result was a one-way ticket to India and Haley's commitment, he'd give her whatever she needed to make that happen. He loved her more than his next breath, and the idea of taking her home with him was the biggest thrill of his long life. But there were complications.

She sat next to him on the couch. "Apparently, I need a *No objection letter* from the U.S. Consulate in India, and I can get that. We have to register at the marriage bureau and wait thirty days."

Jamir took her hand. "Waiting thirty days seems excessive, especially for an anxious groom, but I will do whatever is necessary."

She stroked his thigh with her free hand. "Thank you. I'm not quite through telling you the hurdles though."

Uh-oh. That didn't bode well. "What else must we do?"

"Well, there's the tiny matter of your not having a birth certificate or a passport."

"I imagine some children born in remote villages do not have a birth certificate. And, what is a passport?"

"It's a document inside a folder that people need to travel from one country to another."

He sighed. "More paper. Are you saying I cannot return to India without one?"

"Actually, there might be a way around it. You can get

deported—kicked out of the country and sent home. It can be a long process if you don't want to leave, but if you do, it might be as simple as telling a small fib."

"I do not like to lie."

"It's not an outright lie. We can go to the Indian embassy and you could say you stowed-away on a ship, because you thought you would have a better life here, but you were wrong. When you found out getting a job wasn't possible, you realized you needed to go home in order to support yourself."

He thought it over and nodded. "That is very close to the truth. But is there any other way?"

"Well, you can say you were kidnapped and brought here against your will. But that might bring the police into it. You'll have to leave out the part about being a tiger. "

Neither plan sounded ideal. "Will you go with me when I talk to the consulate?"

She smiled. "You betcha. I'll even offer to take you home to India."

"Do you really think it will work?"

Haley shrugged. "I hope so. I can't think of anything else."

Jamir stood. "Then I will go."

"Not just yet, cowboy. We need to get your story straight and while we're at it, when's your birthday?"

"I do not know the exact day I was born. Shahid is older by three years and he said I was born a few months after our monsoon season."

Haley tipped her head and studied him. "You seem like a Libra to me. Laid back, fair, well-balanced—not to mention romantic."

He smiled, happy she thought of him that way.

"That means your birthday would be in late September or early October. What's your favorite number?"

"Seven," he said without hesitation. "It is an auspicious number in many cultures including mine."

"Okay, October 7th is your birthday. Now we have to pick a year. We sure as hell can't use the real one. How old were you when Vishnu came to you and made you immortal?"

"I am not exactly sure. I believe I was between twenty-seven and twenty-nine years."

She leaned back and scrutinized him. "Yeah, you still look about that age. So, we just count backward…"

"1992. If added together and reduced to a single number, it equals three—another auspicious number in numerology."

"Wow, you're good at math, aren't you?"

He smiled. "Numbers have always come easily to me."

"That's cool. Maybe when we get back to India we can find out if they have something like CLEP testing, and you could get an engineering degree or something."

"Clep?"

"College level exam program. It means you have the knowledge, but don't have the credits. If you pass the exam, you earn the credits. You need a certain amount of credits to graduate."

"Ah. And if I graduate…"

"You can get a good job. I'm guessing with your abilities and a little tutoring from me, you can probably pass the tests for languages and math." She winked. "And you'll probably ace history."

They both chuckled.

"We're getting ahead of ourselves though. First, we have to get you back home."

Haley met Barb and Ronda at their favorite local Bistro on 44th street.

Ronda leaned out from their booth so she could see the door. "Where's Jamir?"

Haley tried to modify her facial expression to look cool and casual. "In jail." She watched as her friend's eyes rounded.

Barb recovered first. "What happened? And why are you so blasé about it?"

She chuckled. "Relax. He didn't do anything wrong. The I.N.S. is simply holding him until they can verify he isn't a wanted criminal, then they'll process the proper documents. He should be out very soon."

"What kind of documents?" Ronda asked.

"Birth certificate, temporary visa, passport, the works."

Barb squinted. "And then what?"

Haley grinned. "And then we get married."

Both women whooped and jumped up to give her hugs and congratulations.

"You could have led with that you know," Barb said.

"I know but it was more fun this way. You should have seen your faces."

Barb crossed her arms. "Bitch."

Haley signaled the waiter. When he came over, she said, "I'd like a bottle of Champagne, please."

He smiled. "You are celebrating something? No?"

"Yes, we're celebrating my engagement."

He grinned. "Congratulations. I will bring you our best champagne."

"How about the cheapest...I'm going to need my money to throw this shindig."

He bowed. "As you wish. All of our wines are excellent."

"We're not picky," Ronda said. "If it has alcohol and bubbles, I'm sure we'll love it. But put it on my tab." She grinned at her friends. "I just scored another big account, and I can afford it."

The waiter left and congratulations were bestowed on Ronda.

Barb sighed. "If only something good would happen to me. I'll have to send *myself* a card at the rate things are going."

Haley leaned her elbow on the table and cupped her chin. "What would it say?"

"Something like, *Sorry all your friends are celebrating great news and nothing has happened for you. Here's a card.*"

"Oh, stop it," Ronda said. "It'll be your turn soon. My granny used to say, 'The sun doesn't shine on the same dog all the time.'"

Barb groaned. "You and your granny's homespun wisdom. You could create your own card company."

Ronda winked at Haley. "Or I could just advertise yours."

"Ha, like I could afford you."

"No charge. Happy birthday."

Barb sat up straight. "Seriously? It's my birthday present?"

"I'm feeling very generous right now."

"Don't question it," Haley said. "Just say 'thank you' and shut-up."

Barb smirked at Ronda. "Thank you and shut-up."

Ronda rolled her eyes. "It's a good thing we know you love us, Barbarella."

Barb winced. "I told you never to call me that. My mother was on drugs when she named me."

Haley laughed. "I promise *never* to call you that, if you'll be in my big, fat, Indian wedding."

"What about me?" Ronda wailed.

"I know you can't leave your job at the drop of a hat, so you get to be my maid of honor in New York."

"Awww…You're the best."

"Bitch," Barb said again.

"What's the matter now? I thought you wanted to see Shahid."

"Oh, I do. I just called you that on principle, because you're getting married in two countries and I don't even have a boyfriend in one."

Haley smirked. "Oh, go send yourself a card."

EPILOGUE

Haley and Barb stood in front of a mirror in the Sepgupta's bedroom, getting her ready for her wedding to Jamir. Soon her friends would be here.

Haley had glanced out the window earlier to see the whole village arriving, the women wearing their most beautiful saris and jewelry. Still she couldn't help feeling that nothing could outshine her in her bright red silk sari, dotted with pearls, and edged in gold embroidered trim. It was stunning. As Barb was brushing her hair into an updo, the door opened and in rushed two of her best friends. Ronda, and Maura.

Haley jumped up, pulling her hair out of Barb's hands, and rushed to her dear friends. She grabbed Maura first. "I haven't seen you in ages. I've missed you so much! However, I hear you've got your hands full with your hot new guy." She winked.

Maura laughed. "Oh yes, he's a handful. You'll have to meet him, I think our summoning worked to find us the best immortals, no matter where we had to go to find them."

Ronda stuck her hand on her hip and said, "Hey, what about me?"

Haley let go of Maura and threw her arms around Ronda giving her a huge squeeze. "I'm sorry, darlin'. I was getting to you with your hug." She giggled. "So, how about it? Did you find your guy?"

Taking a step back and letting her arms drop, Ronda hung her head, "Nope. No new guy for me. I must've done something wrong, the summoning, I mean."

Maura shook her head. "You did fine. It's just taking a little longer for some reason."

"And I'm not completely sure that I found my guy either," Barb said.

Haley grinned at her friends. "Jamir has a brother. And Barb has been… How do I say it gently?"

Barb crossed her arms. "You can say boinking like bunnies, burying the sausage, driving the skin bus through tuna town…"

"Ewww…" Ronda squealed. "We get the picture."

Everyone laughed, including Ronda.

"So, are you going to explore this thing with Jamir's brother, Shahid?" Haley asked.

"I think I'll stick around, and see where it goes." Barb shrugged nonchalantly, but the gleam in her eye and smile on her face gave her away.

"So, it looks like all of you have found someone special. I wonder what's taking my guy so long? And what kind of immortal he is?"

"I'm not sure what to tell you," Maura said. "Except that if you live your life as you want to, and keep your eyes and heart open, I think he'll come to you. We did summon them after all."

"But Haley had to go across the figgin' world." She sighed.

"You may be right," Maura said. "Even though my vamp was right under my nose in New York, I had to go to Romania to meet him."

"So, now that you're all here, let's get this matrimony on the road." Barb elbowed Haley.

"Yes, let's. Do you guys know how to wear saris?"

"I'm the one with the clothing store, remember?" Maura said. "I know how to put one on, and I can help Ronda with hers."

"Great. There are a couple on the bed that should fit you." Barb laughed. "Actually, the six yards of silk will fit anyone."

"I don't see any blouses," Maura said.

Ronda shrugged. "I have a couple of short sleeve T-shirts with me. Will that be all right?"

"Unless Mrs. Sepgupta has something else, those will have to do. I want you guys to have the same beautiful clothing that I get to wear." Haley said.

"And me," Barb said.

As if noticing her for the first time, the girls admired Barb's midnight blue sari with silver trim. Her hair was tied in a braid behind her back, and since it was dark brown, and her Italian heritage made her skin tan nicely, she fit right in with the native women.

"Okay ladies, let's wrap this up." Barb said, and chuckled at her own joke as she picked up both folded piles of silk. Orange will look terrific on you Maura."

"Not my favorite color."

"The other one is pink. Redheads should never ever wear pink."

Maura nodded. "You got that right." She reached over for the orange silk and her eyes popped as she fingered the beautiful gold accents in an intricately woven pattern. "Scratch that. Orange is my new favorite color!"

Rhonda happily grabbed the pink one with silver and green edging and started wrapping it around her middle. "This looks perfect with my brown hair."

Maura laughed. "And what are you going to do when you reach the end?"

Rhonda shrugged. "I don't know tie it off somewhere?" The other three just laughed.

"Hey. I work at an ad agency, not a sari store."

Haley pointed to a dresser drawer. "The petticoats are in there. Second drawer."

Maura opened the drawer and found the matching petticoats to wear beneath their beautiful silk saris. She put her own on first, pulled the ties tight, and knotted it. Then she handed the pink one to Ronda who followed suit. The petticoats were plain and seemed to be made of cotton, but they weren't going to show anyway. Haley watched as her modern friends from New York transformed into beautiful Indian butterflies.

Tears formed in her eyes. "I don't think I've ever been so happy. I have the love of my life, my four best girlfriends, and a whole village of people who welcomed me and have adopted me as one of their own. My heart is so full."

"That brings up a question I had," Maura said. "Where are you going to live?"

"Right here," Haley said, proudly. "The Sepgupta's want me to continue tutoring their children and Jamir will be the grounds keeper, meanwhile watching for any dangerous animals that could wander onto the plantation. They have a couple of outbuildings that were for servants in the British-India days. One of them has been made ready for us."

"And the other?"

Barb had finally put the last pin in her hair. "That's where I'll stay when I come to visit." She began draping Haley with heavy gold jewelry studded with bright colored gems.

"What about that red dot on your forehead thing?" Rhonda asked.

"I'll receive that as a married woman. For now I have a bindi." She touched the small jewel between her eyebrows.

"So that's the Indian version of what? A wedding ring?" Rhonda asked.

"It seems so, but I have a couple of rings that Mrs. Sepgupta's mother gave me too."

The door opened and Mrs. Sepgupta came in with her two children, running from out behind her.

"Oh, Haley! You are beautiful!" The little boy said.

She chuckled. "Well, thank you, Tota. Is everything ready, PimPim?" She asked the little girl.

"Yes. Everything is ready!"

"Including your groom," Mrs. Sepgupta added. "He's very anxious to get started."

"Let's not keep him waiting any longer." Haley smiled. "I'm excited for my happily ever after to begin."

THE OTHER TIGER'S TALE

Barb knew she looked amazing in her midnight blue silk sari with silver embroidery. She had the statuesque height to tower over almost all of the guests, including many of the men. The family and their friends had departed down the stairs, saying as soon as the two of them were ready, they should come on down. Mrs. Sepgupta's mother would use her wedding sari as the tent over the bride as she walked to her fiancé.

"I think it was incredibly sweet the way the Sepguptas have rallied around you, Haley, treating you as if you're part of the family."

"I know. I tutor their children, but that would hardly obligate them to throw me a big-fat, Indian wedding. In fact, the whole village is taking part in the wedding as if half of them were Jamir's family and the other half, mine."

Touched, Barb laid a hand over her heart. She might be thought of as tough, but even she had moments which melted her reserve.

"I insisted they not go into debt, as Indian families often do for a daughter's wedding. Happily they listened. Their own little girl PimPim will grow up someday to want her own big fat Indian wedding."

But Haley's was shaping up to be a sweet affair with plenty of dazzling beauty and delicious foods they could already smell from the kitchen downstairs.

The night before the wedding there was something like a bachelorette party...not a crazy night out, but more of a chill night in. Haley had tried to get her cousin to come from New York, but her uncle who ran the family's Irish bar couldn't spare her for so long. Some of the young women from the orphanage they knew came.

Barb, being an artist, got the job of doing the henna designs on Haley's arms. Even though she'd never worked with the medium, she did an intricate half sleeve from her elbows all the way to her wrists and then on the back of her hand to a point at the base of her middle finger. She joked about just decorating that one finger on each hand, but Haley quickly put the kibosh on it. There was plenty of good natured teasing, so she was sure Haley knew she was kidding.

The following morning, she had to admit her handiwork came out beautifully. There was some sort of Indian superstition that the darker the henna the next day, the better the marriage. Well, on her blonde friend's fair skin that Henna design looked pretty damn dark.

"You know another tradition on the morning of a bride's wedding is to rub turmeric all over her skin to make it glow," Haley told her. "I wanted to allow the Sepgupta women to include as many of the traditional preparations as they liked, but they skipped that one."

"Just as well. You're already glowing." She didn't tell her the women wanted to, but she talked them out of it, because on Haley's fair skin, she'd look jaundiced.

Haley just wanted everyone to be as happy as she was.

Barb was happy too. Not only happy for her friend, but just caught up in the general joy an Indian wedding brings.

Her hair and makeup had been carefully arranged by Barb too. The only thing left for the others to do was to drape her in jewels. Mrs. Sepgupta and her mother took great pleasure in procuring the shiniest bobbles to hang around her neck, from her ears, and even found a gold hoop to hang from her nose without piercing it. They gave her the traditional 21 bangles that represents something or other. Barb couldn't remember all of the stories that went behind the traditions.

Finally they descended the stairs. "You look like you walked into a bling cannon," Ronda remarked.

"A cannon?" Mrs. Sepgupta's mother asked, concern lacing her voice.

"Oh, not a real cannon," Haley explained. "In America they have what's called a t-shirt cannon. At big events sometimes they load a big tube with t-shirts and shoot them into the audience."

The grandmother tipped her head back and forth as if to say, "I don't know what you're talking about, but I'm too polite to pursue it."

The Indian women had tried to prepare them, so they'd know what to expect and when. Barb knew one of the important things coming was a fire ceremony. That Haley and Jamir would walk around the fire seven times. That was supposed to ensure that they would spend the next seven lifecycles together. Jamir had insisted that it was important to him to know he and Haley would find each other again and again.

Barb was really torn when it came to the idea of reincarnation. She was raised by Italian Catholics. And the idea seemed foreign when she first heard of it. It was like getting a do over, and that might prove useful if you remembered your lessons learned...so why didn't we? Maybe next time coming back as a cow would be a lot easier, certainly in India. She didn't know what was a step down or step up.

She was told that she would come back in progressively better situations, if she led a good life. Eventually, once all one's lessons were learned she wouldn't have to come back at all. She would reach Nirvana. She had talked about it with Shahid, and he believed it. But he said he didn't believe in soulmates, and yet maybe he was wrong. It certainly looked as if Jamir had one, but Shahid had never experienced finding a mate during his long life.

So it was finally time for Haley and Jamir to come together. Half the village was on the outside of the house already and the other half on the inside. Everyone filed out, leaving Haley, Barb and the Sepgupta family to come out last.

Barb was just about to walk outside when she felt Shahid's presence. She could feel, more than see him. Everyone else was facing away from her and she looked over to see what they were staring at. Her eyes popped. A giant elephant was lumbering toward them, with Jamir riding on its back.

She recoiled at first. The huge animal looked her right in the eye, and something fluttered in her chest. She had never seen anything so big...nothing alive anyway. She recognized her feeling as fear. She wasn't sure she'd be this afraid of an armed mugger in New York.

Jamir was dressed like a prince. He had a long white tunic that was embroidered in gold and wore matching white pants. He slid off the side of the elephant and met Haley. Taking both of her hands in his, he grinned.

Barb just couldn't take her eyes off that elephant. She had all but forgotten the bride and groom until finally Shahid came over and put an arm around her back, to escort her to a place just outside the priest's tent.

She forgot about the elephant when she finally looked at Shahid. He was also dressed in the kind of finery she didn't see every day. Another long tunic but gray with silver embroidery and matching pants. He looked very handsome. He was slightly bigger than Jamir and a little more rugged looking, but that's exactly how she liked her men—big, rugged and good-looking.

She took his hand and walked over to the tent still squeamish about the elephant, but hey, every culture has its quirks, right?

She leaned in towards Shahid and asked, "Isn't anyone going to hold onto that thing?"

Shaheed looked down at his pants and grinned. "What? Are you offering?"

She elbowed him. "Not that, you goober. The elephant."

"Are you afraid of elephants?" he asked, still smiling.

"I never realized I was until now. They seem awfully big and unpredictable."

"What makes you say this elephant is unpredictable?"

She shrugged. "I don't know. It's just a feeling…"

Even though she couldn't understand much. Barb really enjoyed the beautiful looooong ceremony. She had just begun learning to speak Hindi and write in their beautiful Sanskrit. Haley was probably picking it up faster because of her affinity for languages, but Barb was also excited about learning something new.

If she wanted to stay, she could try to adapt her snarky cards to Indian culture, eventually. Although, people here seemed the opposite of snarky. She had a lot to learn about that first.

Meanwhile, she sat near the tent and held hands with

Shahid. He glanced over at her once in a while and smiled when their eyes met. He seemed proud and happy.

Barb figured it was because he was attending his brother's wedding, which was even more of a big deal since they claimed to be soul mates who had found each other again. He was genuinely happy for him and Haley. When there came a pause for a subtle whisper she leaned over to Shahid and asked, "Do you believe in soulmates?"

He leaned back and studied her face for a moment. "I have not experienced it. I doubt I ever will. You? Do you believe in soulmates?"

Barb snorted. "No, I don't. I think I could probably make a relationship work with any number of people, as long as they're willing to put up with me. I'm no walk in the park."

Shahid laughed, but stifled it quickly. Apparently the ceremony was at a serious part.

Jamir and Haley were separated by a scarf, so it didn't seem like a terrible time to discuss the beliefs of Hindus.

"So, you're saying you're not hundred percent sold on the idea of reincarnation?"

Shahid's eyebrows shot up. "Of course I believe in reincarnation. What made you think I didn't?"

She shrugged slightly. "I... I figured just because you've been around 300 years. That would kinda make it hard for you to change lifecycles and all that. Right?"

His expression became pensive. Then he shook his head. "None of us can know what the gods have in mind. Such as why they chose my brother and I to guard the temple for 300 years, and then replace us with two other shape shifters. Jamir is convinced it's because Haley returned to him one hundred years after his chaste love, Helen was taken away. He longed for her and mourned her absence for so long, the gods probably got as sick of hearing him moan as I was. Or perhaps it's because you breached the Temple's entrance before I could drag you away."

"Hey, I saw three tigers... That meant if you were one and Jamir was another, then the third one had to be a real-ass tiger! The temple was the only place to hide."

Somebody hushed them from behind.

Fine. She stayed quiet for another long stretch. Just as she was getting sleepy, Shahid leaned over and bumped her shoulder. "Because neither one of us believes in soulmates, perhaps that's what makes us soulmates. Did you ever think of that?"

It was her turn to laugh. Then she quickly covered her mouth and tried to look serious again. "I never thought of that, but you may have a point."

It was time for the fire ceremony. The priest blessed something in the fire pit and threw what looked like herbs and flowers into it. It wasn't exactly a fire pit, as much as a metal container, but something caused a spark.

The spark spooked the elephant. Barb jumped up and ran. Unfortunately, she rushed right into the path of the stampeding elephant. She looked over her shoulder to see the gigantic beast coming right up behind her and fell to the ground. A sharp pain was followed by seeing stars, and then everything went black.

Barb awoke to shouting and another sound she wasn't familiar with. Metal on metal. Clash, clash, clash. Men were groaning and sometimes, screaming. When she opened her eyes, she took in the chaos of a squash-buckling swordfight!

These were not the gentle people of India. And she wasn't looking up at the top of a white tent. Instead she gazed at white sails, a wooden mast, and heavy ropes.

When a wave hit, she rolled onto her side and realized she was laying on a wooden floor. *I'm on the deck of a friggin' ship!* Or was it a frigate? She not only didn't know her ships, she certainly didn't know this one or why she was here.

Pushing herself to a sitting position, she was able to see more of the deck, as well as her drab pants tucked into a pair of black leather boots—and a Jolly Roger flag waving over the bow.

Shit! I'm on a friggin PIRATE frigate.

"Stay down!" a familiar voice yelled from directly behind her. A strong hand on her shoulder pushed her hard and she resumed her earlier position.

The voice had a body and it was coming into view—straddling her. Swords clashed right over her head. And something else was hovering right over her head. A pair of breeches, which looked to contain an impressive...

What is the matter with you, Barb? You're thinking about a man's junk at a time like this? She almost giggled. *Almost.*

The man with the impressive package pushed his attacker farther and farther away from her. As soon as she was clear of his—ahem—she'd do what she could to get out of the way.

At last a guttural bellow indicated one of the fighters had just met the business end of Mr. Sharp and Pointy. She struggled to her feet and backed up to the side of the ship where there was a rope she could hold onto.

The fighter who'd just protected her reached down, picked up his attacker's sword and tossed it to her. "Here, Bonny! Help fend off these fuckers."

She caught the heavy sword by the hilt as if she'd done it hundreds of times. Oddly enough it felt comfortable in her hand.

"Thanks, and by the way, my name isn't Bonny!"

He laughed. "All right, Anne, then."

Anne Bonny. Where have I heard that name before? And furthermore, where have I seen that pirate before?

An attacker in a red uniform came at her. She swung the sword, easily separating his head from his neck.

"Oh my God!"

"Well done, Bonny! I mean, Anne." The pirate grinned at her.

She'd know that lascivious grin anywhere. "Shahid?"

"Anne Bonny?" a soldier yelled. "Men! It's the famous female pirate Anne Bonny! Capture her at any cost!

A moment later she was set upon again, and this time another red coat joined in the fight. Swinging the sword with both hands she fended off one attacker and then the other, but the first one recovered quickly and came at her again, as if to run her through.

Shahid was there in a split second, skewering the man before he could reach her.

"Jesus! Thank you!"

"Jesus had nothing to do with it," he said. Grabbing her around the waist he yanked her against his hard torso and kissed her. She stumbled backward and fell, hitting her head against the hull as she went down.

When Barb opened her eyes she was looking at the sea, but from a beach in a totally different location. Someplace damp and cold. Definitely not India or the Caribbean.

She managed to stand, but with her head aching and dizziness overtaking her, she stumbled backward a few steps. Leaning over, she grabbed her knees and steadied herself. The shoes on her feet were different! They had buckles on them and they were chunky and black.

Her dress was long and black too. She straightened up

and saw that she was wearing some kind of white apron. She touched her aching head and felt something like starched linen. She surmised she must be wearing some kind of hat or bonnet. Gazing out at the scene, she saw a pebbled beach and a ship anchored a ways off shore. It appeared much older than sailboats of this day and age... *that is if I'm even* in *this day and age.* Looking down at herself, she doubted it. She turned toward land and noticed trees behind her. And somewhere in the trees was movement. She froze when Indians emerged—and not the ones she knew in India.

"Did I just come over on the Mayflower?" she asked herself out loud. The Indians didn't seem to pay much attention to her. They sought out and were speaking with a man. Someone dressed similarly to what she would expect of a male pilgrim. *What the heck?*

She found a large rock and rested her butt on it. "This can't be..." She just wasn't prepared for this kind of dream... or whatever. It felt all too real. The bottom of her dress was wet, her feet felt damp, and there was a distinct chill in the air. Right now she'd give anything for her tiny heated apartment back in New York. Her place might be small, but at least it was cozy. She didn't feel cozy here at all.

The man speaking to the Indians stopped suddenly when he caught sight of her.

"Ye, there... Why are ye not with the women, preparing to break our fast?"

"Um... Because I'm a rotten cook?"

"Ye dare cook something rotten? After so many have died here? Take me to these stores of rotten food."

"Oh! There's no rotten food. Uh... Not anymore. I just threw the bad stuff out. In the ocean."

He walked over to her slowly, appraising her. "I do not remember ye. What are ye called?"

She was about to say, Barb, but 'Beatrice' popped out of her mouth. *WTF?*

She needed to know a few things too and asking might distract him from his line of questioning. "I seem to be a bit disoriented. What place and year is this?"

He reared back and his jaw hung open. Then as if remembering himself, he snapped it shut. "Why, t'is 1621, and ye are in the new world. Do ye have a fever?"

"No. Not at all. I'm healthy as a horse."

"Ye speak strangely."

Her usual snarky self would say, 'so do you, buddy,' but she caught herself in time.

"Who is thy sire?"

Uh oh. She wasn't sure if he was asking about her father or husband. *Damn, why didn't I pay better attention in my history classes?* "To tell you the truth, I have no sire with me. I came here on my own."

He seemed momentarily stunned. "Do ye mean to tell me ye sailed from Europe to a faraway land—by thyself?"

"Uh, sure."

"Preposterous!"

They stared at each other for a long moment. Barb wasn't usually one to back down, but she had to do something before this guy called her a witch and planned a beach barbeque.

"Kidding! Ha ha. I was just making a joke. You know, something to lighten the mood. Of course I didn't row over here all by myself. I, uh…stowed away."

"On my ship?"

"On your ship—or the other one." *Were there others? I seem to remember three names. The Nina, Pinta, and the Santa... Ohhh dear. That's right. I'm thinking of Columbus. Wrong century.*

"Ah, the Speedwell," he was saying. "It was Dutch, which explains thy odd manner of speaking. Did ye not give thy name when ye came aboard my ship after the Speedwell was deemed unfit to make the journey?"

"Uh, yeah...no. I didn't."

"Well, Beatrice, ye may have come with no sire or mate, but with only twenty-eight women to have made the journey and nearly one hundred men. Ye will have no trouble finding a mate. And then ye can cook, sew, and clean the fine houses we will build."

Lovely...

One of the Indians stepped closer and for some reason Barb didn't shy away from him. He seemed familiar...

Holy shit. I'd recognize whose eyes anywhere. It was Shahid.

He spoke a few private words with the English gentleman. The man eyed her and nodded.

Shahid grabbed her and tossed her over his shoulder. As he ran into the woods, her head spun again and she fainted.

"The Spanish murderers are coming!"

"What murderers?" the king asked.

"Cortez. It is said he conquers the Aztecs in the name of New Spain."

The king let out a huge sigh. "Fine. Let's sacrifice another virgin."

Barb was overhearing this conversation from a small stone enclave. By now she realized she was going progressively further and further back into her past lives.

Virgin sacrifice, huh? It's a good thing I'm the furthest thing from a virgin... at least I was in the twenty-first century. But what about now?

She glanced around to see if there were other women nearby. She appeared to be alone.

"Who is the lucky woman to be so honored?" the messenger asked.

"Xoco. She is in the next room."

Next room? Hopefully there were a lot of next rooms and they weren't coming for her.

A black haired, tanned man, with a square face and almond eyes rounded the corner of her alcove and said, "Oh, Xoco... Want to come with me and get a little snack? We have plantains..."

Shit. He's talking to me. "No thanks. I'm not really hungry."

"All right," he said.

He gave up surprisingly easily.

"I have something even better. A new drink the king just invented. It's made from oranges left in his chamber for many days. During that time, the Gods infused it with the most wonderful qualities. It will relax you and make you feel wonderful at the same time."

"Are you talking about booze?" *It sounds like early fermentation, and I think I remember hearing about the Aztec civilization going downhill after its discovery.* "I'd stay away from that stuff, if I were you."

The king joined them. He wore similar scanty clothing and a cape, but with more adornments. Barb hadn't even taken a good look to see what she was wearing. Glancing down, she had on a beige skirt and blouse with a few wide red stripes, which seemed to be made of woven material, and it itched.

"Come Xoco. I will allow you to stroll through my gardens as we drink our orange nectar."

She looked up into the king's eyes and saw—*Damn, not again... Shahid?*

She rose and threw herself into his arms. "Oh, thank goodness it's you! I know you'll save me from being sacrificed."

King Shahid—or whatever his name was in this lifetime—just stared at her.

"You will, won't you?

He glanced over at his messenger. "Let us have that drink now, shall we?"

He bowed. "I will send a servant to retrieve it right away," he said.

As soon as he was gone, Barb said, "I'm not the virgin you're looking for."

He simply stared at her.

Damn, that worked in Star Wars. Then Barb sidled up next to him and reached for his loin cloth. "You wouldn't want to waste this fine body on a cold slab, would you? We could drink that special juice and have some fun..."

He grabbed her hand before she got a hold of his lingham —or cock, depending on which language was in play at the moment.

She sighed. If she was a virgin sacrifice in this lifetime, it would explain a few things about her current lifetime.

The servant entered the chamber with two cups of orange liquid.

"Oh, man. I'm going to need that." She grabbed one and downed it. Then she reached for the other. The servant swiveled away from her sloshing some of the liquid over the side. "This is not for you," he said, angrily.

"Let her have it," the King said.

"Very well." He handed the cup to Barb.

She sipped it this time. *Maybe I can draw this out until the king changes his mind.*

No such luck.

He snapped his fingers and two large men entered the room. "Take her to the sacrificial altar."

As soon as they grabbed her, she fainted.

Oddly enough when Barb came to, she seemed a little too comfortable to be laying on a cold altar. Was she going back to yet another terrible lifetime? Even with her eyes closed and lying down she felt as warm and comfortable as if she were in a bed.

Letting her eyes flutter open just a crack, she hoped this life wouldn't be as dreadful as the others, but if she was going backwards in time where could this comfortable bed be?

If only she could decide where she wanted to go…

Someone was shaking her arm. "Barb? Barb!"

Hey, someone is calling me by my real name and it sounds like Haley.

Opening her eyes fully, Barb focused on the faces above her. She saw Haley, Jamir, and Shahid, All looking very concerned.

"Are we in the 21st century?"

"Where else would we be?" Haley asked.

"I hate to tell you this, but I think past lives are real. I just had a chance to experience three of them."

Shahid and Jamir exchanged a look that said, "Wow."

Haley sat on the bed next to her and took her hand. With her other hand, she felt Barb's forehead.

"I don't have a fever. By the way, aren't you supposed to be getting married?"

Haley just shook her head. "Making sure you weren't terribly hurt, took precedence. We can get back to the wedding at any time."

"What's everyone doing in the meantime?" Barb asked.

Shahid grinned. "Partying. They're serving food and tea early, and everyone is dancing. I was hoping you would be all right and able to enjoy the festivities, but it can wait until you feel better."

Barb sat up and crossed her arms. "Oh, now you're all concerned for my well-being. Do you know you allowed me to be a virgin sacrifice? Not just allowed it...you ordered it!"

"A what?" He burst out laughing, then coughed to make himself stop.

"And after that, you were an Indian—the American kind, and apparently you captured me and took me away from the Mayflower. But since I was a stowaway, I don't think they cared all that much."

Haley had to laugh at that one.

"And if that wasn't bad enough, you had me in a sword fight, on a pirate ship. When I was on the ground. You were nice enough to defend me, but as soon as I got up, you threw me a sword and told me *to defend myself.*"

"Was I there in any of these past lifetimes?" Haley asked.

"No."

"Was I?" Jamir asked?

"No."

Shahid just grinned. "So what you're saying, is that we, you and I, have been together in three past lifetimes."

"Hmmm..." She knew what he was getting at. "But I thought you didn't believe in soulmates," she said.

He shrugged. "Maybe I do now."

"So you think all those lives were real? Are you going to be that selfish and callous again in this lifetime?"

"You have given me a chance to see where I went wrong. If I make it right in this lifetime, my circumstances will improve in the next."

"But I thought you were immortal."

"Since we were permanently replaced as guardians of the temple, we haven't been able to shift," Jamir said. "I think our immortality is over."

Barb stared at Haley. "Did you know about this?"

"Yes, Jamir told me. I didn't think it had much to do with you or that you would care."

"How could you think I wouldn't care? Shahid may not have been perfect in past lifetimes, but he's perfect enough for me now."

"You and Shahid? I thought you were just, you know… friends with benefits," Haley said.

Shahid grinned and leaned down to kiss her. Barb returned the kiss at first, then pushed him away.

"What's wrong?"

"All those things you did… What do you have to say for yourself?"

"I'd say I've already saved you from being a virgin sacrifice in this lifetime by making damn sure you're not a virgin."

Haley and Jamir burst out laughing. She slapped Shahid's arm. "Very funny."

"I won't carry you away from your people, because you've already carried yourself away by your own choice. And as far as handing you a sword to defend yourself, I don't see what was wrong with that."

"Seriously? I was trying to fend off two uniformed soldiers!"

"What happened? Did they kill you?"

"No."

"You seem pretty independent and capable of defending yourself, but if it comes down to your needing my help, I will be there. I promise."

She relaxed and smiled. "I believe you. You'll probably mess up something in this lifetime, but it's good to know you're going to try not to."

"That's all any of us can do," he said. "Now let's get these two married, so we can dance and enjoy each other's company—for perhaps another lifetime."

EPILOGUE

As Barb came through the door of the hut she lived in near the village, Shahid smiled. "How was your day?" He slept on a mat outside, but the mat was missing at the moment. Maybe he had washed it and left it near the river to dry.

"It was good. Now that Haley is tutoring the Sepgupta children again, the orphanage said I can be an English teacher there. The pay isn't great, but it beats no pay at all."

"That's wonderful!" He rose and embraced her.

"And how was your day?"

"Oh, you know… Jamir and I planted some more tea on the empty hillside near the temple."

"Near the temple? Aren't you afraid the tigers will scare away the villagers who harvest the tea for the Sepguptas?"

"No, because we will be the ones doing it." He winked. "I believe you call it 'built in job security'."

She chuckled. "So, we're still the only ones who know the tigers there are shapeshifters?"

"Unless a real tiger shows up."

She shuddered. "Please don't scare me. There are enough wild animals in this country to keep me sleeping with one eye open."

"Ah, speaking of that…" He held out his hand to her.

She took his hand and stared at him curiously. "What's going through that devious mind of yours?"

"Come. I'll show you."

He held open the tent flap that covered the hut's door and she followed him out. As soon as they were standing outside in the warm evening breeze, he took her hand and began strolling down the road toward the Sepgupta's tea plantation. They enjoyed the warm breeze in companionable silence most of the way there.

When Haley and Jamir's home behind the main house, came into view, Barb asked, "Are we visiting?"

"Not yet. Perhaps later."

"Hmmm…" *What could he have to show me?*

At last she noticed a new outbuilding next to the one Jamir and Haley lived in. Pointing to it, she asked, "Has that been there long?"

"No, not long. In fact Jamir and I just finished it this afternoon."

"Finished what? Building it?"

He stood proudly in front of the small but sturdy looking building. "Yes. Do you like it?"

She leaned back to take in the details. There was a wooden porch along the front with a thatched overhang to keep the rain off anyone standing outside during the Monsoons. An actual door and glass windows would keep the building safe from predators.

"It's nice," she said.

"Nice? That's it?"

"Well, no… It's *very* nice. Why did you build it?"

He gave her a sly smile. "We built it for you."

Her brows rose. "Me? I'm going to live here?"

"*We* are going to live here…unless you'd rather stay in the hut. In that case, we can probably sell this—"

"Don't you dare say another word!" She threw her arms around his neck and hugged him. "Thank you," she mumbled into his shirt. "Thank you so much."

"I knew you'd feel a whole lot safer with wooden walls and doors. There's only so much I can do to protect you from tigers, snakes, crocodiles, and whatever else may try to eat you...except me." He winked.

She let out a deeply held breath. "You have no idea how much this means to me."

"Oh, I think I do. I'm sure you had your doubts about your own sanity living in a bamboo hut with me on your doorstep."

"Living in a hut, yes. But with you? Never. I have no doubt at all that I belong with you. I was just worried about what would happen to you when the monsoons came."

He pulled her close and murmured in her ear, "I appreciate your being worried for me. I know that I belong with you too, and I didn't want to give you any excuse to leave me before our next lifetime."

"Why would I leave?"

"Ha! You would probably lose your job saying, *Propriety be damned!* and insist I sleep in the hut with you. I thought it would be much better if we were married and living in a nice house."

She leaned far enough away to see his face. "You mean that, don't you?"

"Yes. And if we're to be together for the rest of our lives, I don't see why we shouldn't get married like Jamir and Haley did. I don't have a birth certificate, but it's what's in God's eyes that's important."

"And the villagers. We don't want to give the nuns at the orphanage any reason to fire me, now that they can."

"True. So you are agreeing to marry me?"

"On one condition."

"What is that?"

"Absolutely, positively, NO elephants at the wedding."

He laughed. "I will ride in on a donkey, if that is what you wish."

"How about walking on your own perfectly good feet?"

"I can do that too."

They shared another long kiss and Barb reveled in the warmth and love of her soulmate's arms surrounding her.

"Let's go tell Haley and Jamir," she said.

He wrapped his arm around her waist and led her next door. She knocked, and after only a few seconds Jamir answered the door.

"May we come in?" Shahid asked, already removing his shoes.

"Of course." Jamir stepped aside to let them pass.

Barb removed her shoes too and set them next to Shahid's. "Is Haley here? We have something to tell you... Both of you."

Haley came into the main room from the kitchen, drying her hands on a towel. "Hi, you two. I thought I heard your voices."

"Did you know about this?" Barb asked her, pointing in the direction of the building they'd just come from.

"What? You mean the source of all that sawing, hammering and cursing? No. I have no idea what you're talking about."

"Ha ha. Did you know your husband and my fiancé were building the house next door for me?"

"Did you say 'Fiancé?'"

Barb grinned and glanced at Shahid who was grinning at his brother. "Yeah. I did say that."

Haley threw herself in Barb's arms and shouted, "Congratulations! I'm so happy for you. Screw that. I'm happy for *me!* Now I know my best friend won't leave and move back to New York."

"I have no desire to go back there. Do you?"

"Nope. Come with me to the kitchen...so when is the wedding?"

She shrugged. "We could wait a few weeks, months or a year. It doesn't matter, if we're soulmates, right?"

"Right. Oh crap! I can think of one person who won't be happy."

"Who's that?"

"Ronda! With Maura in France and the two of us staying here, she'll be all alone."

"Yeah, she'll be surrounded by eight and a half million people, but all alone," Barb said, sardonically.

"Why don't you call her and tell her right away?"

"Um, because it's the middle of the freakin' night there."

"Oh, right. You can call Maura. It's morning there."

"That can wait too. Right now I'd rather enjoy this with the two of you instead of hearing them moan and groan about how they have to make another trip to India."

"I don't think Maura will mind. After all she has Mr. Tall, Dark, and Devilishly Handsome to keep her company on the long trip. I worry about Ronda though."

"Ronda hasn't met anyone yet?"

"Nope. I was just talking to her last night. She's not in a good headspace either. Her parents died in a Cessna crash, and she's moving back to their home in Maine."

"Oh, no! When did that happen?"

Haley picked up the dish rag and resumed drying and putting away the dishes. "About a week ago. She's quitting her job at the ad agency too."

"Really? I thought she was pretty successful there."

"I guess she wasn't as happy with the work as she was

with the paycheck. Now she shouldn't have to worry about either one."

Barb shook her head. "Gee, I feel badly about saying she'd be all alone in the middle of millions of people. How many people live in Maine? Half a dozen?"

Haley snorted. "No, you jerk. There has to be at least a couple hundred."

"I'm sure she'll find someone...eventually."

"Look, I know she'll be happy for you. And weddings have a way of being contagious."

"What... You think she'll come to another wedding and break out in bridesmaids?"

Haley pushed her shoulder. "Same old snarky Barb."

"You wouldn't want me any other way..."

"That's for sure." Haley grabbed her for another hug just as Jamir and Shahid joined them in the kitchen.

"How shall we celebrate this momentous occasion?" Jamir asked.

"I have a little something stashed away," Haley said. She pulled a chair over to the counter so she could reach the cabinet above it. Jamir had built her a few cabinets with doors on them, instead of the usual open shelving. Now Barb knew why. On the top shelf was a big bottle of Irish Whisky.

"Oh my God. Isn't that the stuff Maura had us drink, so we'd go through with the summoning?"

"Not the same bottle, but I believe we got very drunk on whisky that night, yes."

Barb rolled her eyes. "It seems appropriate somehow, since that's what started this whole mess."

When each of them had a glass with an inch of the rare liquid ready, they raised their glasses. "To your health and happiness," Jamir said.

"Sláinte!" Haley added.

"Cheers!" Barb exclaimed.

"Are there any other words you'd like to toast to, brother?" Jamir asked.

"To my beautiful bride," Shahid said.

With an audible sigh, Barb clinked his glass and swallowed the amber liquid, not even complaining when it burned all the way down her esophagus.

BIOGRAPHY OF ASHLYN CHASE

Ashlyn Chase describes herself as an Almond Joy bar. A little nutty, a little flaky, but basically sweet, wanting only to give her readers something yummy that leaves them smiling.

She holds a degree in behavioral sciences, worked as a psychiatric RN for 15 years, and spent a few more years working for the American Red Cross.

Most authors, whether they know it or not, have a theme—something that unifies their whole booklist. Ashlyn's identified theme has to do with characters who reinvent themselves. After all, she has reinvented herself many times. Now she is a multi-published, best-selling, award-winning author of humorous paranormal and contemporary romances, represented by the Seymour Agency.

She lives in beautiful coastal Florida with her true-life superhero husband who looks like Hugh Jackman if you squint. She and Mr. Amazing have been adopted by two beautiful cats.

Where there's fire, there's Ash
    Sign up for my newsletter here: https://bit.ly/2xDwjPe or right from my home page: www.ashlynchase.com
    Join my facebook fan page: https://www.facebook.com/AuthorAshlynChase

Follow me on Bookbub: https://www.bookbub.com/authors/ashlyn-chase

I occasionally tweet as GoddessAsh. https://twitter.com/#!/GoddessAsh

Instagram https://www.instagram.com/ashlynlaughin/

Pinterest https://www.pinterest.com/ashlynchase/

ALSO BY ASHLYN CHASE

For more books go here, https://www.books2read.com/ap/ngobln/
Ashlyn-Chase

A Phoenix is Forever; print, ebook, and audio [Phoenix Brothers
series]

More than a Phoenix; print, ebook, audio [Phoenix Brothers series]

Hooked on A Phoenix; Available in print, e, and audio [Phoenix
Brothers series]

Never Dare a Dragon; Available in print, ebook and audio [Boston
Dragons series]

My Wild Irish Dragon; ebook, print, and audio [Boston Dragons
series]

I Dream of Dragons; ebook, print, and audio [Boston Dragons
series]

Wonder B*tch; ebook only

Laura's Upcycled Life; ebook only

Heaving Bosoms; ebook and print [Heaving Bosoms/Quivering
Thighs duo]

Quivering Thighs; ebook and print [Heaving Bosoms/Quivering
Thighs duo]

Thrill of the Chase; 1 author anthology, ebook and print

Guardian of the Angels; ebook only

Immortally Yours; 1 author anthology, ebook and print

Vampire Vintage; ebook and print [Be Careful What You Summon series]

Love Cuffs; ebook and print

Out of the Broom Closet; ebook and print [Love Spells Gone Wrong series]

Tug of Attraction; ebook and print [Love Spells Gone Wrong series]

The Cupcake Coven; ebook and print [Love Spells Gone Wrong series]

Gods Gone Wild; 2 author anthology; ebook and print

Kissing with Fangs: ebook, print, and audio [Flirting with Fangs series]

How to Date a Dragon; ebook, print, and audio [Flirting with Fangs series]

Flirting Under a Full Moon; ebook, print, and audio [Flirting with Fangs series]

The Vampire Next Door; ebook and print [Strange Neighbors series]

The Werewolf Upstairs; ebook and print [Strange Neighbors series]

Strange Neighbors; ebook and print [Strange Neighbors series]

Thank you for reading my books! If you enjoy them, please leave a positive review. Reviews sell books. Sales feed authors. Well-fed authors write more books. *Thank you!*